*Sakeema, bond brother, answer me!*

Something — something strange. No mindspoken answer, yet I sensed a passion I could not name. Something.

*Sakeema!*

Moving warily, somewhere near.

*Sakeema! Help me, help us all!*

Even the Fanged Horse Folk? Yes, if the world were to remain, they would have to be on it.

*World brother, come to me. It is all ending, I need comfort.*

But Kor would not have been afraid to come to me. Perhaps Sakeema had been only in my dreams too, all this time.

*Sakeema.*

I mindspoke, not in pleas any longer but in heartache. And with great clarity and tenderness someone answered me.

*Be still. I am coming.*

Also from Orbit by Nancy Springer:

CHAINS OF GOLD

THE SEA KING TRILOGY:
MADBOND
MINDBOND

NANCY SPRINGER

# Godbond

Sea King Trilogy 3

An Orbit Book



First published in Great Britain in 1990 by
Futura Publications, a Division of
Macdonald & Co (Publishers) Ltd
London & Sydney

*All characters in this publication are fictitious and any resemblance to real persons, living or dead, is purely coincidental.*



ISBN 0 7088 4439 1

Reproduced, printed and bound in Great Britain by
BPCC Hazell Books Ltd
Member of BPCC Ltd
Aylesbury, Bucks, England

Futura Publications
A Division of
Macdonald & Co (Publishers) Ltd
66–73 Shoe Lane
London EC4P 4AB
A member of Maxwell Pergamon Publishing Corporation plc

*(One there was, the enemy,*
*Who bore away the tree.*
*Two there came who sundered the fruit*
*Amid earth and sky and sea.)*

*Two there were who came before*
*To brave the deep for three:*
*The rider who flees,*
*The seeker who yearns,*
*And he who is king by the sea.*

*Two there were who came before*
*To forge the swords for three:*
*The warrior who heals,*
*The hunter who dreams,*
*And he who is master of mercy,*
*He who has captured the heart of hell,*
*He who is king by the sea.*

TASSIDA'S SONG

# Prologue

I am she, the enemy, the cormorant goddess in the depths of the sea; but in the days of which I speak I arose from the sea, I flew. I am she whom men called great glutton bird, all-devourer, destroyer: Mahela. Even the wisest of them all, my beautiful young Korridun, knew me by no other name.

My weapons were potent, but few enough. I could hurl the sea against the land. I could reach forth with black hand of storm. At the time I had seven of the devourers still. They were stupid, clumsy brutes, fit only for the taking of soft-willed creatures one by one, but loyal, as befit my creations. I had made the devourers myself, out of lonesome sleep and the stuff of my thwarted dreams, when my fertile time had long since passed and I had thought I could make living things no longer. They themselves were as ugly as my bitterness, but many were the pretty pets they had brought me, gleaning the world for me. Mortals feared them worse than waking nightmare. Puny human weapons, knives of stone and bone and shell and obsidian, were of no use against a devourer's cold, gray flesh, nearly as fluid as seawater. Nor were spears and arrows tipped with bone or blackstone.

But Korridun and Dannoc and my winsome Tassida feared the devourers no longer, for those three bore the three swords and had learned the courage to use them. Against those three I had to bring forth my only remaining weapon, the one that hurt me worst: despair.

Of the ways of despair, I knew far more than they.

For I was once one, like Korridun King of the Seal Kindred, who could feel what moved in the hearts of my people. But I was far older than he, I remembered back to legendary times, the days when the sensate swords were forged, when kings wore crowns and ruled kingdoms, when people swarmed the world with their numbers, building cities of stone and tall-masted ships and ever-more-clever weapons of war; and the knowledge of the hatreds, the shames and pettiness and greeds and perfidies of mortals had long since driven me to desperation. Feeling their envies and their needfulness as my own, as I did—it would have driven me to death. So, to survive, I had learned to harden my heart, to turn those passion-spears away from me. Now it was I who pierced the hearts and minds of others with my own pain.

All the more pain, since Korridun had forsaken me.

Rousead, I flew forth. In black cloak of storm and wrath and desolation I flew to Seal Hold, where Korridun had gone.

He and Dannoc, always Dannoc. How it smote me with jealousy, the way the two of them cleaved together, friends who would be remembered in legend, should the world live so long. They had bonded each other to brotherhood in blood. Together they had fought Cragsmen and Fanged Horse raiders and devourers and heartache. They had faced torture and hotwind wildfire and the passionfires within. They had ventured to the greendeep in seal form and brought each other back from the realm of the dead—my realm. Korridun loved Dan above anything, nearly above self and certainly far above me. I had to part them.

They had grown too powerful, I told myself.

And Tassida. Worse yet, Tassida had been with them since their return from the sea, though she loved them both, heart torn between them, and always before she had fled from their passion for her. Tassida, Korridun, Dannoc, all three together . . . it could not be suffered.

I laid my cold touch heavy on the minds of all of them, to sunder them. I made them feel my own jealousy and despair. And amid storm and lightning flash and the coming of night I flew over them where they stood. Battered by wind and lashed by rain on the rocky headland of Seal Hold they stood, while all others cowered within the cave.

Dannoc demanded of his bond brother, "Why did you not kill her, the great glutton who eats us all, while she lay sleeping under your hand?"

And Korridun gave a low, hard laugh, more dangerous than a shout. "What, slay the only woman who has ever preferred me to you?"

Korridun, king by the sea, my fair young bedmate, in sealskin breeches and faded tunic of wool, not even an armband on him for glory, yet fairer to me than the jeweled and crowned kings whom only I remembered. Korridun, my passion, the smooth skin of his face shell-tan, his hair seal-dark, his eyes dark and ever-changing, like the wash of the sea. Korridun, who had died three times and found his way back to life; not even I who ruled death could keep him close to me. Korridun, sea king, master of mercy. I had dared to hope that in his mercy vast as the sea he could love me. But after the one night in my bed—and by our bliss I had thought us forever wedded—he had left me. Looking on him again, I hated my own stubborn hope.

And close by him, Tassida, my willful Tassida with the lean, tough body of a warrior, the farseeing gaze of a visionary, the proud, dark-browed face. Face like mine. Tassida, my little daughter, how I loathed her. Had I not taught her, as a mother ought, to stay far from men? Had I not taught her fear? Yet there she stood between Korridun and Dannoc, one of her hands reaching toward each. She had taken Dannoc as her bedmate, and Korridun knew it, and I battered his heart with jealousy, with hatred for them both, with my own misery—for I knew that at his center Korridun yet loved her as he refused to love me.

Dannoc. Spear-tall, spear-straight and stormwind-strong, he was all a spear-point of seeking and vision and desire. Many were the men who called him mad, but had any woman ever looked on his hair the color of lightning, his bare shoulders and his dreaming blue eyes without wanting him? He had done murder, yet he loved Korridun better than a brother, and he had heart in him to love a lifemate unto world's end. I preferred Korridun, for the sake of his mercy, but I knew to my center why Tassida had chosen Dan, and the knowledge troubled me. They were strong, far too strong, together.

How much stronger, then, the three of them together?

I pierced their hearts and minds with knives of my own embittered passion, twisted the blades, and Dan and Korridun broke out in bitter quarrel.

"You defeated king!" Dannoc railed. "All the great things I had thought of you, and now you have given up!

You coward, fleeing Mahela's realm like a kicked cur! You left your own mother there, whom we had come to save, and my—my father, there, in that deathly place, forever!'' Dan panted with fury and struck out at Korridun with his fist; Tassida caught his arm to prevent him. She came between the two of them, pleading, but I was still stronger than she.

Kor said, ''I should have left you there as well.''

Korridun's anger, quieter, more silent, more brooding and lasting than Dan's, always. Quarreling was in the two of them, I could not have made it out of nothing, but I urged Kor's hard words out of him amid stormwind, I lashed Dan's rage with stinging rain.

''Betrayer! You limp thing, flattened to the sand by a storm! Rad Korridun, noble king, what is the good of you?'' Dannoc mocked, or begged. ''The whole mortal world is dying around us, and will you not lift a hand to save it?''

And in terrible sorrow Korridun cried out, ''I am not Sakeema!''

The god Dannoc had been seeking all his life. The god he deemed could save his dwindling world. For a brief while, a season or two, he had thought he had found his god in Kor.

''I know that now!'' he shouted amid the shrieking of stormwind, and Korridun felt his heartache, felt it in his own body, as always, and the force of it staggered Kor and turned him white under the flare of lightning. Dannoc saw, and then there was no anger in him any longer, only a deathly weariness.

Tassida put one of her arms around his shoulders, one around Korridun's. ''Leave it,'' she urged. ''Come in, before you are swept away.'' And Dannoc would have gone with her.

But there was bitterness aplenty left in Kor. ''Go ahead, Dan,'' he said, his voice low, grim. ''Take her to your chamber. Tass, the only woman I have ever loved. Whisper her name in the darkness and wish you could see her face—''

Dannoc's head snapped up, his hair flying lightning-pale around his face first pale with rage, then flushed dark. ''Draw!'' he commanded, and he crouched and reached for his weapon. Kor did the same, but Tassida stepped between and pushed the two of them apart so that they staggered backward.

''No!'' she cried, her proud face full of horror. Kor glanced at her, a single angry look, and something passed between them—I did not at the time understand mind-speak, to know that Tassida had just suffered what she feared worst in the world: invasion by force. But I saw her dark eyes open wide with terror, and I was glad. She turned and ran, found her horse and rode away at a reckless gallop amid night and storm.

Dannoc swore. ''Son of a whore!'' he raged at Korridun. ''You piss-proud, jealous worm! You might as kindly have raped her, and had it done with!'' He lunged at his bond brother, and the two of them grappled beneath the black sky.

They had not, after all, drawn weapons on each other. They fought like impassioned children, sprawling on the rocks, trying to hurt each other with fists, knees, heads, bloodying each other's faces. After a while they staggered to their feet, panting and glaring at each other.

''Sakeema!'' Dan shouted, not so much at Kor as at earth and sea and sky. ''The whole world is coming apart in shards, and can you do nothing?'' His voice rose so high that like a stripling's it cracked.

Kor raised a curled fist and struck his bond brother full

force on his nose, breaking it. Blood rushed down amid the rain. And the water on Korridun's face, not rain entirely; he was sobbing. "If you have thought I was a god, it was your own folly!" he screamed at Dannoc. "I have told you a hundred times, I am not—our savior."

Then I saw tears trembling in Dannoc's eyes, and I knew the quarrel was over, for I felt the love in them, and I thought surely I had failed. They would embrace, now. Nothing could ever part them. But Dan did not move toward his brother.

"Then I had better go find the god and awaken him, wherever he sleeps." Dannoc's voice trembled. "For no one less can save us now."

And he went away, took horse and rode into the mountains without touching Kor even with the glance of his eyes. And Kor sank down on the rocks and lay where he was, under a black cloud of my making.

I shouted in the tempest, triumphant. The three sword bearers had gone their separate ways. The innocent fools, they had let my stormwinds sunder them, scatter them like three dry leaves. Together, they could have resisted me. Even—no. I would not say that I could be defeated.

I returned to the sea, I rested. Storm abated. But within the turning of the day, a longing grew in me again to see the land. The one brief sight of the storm-lashed rocks and twisted spruces of Korridun's headland had not been enough. I took form of a bird, a petrel, swift and strong and light as a swallow, and I flew far over the dryland world.

Heartbreaking, how beautiful it all was. Because of the heartbreak I had kept myself away for so long, hiding myself in the greendeep. . . . How beautiful, the seaside cliffs where the cascades sang, wild with springtime snowmelt, amid crags greenfurred with moss, where the Otter River ran down its canyon, shouting, to the sea. I had forgotten how lovely, I pressed on, I had to see more. . . . Beyond, beyond, up in the highmountain meadows where the deer had once grazed, the pale spikes of dwarf willow still pushed up through the skirts of the eversnow. And down the mountain flanks, the way that greathearted fool Dannoc would go, the forest floor was a froth of windflower and white violets and larkspur amid bracken. And the aspens, putting forth yellowgreen leaf, and the bright branch tips on the blue pines. . . . Seeing was no longer enough for me. I set my feet on the damp earth, I touched twig and leaf, I stooped to smell the small yellow springlilies. And I remembered all that lay beyond the snowpeaks: the austere sweep of the steppes, the tallgrass prairie, the rumpled uplands thick with hemlock and glinting with shallow lakes, the blackstone thunder cones. On the cindery flanks of the thunder cones, the tiny flowers with stems no thicker than a hair would be blooming, as they did once a year, covering that harsh rubble with an amaranthine mist. I knew, though I did not go there to see. How well I knew.

And beyond the thunder cones, the plains vast as the sea. . . . What lay beyond them, I knew, though no mortal knew. But it did not matter. The six dwindling tribes all huddled between the plains and the sea, and no other folk trembled anywhere, any longer. It was with these six tribes of wretched, stubborn humans that my business lay, and with seacliffs, river, snowpeaks, steppe, upland demesne and plain. Except for humans, the creatures were already gone, or nearly all. My devouring servants had brought them all to me.

Night spread like a dark flower in the dome of the sky. I circled back toward the sea.

Below me on the mountain's flank, a spark of light, a campfire. I darted low to see. Men, by the fire—

Korridun, my Korridun, and Dan, together again. And lying at their feet, a silver wolf.

A wolf! There could be no wolf. There had been none for three generations of mortal life. I had them all. Folding my wings, I glided to a perch in a blue pine, my heart shaking my feathered breast with its pounding. I would castigate my servants and send them forthwith to take this handsome silver oversight—

But as my eyes caught on Korridun, I forgot the wolf. Tears on the sea king's bruised face, shining in the firelight, nor did he turn aside to hide them, or trouble to brush them away. On Dannoc's face also, tears, unashamed. Their right hands, clasped, passing the grip of their bond brotherhood. Their heads high, their eyes meeting, and I knew for certain, watching, what I had sometimes suspected: they were speaking to each other without words, mind to mind. Dannoc's eyes, blackened by blows, swollen almost shut; he closed them, let his head lie for a moment on his bond brother's shoulder.

My own heartsore longing for Korridun made me feel weak and sick as no wound had ever done. *Ai*, how I wanted that closeness with him, the tears on his face, the touch of his hand, the touch of—his mind. Lovesickness left me no more strength than a winterstarved dove. I could not drive Dannoc away; yet I could not bear to see him stay. Sleep, I willed him. I am the goddess of death, and sleep is a portal to my realm; I have that power.

Exhausted, he did not combat me. He lay back where he was and slept. Korridun got up and brought a riding pelt to cover his naked shoulders, and Dannoc stirred drowsily under it. "Heartbond came first," he murmured.

"I know, my brother," Kor answered him softly. "Rest well."

Kor rested by his side, sleeping not quite so deeply, and

the fire burned low, embers blackening into ashes, and the wolf slipped away, a shadow in the night, to do its useless hunting. Useless, for few mice rustled in that night, few pika squeaked, few rockchucks quarreled, few voles crept. I am the goddess, and what I will, I do; with my loyal servants I was taking them all. And in the trees of that place no birds stirred but I, where I perched as if tethered by the leg.

Go to him, I willed myself.

If I had taken my human form, I would have been a naked woman, my body warm, comely, I knew how comely. Fit to show him—tenderness. . . .

Tenderness would have been surrender. I could not move.

Go to him, I told myself fiercely. Or else go away, and make war on him, and cease looking on his face.

I could not do either that night.

He stirred restlessly in his sleep, my Kor, he moaned, and all night, small and winged and hidden in darkness, I looked on him and could neither go to him nor go away. And before first light he came fully awake, sat up and put his head in his hands as if he could not face the day.

Then he got up, moving about quietly so as not to awaken his sleeping brother, and divided Dannoc's gear from his, leaving Dannoc's on the ground. He readied his own horse for travel. When he was done, he stood and looked at Dannoc's face, the bruised and lidded eyes very still in sleep.

"I will endure, apart from you," he said, aloud but softly so that he would not awaken the one to whom he spoke. "I have made myself a pact to be strong. But I cannot bear this leave-taking."

They had come together, then, only to part again? In the stillness before dawn, perched very small amid towering mountains, in that hush and chill I clearly knew the truth. It was not force of my spleen that was sending Dan away from Kor; it was the power of his own yearning dream.

Kor said to him, very softly, "If any mortal can find and awaken the god, it will be you. Seek well, great heart."

He seemed about to turn away, but did not move, and in the gray breaking of day I saw the struggle in his face, and I fiercely willed Dannoc to slumber soundly, not to awaken.

Kor said, "So—so much I never told you." He wished Dan to hear, in a sense, I felt sure of that. He more than half wished to wake him. "My brother, I remember the first time I saw you, stark mad, riding into the lodge on a lathered horse, your great knife raised to slay me—and I betrayed all my promises to my people, I wanted your love even then. It was as if I had found something that had been lost since before I was born. As if I had found a part of myself."

Though I would not let him wake, Dannoc stirred in his sleep, turning toward Kor, stretching a hand toward him for a moment before it stilled and lay slack on the ground.

Kor went and kneeled beside him. Intensely he said, "Have you not felt it too, Dan, how there is something odd, fated, about us? The two of us, and Tass. Dan, remember how she stared when she first came to us? As if she recognized us, though she had never seen us before?"

He touched his bond brother's hand, but I willed Dannoc deeper into sleep.

"*Ai*, but you are exhausted," Kor murmured. "And small wonder. You ventured . . . you came so close. . . ." The tumult in his face stilled as he gazed at Dan, remembering something of which I knew nothing. "Mindbond," he whispered, and his eyes had grown calm and full of courage.

He took Dannoc's quiet hand in his and passed the grip of their bond brotherhood, kneeling by his sleeping brother's side, as still as the sleeper, and in their stillness I sensed mindspeaking. Then Korridun laid his brother's hand softly down. He bent and kissed Dan on the brow, the kiss of a king. Then, letting his touch not linger, he got up, mounted his horse and rode away, bound toward Seal Hold.

He had come to the mountains to find his brother and bid him a fitting farewell. That done, he went back the way he had come, to the place where his duty lay, where his people and their quarrels awaited him.

I watched after him, knowing I would not allow myself to look on him secretly again. I lost all strength, all resolve, all warrior hardness, doing so.

Then I waited where I was. The sun rose high before Dannoc awoke, looked around him, then got up and moved about softly, silently, as if remembering a good dream.

In truth, he was very comely, even with his blackened eyes and broken nose, for he was tall and strong of bone, nobly browed and fair of face and goodly, like the mountains he loved, and I could not entirely hate him, though I wished to. We were too much alike, he and I. Like me, he loved only one thing more than Korridun, and that was—the world itself.

And I would have it, and I would fight for it, and I would kill him if need be, to take it.

He rode away, upmountain, eastward, his back to the way Korridun had taken, and I watched after him, and saw a flash of silver amid the blue pines: the wolf, keeping its distance from him, yet trotting along with him.

It was as well, perhaps, that Korridun's people were

quarreling with the Otter River Clan, and that the Fanged Horse Folk would come raiding. It was as well that Dannoc would face starvation and the enmity of the Cragsmen. It was as well that Tassida would face mortal dangers as well. My fiery Tassida, wherever she had gone.

It was well that—that other enemies might kill them, that I might not have to slay—these three whom I loved. . . .

For slay them I would, I vowed within myself, if they came in the way of my plan.

I flew away seaward, swiftly, and plunged to my undersea realm, and took my proper shape as goddess of Tincherel, and sent my fell servants forth to harry the swordbearers, all three of them, but especially Tassida, should they find her, for she needed to be kept afraid. Dannoc and Korridun might meet again, it would not surprise me, but if Tassida joined them, I would have no choice. . . .

And as an afterthought, I bade the servants bring me the wolf.

# Chapter One

I am a madman, a murderer, a mystic, and above all, Sakeema's fool. Always, Sakeema's fool. I am he whom folk called Dannoc, the dreamwit who left his bond brother in search of the god.

And I found him soon, in a way. I starved, those early days of the journey, for there was scant food to be found on the mountainpeaks, and at the Blue Bear Pass, as I lay weak from hunger and chilled by the thin air off the ever-snow, he came to me.

His head crowned in skyfire glory, he looked down on me. Lying on stony ground, blinking up at him, I could not see his face.

"Sakeema?" I mumbled. I had seen him so once before, in vision.

"Don't call me Sakeema, Dannoc!" A well-beloved voice, annoyed as always when I addressed him by that name. For a time I had thought he was the god. It was my bond brother, Kor.

But when he kneeled beside me, helping me to struggle up and sit with him, still I could not see his face. I badly wanted to see again his quiet, dark-eyed face. But it was hidden by the blaze of light around his head, and I felt as if the god held my shoulders in his hands.

"Are you sure?" I murmured. "You look so much like him."

"Dannoc, you are lightheaded." And no wonder, after the many days without sufficient food. "Come on. I will take you back to Seal Hold."

Only the world's peril could have made me leave him as I had done. The vast, wild world, mountainpeaks, meadows, pine forests, plains, all dying, falling bit by bit into Mahela's maw. To my soul's center I wanted to go back and be with him again, yet I could not. "Must go find Sakeema," I muttered, and his hands sagged away from me.

*Seeker,* he mindspoke me, *how do you expect to find Sakeema until you have truly found yourself?*

He cast aside a king's distance, mindspeaking me, he was all candor, his soul bared to mine. Though there was never less than truth in Kor, ever. . . . But I did not heed him, I snorted in scorn, deeming that I knew myself well enough. What was there to know? That I was the only one in the six tribes crazed and foolish enough to go off in search of the god?

Kor—if it was Kor—the one with the face I could not see against skybright glow—he lifted one hand and touched my forehead in answer to my scoffing.

"What is your name?" he asked aloud.

And I could not remember. I was madman, murderer,

once again in the prison pit and utterly at his mercy, but unafraid. And I could not remember my own name.

"Of what age were you when you took your name vigil?"

The same question he had asked me once before, but this time I remembered the answer. I had been thirteen, and my father had braided my sunbleached hair for me into the two braids of a Red Hart adult and warrior. How I had loved him in those days, my father, king of the Red Hart Tribe. . . . He had turned back and embraced me yet one time more before he had left me. I remembered clearly enough the days alone on the crags up amid the eversnow, where the air was thin and nothing came but wild sheep and the black eagles soaring. I remembered the fasting, the lightheaded weakness that had come over me, the same hunger-weakness that I had felt all too much of late. . . . And I remembered, or relived, the vision:

A hunter, a proud Red Hart hunter in deerskin lappet and leggings, bare-chested, with the yellow braids lying long on his weather-browned, battle-scarred shoulders. His head high, his blue eyes keen. Myself, when I grew older, I had thought or hoped as a stripling of thirteen summers. The hunter kneeled to study the ground, finding his way along a faint trail. Then he stood and scanned the land intently, and I saw that he had ventured to a mountain-peak, and that his blue eyes, deep as highmountain sky, searched crag and eversnow and meadow, spruce forest and pine forest and fir forest and distant shortgrass steppe, hilly uplands and river valleys and even the vast plains and the vast sea—all the world he scanned, searching. He carried a well-curved bow, and he raised it and shot a red-fletched arrow, far, far, so far I could scarcely follow its flight. I lost sight of the hunter and saw only the arrow—but no, the hunter was the arrow, its sharp stone head wore his keen-eyed face, his long braids streamed in the wind of its passing. It pointed sometimes downward toward the belly of the earth and sometimes upward toward the sky, but it never fell to earth, and its red feathers beat like the wings of a red bird. And it shone like the sun, its seeking head and feathered shaft aglow with sunyellow glory, and then, as if it had just seen me, it shot straight at me to bury its sharp stone head in my heart, or so I thought. It sped toward me, the face of the hunter turned eagerly toward me—but I gasped for breath, seeming already to feel that bolt in my gut, and I blinked, ending the vision.

Dannoc, Dannoc, Dannoc. My name was Dannoc, "the arrow."

I looked at the shining head and shadowed face of the one next to me. "Dannoc is my name," I told him.

"Are you certain?"

Such nonsense. It had been my name for years. How could I be less than certain? The image of the arrow had filled my sight. "Of course I am certain."

"Of course. Are you ever less than sure?" Affection along with the gentle mockery in his voice. "But I think it is not your true name. Call yourself, rather, Darran, 'the seeker.' The hunter, the one who follows the faint trail."

I gazed with caught breath, struggling to understand what he was saying.

"Luckily, 'Dan' will do for both," he added in a voice both tender and oddly aloof. "Farewell, Dan, my friend. Seek well. I will miss you while you are parted from me."

"Kor! No!"

Like the arrow in my vision he took flight, soaring skyward and away from me, shining like the sun.

"Wait! Kor!" I cried out, struggling to rise, falling back on the ground instead. Odd, that I was so weak I could not stand. Hunger had not yet made me so weak. . . . In desperation I mindcalled him. *Kor! By all the bonds that join us—*

It was no use. Mindspeak carried no farther than tongueshot, in my experience, and already he had dwindled to a light like a daytime star, and then he was gone. Far, far away from me.

I must have been weeping. My face, wet with tears—but tears did not rub so. Something warm and wet scraping my face. . . .

I came to myself and cursed myself for a wanhope. It was the wolf, my companion, licking my face to rouse me from my sleep, my dreaming. As soon as it saw I was awake, it backed away from me so that I would not touch it.

Shakily I got to my feet. Chill, rocky mountainpeak and eversnow all around. Anything else had been all dream, or vision brought on by my starvation, like that namevision years before. . . . Of course Kor had not been with me, no matter how much I longed for him. He was with his people in Seal Hold. I, a willful blunderhead, had left him there.

"I was dreaming of Kor," I said to the wolf, my voice trembling like my legs.

I bent as slowly as an old woman to pick up my bow and arrowcase, so weak with hunger and longing that I had to steady myself with a hand against the ground.

"What a halfwit I am," I told the wolf after I had straightened. "Kor would never hide his face from me. He does not—he does not fly like a god. . . ."

Yet the things he had said had seemed so true, I would have put my hand in fire for them. I had walked through fire once for his sake.

"The dreamer in me wants to say it was Sakeema," I muttered to the wolf.

It listened solemnly. I noted, with the pang I felt anew every day, how thin it had grown under its graysheen fur. Sakeema in vision was of no use to me or to my dying world; I had to find him in flesh and in fact, alive and waking.

I slung my arrowcase onto my shoulder. Alar, my blade, rode in her leather sheath on my hip. At no great distance stood my fanged mare, Talu, pawing at the scree and butting with her oversized nose, hunting for something good to eat, an adder perhaps. She swung her bony rump toward me in a bored way when I walked toward her, threatening to kick or make me chase her, but on that day she let me take hold of her readily enough. A good thing, for I could not have caught her otherwise. I had to steady myself by her headstall as I led her to the place where my riding pelt lay, and she gave me a contemptuous look.

"Fathead," I accused her, though in fact her head and all parts of her were anything but fat. She was rawboned and slab-sided, my Talu, her hide scarred by many battles, her fangs sharp and her temper sour. Ugly as the Fanged Horse tribesmen who had reared her. I slung the riding pelt and my empty food bags on her back, fastened the surcingle, and struggled onto her.

Eastward I rode, on a horse the color of dry dirt and thunder-cone grit, with a wolf by my side, down the mountain flanks toward the place where I judged Sakeema's cave might lie if the legends of my tribe spoke truth.

Heartbreaking, how beautiful it all was still. The very rocks, lovely with gaywings and doveflower twining down. Spring was at its wild, dewdrenched height, and the wrens and warblers should have been trilling as loud as waterfalls leaping with snowmelt. But I heard no song of any bird except the whimper of sorrowdoves and, once, the dark calling of a raven. All the way up the Blackstone Path from

Seal Hold I had seen no creatures moving, I had ridden through silence except for the rush of cascades. No chirring of squirrels in the blue pines and firs, no whistle of marmot or squeal of pika from the rocks, no thrush's song. Not even so much as a wretched sparrow was to be heard any longer. Mahela had taken all the creatures into her maw.

I had learned to eat grubs from rotting logs, potherbs, sparrow grass, even the lichens off the rocks. I had eaten vipers as my fanged mare did, stealing them from her after she had killed them. Talu would munch nests of asps, not minding the stings. Perhaps it was the poison that made her temper so vile. . . . In the highmountain meadow there had been nothing to eat, not even snakes, for the horse and the wolf and me.

The nature of the land changed as I rode down the eastern slopes of the mountain called Shaman. No cataracts any longer, no spruce and blue pine. I rode through spearpine and towering yellow pine, saw the grass growing thick between the thin-branched, spice-dry trees. These were the reaches of the Red Hart Demesne. My people came here to hunt the deer. But I saw no herds fattening on the lush grass. I had seen no deer, not so much as a solitary stag, since the year before.

I left the trail and rode aside, casting about, searching for a certain cave, which I had never seen except in a vision, which no one had ever seen, the cave where legend said Sakeema lay. Looking for the cave, or for those who could show it to me. The folds and steeps of the mountain flanks went on and in and up, vast beyond thinking, so vast that generations of my people had not explored half their indeeps. Even I was not fool enough to think I could find the secret place by myself.

But once in Seal Hold I had dreamed of a white hind, and I had dreamed of her again on the journey since.

In the dream I had heard the howling of wolves and the lamenting of birds, all the creatures of Sakeema mourning because Sakeema was dead. And I had seen the cave, a tall crevice in some wild mountainside, the entry shaped like a narrow fir tree, aspiring upward, with a cataract pooling by the threshold. And I had seen Sakeema's body borne up the mountainside on the backs of stags. The deer were bringing his maimed body home from the hands of the torturers, home to his birthplace. Somewhere the kings who had killed him rejoiced, but every creature in the world hung its head in mourning.

Hinds stood in a trembling cluster before the cave. And when the bier approached them, they went to Sakeema, and their soft muzzles touched the body of Sakeema, and they turned human, naked but covered with soft fur like that of fawns. And they wept. Weeping, they carried the body within the cave and laid it there. Then the white hind, she who had suckled Sakeema as a baby, the white hind in her deer form stood over the dead god and wept through the day and the night. And with sunrise Sakeema lay healed, alive and whole. But all the deer's nuzzlings could not awaken him.

His face—I knew it well, we had met before, yet I could not remember it when I awoke.

Therefore I searched for the white hind or for the cave I had seen in the dream.

I found nothing, neither cave nor hind and least of all the god. Or food. Nightfall came, and I slept while the wolf watched over me and hunted by turns. Perhaps it found itself a toad or a lizard lurking in the dark. I hoped so. At sunrise I groaned and got up and mounted Talu. I had scarcely strength to struggle onto her. If it were not for the horse, I would have been able to go no farther. But once on her, I rode grimly. Until sunset I searched, riding in broad zigzags across the mountainside, and I rode on into the dusk, for it is at dawn and dusk that deer are mainly to be seen.

"Look," I whispered suddenly, gladly, to the wolf trotting by my side.

It was a deer. Not the white hind, but a red deer, a mere yearling, scarcely more than a fawn, standing at the verge of a thicket and watching me with slender legs drawn under it, poised for flight. I stopped Talu and looked, for the sight of the young creature, stare of dark eyes, great quivering ears, smooth flanks and the creamy fur of neck and belly—the sight of it gave me a dim sense of hope, however witless. Hungrily I gazed—it was heart hunger. I had no thought of food for my belly, and though my bow hung close by my hand I made no move to use it. In that twilight moment I knew that I would gladly have eaten greens for my life's time just to keep one such beautiful creature alive.

For the span of a few precious breaths the deer stared at me as I sat Talu. Then a shadow came slipping over my head, out of the west, and even before I looked up I flinched and cowered, knowing what I would see.

Devourer!

No matter how often I saw the cold, foul brutes, I could never constrain that first panicky jolt of terror. Or—sheerest loathing as much as terror. Even at the distance and in the sweet, open air I seemed to smell the thing's reek, that most horrible of all odors to me, smell of—woman, of lovemaking, turned to slime and decay. Even at the distance I seemed to feel the monstrous breasts at my face.

Rippling wings of fish-gray flesh swooped overhead, huge, blocking out the day's dying light. The single eye peered whitely just above the headless thing's hard dugs. I saw the—clam, the cleft, swollen like that of a bitch in heat, just beneath the monster's thrashing tail, and in the midst of that vast bulk, the maw, ringed with spearpoint teeth, wide open to take in whatever the mindless thing's cold mistress had commanded.

Alar sprang out of the scabbard to meet my hand, her pommel stone blazing, for she liked the minions of Mahela no better than I did.

Scudding over me, the devourer bellied down on the deer.

I shouted and sent Talu leaping forward, lifting my sword, more enraged than if the monster had attacked me. I should have known its errand was not to me. It would attempt me in the dark of night, sometime when I had moved in my sleep and my hand lay far from my sword. The mindless thing, it yet had cleverness enough to fear my sword. And by Alar's soul, she and I would not let it take a yearling deer!

But all was over even as I shouted. The deer had only time to bleat once and take a single leap before it was gone.

Gone, as if it had never been. Taken into that great maw, taken away for Mahela, another captive for her undersea court of death, the chill place she called Tincherel. She liked lovely things, Mahela, such as this deer, and the soft-eyed creature seemed to have no will to resist the monster for even a few moments. The devourer lifted upward and flew away westward, swimming in air, its flattened snake of a tail flailing like an eel. Swimming heavily but well out of my reach, it bore its prize away, and in my hand Alar shook, her pommel stone flaring the color of lightning, as angry as I.

"Slime of Mahela!" I swore to any listener. Then a

trembling took hold of me that would not stop, a weakness that lay on me heavy as a devourer, my own hunger devouring me, I could not center myself, I could scarcely put away my sword. My head spun, and I slid off Talu, thumped to the hard ground and lay there, not much aware of anything.

# Chapter Two

Some time later I awoke to find myself blinking into fire-light, with a pungent taste in my mouth and my head resting in the naked lap of a full-breasted deer maiden, pillowed on the springy hair of her merkin.

Oddly—for I had never been a slowcome with women, no matter how weak and wounded I might be—I felt no lust for her, not even gazing up at the sway of her russet nipples as she moved her arm to bring the liquor to my mouth again. It was some sort of hard berry wine, very bitter, and I coughed on it and sat up in protest. My eyes met many smiles. There were other deer maidens bending or sitting all around me, their large eyes glowing warmly in the firelight, their glossy fawn-furred bodies close to me, red-brown hair cascading down to their backs and shoulders but failing to hide their full, round breasts. And still I felt no desire for them, though the last time I had encountered them I had gone so moon-mad with aching for them that Kor had feared I would sprout antlers.

It was because I was so weak with hunger, I decided, and filled with despair—no. Suddenly I knew what was keeping my cock so unwontedly quiet. Tass. My love for Tass. I had consummated it with her, and now I was hers utterly, forever. The knowledge gave me a pang of yearning and unease. Long ago Kor had told me that he was in thrall, that he wanted no woman but Tass, then or ever, and I had not understood or believed. If he felt that way still, which I judged he did, how had he forgiven me?

I looked at the naked, lissome damsels smiling all around me, answering their smiles only with my own, glad of their friendship, quelling my aching thoughts of Tass, of Kor. At least, I told myself, there was no danger any longer that I might become like Birc—

And there he was, striding up to kneel beside me, shyly smiling as of old to greet me, the shaggy hair of his forehead stirring and parting to reveal knobs and spikes in velvet.

The wolf trotted into the circle of firelight at the same moment, making the deer maidens jump up with bleats of fright, then turn into hinds within a heartbeat as they fled. Birc stiffened and quivered but did not change form or flee. He was courageous, Birc, as he had been since the first day I had known him, one of Kor's guardsmen at Seal Hold. He watched the wolf narrowly as it lay down beyond the fire, then let go of fear and sat beside me, offering me a seedcake such as the deer people are accustomed to eat.

I gave him a one-armed embrace as I accepted it. The seedcake was an awful thing, as I knew quite well, made of millet coarsely ground and nearly as bitter as the liquor. Nevertheless, I ate it within the moment. Birc gave me another, snatching it from the hot stones near the fire, and when I had finished it he offered me a third.

"No, thank you," I said. "My gut is aching." Two of those things would be enough to either strengthen me or kill me.

Birc extended a hand toward me in silent inquiry. He could not speak, of course, any more than a sylkie could, and I had to guess what he wanted. He was wondering why I was not with his former king, probably.

"I had to leave," I explained. "I must find Sakeema."

Birc's brows arched high.

"I must find Sakeema!" I repeated more fiercely, "or the whole world seems likely to slide down to ruin. But Istas has died, and Kor had to stay at Seal Hold. . . . Birc, you know I could not have left him for anything less."

He was still looking at me, quizzical. I tried again.

"Kor was well enough when I left him. As long as there are mussels on the rocks and fish in the sea, he and the Seal Kindred will not starve. But I know he will soon be hard beset." I felt my shoulders sag. "The Fanged Horse Folk are in ugly humor, and they threaten. So does the Otter River Clan. If only I can find the god quickly and go back to him. . . ."

Something moved white in the night. The fair white hind, Birc's mate, walked up to him on dainty cloven hooves, nuzzled his ear, and changed with the touch into her human form, the fine fur of her body creamy pale, her glorious mane of hair the color of a red deer in sunset. She gazed at me with herb-purple eyes. I had once been afraid of her, for men turned mute and grew antlers for love of her. But whether from desperation or folly, I feared her no longer.

"Can you help me find Sakeema?" I asked her, the first

time I had spoken directly to her. "Can you guide me to his cave?"

She and Birc looked at each other, then tried to tell me with gestures something that I could not understand. They were anxious, they made small bleating noises such as deer do. I asked again to be taken to the cave, and again they looked at each other, conferring, and this time they nodded me a grave-faced agreement.

With the dawn they set out to take me there—the wolf was nowhere to be seen, for it was a courteous creature and knew that these strange deer-humans could not abide it, nor were they to be hunted. And they were all in deer form, my friend and his eerie bride and all their retinue. Birc made a magnificent hart, his dark eyes flashing, kingly even though his antlers were only in their first springtime growth. The white hind and her maidens leaped and darted, all aquiver, taking every step airily, and Talu plodded sourly along the ways they led us. It was a hard, two days' journey over rough, craggy mountainside, and my winsome mount took every step of it with her ears flattened back in ill humor. Perhaps the beauty of the deer annoyed her.

The pathless way led southward and westward, into a fold of some nameless mountain's flank, a fold that led on and inward, bend upon bend and crag after crag, until I was well out of any demesne I had ever explored, in unknown land somewhere near the headwaters of the Otter River. The second day we climbed a dry gorge so steep and rough that I had to leave Talu and go afoot, though the deer folk leaped up nimbly enough. And I was glad that I had been eating their foul seedcakes all the way, for I would never have found strength to manage it otherwise. Sometimes when the sunset had turned sky and snowpeaks blood red, when I was streaming sweat despite the chill air crawling down from the icefields, I looked up and saw what made me forget any weariness, any hunger except the hunger for Sakeema.

The crevice, pointing skyward. The very cave I had seen more than once in a dream.

Birc and the damsels, still in deer form, awaited me near the threshold as I came panting up. They looked at me with eyes that seemed ready to weep—but then, the great dark eyes of deer seemed always like pools of deep water, or jewels made of tears. I walked past them and stood at the entry, quieting my breathing, trying to center myself, trying to calm my heart's wild clamoring, Sakeema, Sakeema, Sakeema. . . . Be still, the god had said to me once in a vision, and if you feel even so much as the flying of a midge in the night, I am yet with you. I stood until I found the stillness of Sakeema, the quiet made of leaf rustle and insect voice and breath of—

Breath of my god. Someone breathing, inside the cave.

Awed, trembling, with slow steps I entered.

I could see—shape, shadow, in the dim indeeps of that place a man's form. Not asleep, but erect, silent, awaiting me. I stood shaking and gawking like a dolt. I could not—I could not see his face. Sakeema, my god, if only I could see your face, I would remember, I would know you. . . .

He moved a step toward me, into the dying light from the doorway, and raised his spear in his hand, and grinned.

My demon-possessed brother Ytan.

"Scum of Mahela!" I roared at him, and he laughed aloud.

He expected surprise and fear to freeze me a moment so that he could gloat—for Ytan must gloat, always, or he could featly have killed me from the shadows. He deemed he would kill me now, within a breathspan. His strong hand drew back the spear—

I had been so much in hope that the sight of him drove me wild. I had not even sense enough to be afraid. I bellowed, and Alar leaped to my hand, and I charged him, slashing with the sword. He let fly his spear at the moment I moved—its blackstone head parted my loose hair, then chimed against the wall. Facing me good as weaponless—for no stone knife can withstand Alar—Ytan hissed in breath between his grinning teeth and ducked away from in front of me, dodging back into the shadows.

"Where is Sakeema?" I bawled out, my voice echoing around my ears in that closed space, so that I sounded like a hundred wounded bison. Nor did I give Ytan time to answer, but charged him as if he might somehow be hiding the god behind his back. I attacked him furiously with the sword. If I had not been too distraught for any proper skill, I am sure I would have killed him without a second thought. But I swung as if hewing trees, and never struck him. He slipped under my crazed blows and darted out the entry. I blundered around the walls of the cave, snatching at the shreds of my hope, thinking vaguely, frantically, that there might be some passageway, some recess, some cranny where the god had lodged like a windblown seed. There was none. The place was small, and quite empty. If ever Sakeema had been there, he was gone.

I plunged outside. The deer people were gone, had scattered, and in a heartbeat I saw why. Ytan stood on a low crag, near at hand but out of reach of my sword, and though his spear still lay in the cave, he had found—

I dove, and heard the faint whirr as an arrow skimmed over my back, the *thwock* as it lodged in the resinous trunk of a yellow pine. I snatched a glimpse of it teetering there, a crude shaft, poorly fletched, as I landed on the ground, rolled, and scrambled for shelter. Even as I came to my knees behind the pine another arrow thudded into it, and I heard Ytan laughing again.

"Where is Sakeema?" I bellowed at him. The more fool, I. As if Ytan would tell me, even if he could.

"Whose face did you see, Dannoc, when you stood shaking and found me?" he replied, and then he shouted with laughter, yell after yell of mocking, moon-mad laughter. He stood on his crag nearly helpless with laughter. I set my teeth, slipped my own bow off my shoulder, made shift to ready it without standing up.

"Who has knocked your nose askew, my brother?" Ytan cried crazily.

There on his vantage he stood, with the mighty peaks looming behind him, shining in sundown light—seemingly as tall and goodly as the mountains he stood in deerskin leggings and bisonhide boots, bare-chested and mighty-shouldered, his drygrass-yellow braids hanging long, as befits a Red Hart warrior. And a Red Hart's strong, beardless, fair-browed face. . . . But for the braids, Kor had once told me, I looked enough like Ytan to be his twin. And all the more so, Ytan seemed to be saying, now that my broken nose had skewed my face, making me resemble the bent-from-true, leftward thing he was.

"Tell me who has hurt you! I will avenge you, brother mine."

"Mahela take you," I muttered, setting arrow to my bowstring.

"It was Korridun, was it not? Why are you not with your beloved Kor?" He needs must taunt me by those I loved. . . . "And where is that dark-browed warrior maiden? The haughty rider on the pied black gelding? Castrated it herself, she did. How proud of her you must be. What is it you call her? Tassida My Love?"

I felt my throat close with a spasm, more in heartache

than in rage any longer. How had he come to know so much? The devourer in him, it had taken his cleverness and turned it dark, evil.

I had let a devourer out of my father's body with my sword. Mind had often told me to do the same unkind favor for Ytan. But first, I had to get near him.

I had nocked an arrow to my bowstring. Rising, I took aim. "This is meant for a feather in your hair, Ytan," I shouted as I let fly, for I wanted him to know that my aim was true.

He jumped aside, but the arrow was far more swift. It stopped his laughter, piercing the braid by his ear, as I had intended it to do. With an angry yell he broke it and pulled it out, and I stepped forward, another shaft at the ready.

"You should have kept that, Ytan," I mocked. His arrows were crude things, likely to fly astray, for he had never been much of a craftsman, Ytan. His bow, I saw, was made of bent ashwood, less powerful than my sinew-and-hartshorn one. He was not unskilled as an archer, and I knew it, but I had the better weapons.

He knew it too, and let fly with words instead of bolts. "Has Tassida left you, Dan? The rotbottom wench, how could she? Yet I thought I saw her galloping off like a hellkite, one night in a storm."

The piss-proud cock, spying on me. . . . My jaw hardened, and I eased closer to him. Seeing me coming, he grinned anew.

"I have a plan, Dannoc," he told me in a friendly way. "I know what I am going to do. I am going to find her before you do, that proud Tassida. And I am going to lie with her. If I let my hair hang loose, and come to her in the dusk and whisper her name, she will think my name is Dan."

My fingers jumped on the bowstring. He saw it and barked aloud with laughter.

"Go ahead, kill me! Why are you waiting? I will kill you as soon as I can. Then your doughty Tassida will be mine for as long as I choose to keep her."

"By Sakeema's blood," I told him between clenched teeth, "I would like to kill you."

"But, dolt that you are, you will not." Smiling, he raised his bow. "I will kill you and go to Tassida. When I abandon her, she will say it was Dannoc who brought her low."

I stood close enough to him to see his eyes, blue as highmountain sky over eversnow, to clearly see his face, very comely, straight brows and a strong chin, and only his leer showing how shadowed was his soul. . . . And I knew I had been badly mistaken to count on the might of my weapons to cow him, for mine was an empty threat. I could not kill him, and he knew it. I had loved him too much, the good days gone by. . . . My hands shook so badly that I could not let fly even to maim him. I stood in the clear, nothing nearby to dodge behind. Like the dolt he said I was, like a deer drawn to the deer of straw, I had put myself in deadly peril.

I saw his blue eyes, so much like mine, like our father's, saw them glint and narrow to slits as he pulled back his bowstring—

A growl fit to chill the blood, a graysheen blur, and from the laurel thicket that flanked the crag the wolf leaped, a flash, teeth shining. Fangs struck. Jaws fit to fell an elk closed on Ytan's right arm, and the wolf snarled into his flesh, tearing at him. The force of the attack nearly knocked him off his feet, wolf's weight pulling him downward, but Ytan was strong. He yelled with fury, flung up his arm—it took the wolf wholly off the ground, but still the creature hung on, eyes blazing, Ytan's blood splattering its fur. Ytan struck with bow and booted foot to no avail. Then he dropped the bow and fumbled for the stone knife at his belt, left-handed. He found it—

My own leap had carried me up the crag, and before he could strike I toppled him, laid him prone on the rock, kicked the knife away and held the point of my sword at his throat. The wolf loosed its grip, shook itself, ran its pink tongue around its muzzle, then began hungrily to lap at Ytan's blood. He cursed it and glared at me, but I would not let him move until the wolf had supped its fill. My brother knew I would not kill him, but by Sakeema he could see it in my eyes that I had in my heart to hurt him exceedingly if he vexed me. . . . When the wolf turned away, I stepped back, taking care to tread on Ytan's wooden bow and break it.

"No need, Dannoc." He spoke with nothing in his hard blue stare but hatred, poison of Mahela. "I will no longer try to kill you. There are ways to hurt you worse. When I find the woman I will slit her nostrils with my knife, and notch her ears to match yours, and slash her breasts. All this before I have had my way with her. Then—"

My sword moved in my hand, and for a moment he must have seen something in me that truly frightened him, for with a sharp intake of breath he stopped speaking.

"No such bold boasts, Ytan," I told him. "It is true, I am loath to slay you, for I remember the days when we tamed the curly-haired ponies together and scouted the deer. But I might not be so slow to cut off a hand or two, if you menace. Or lop off other parts of you and feed them to my friend here."

The wolf panted in wordless approval. But Ytan grinned as toothily as the wolf, for already my bloodthirst had left me, and he could see that. It is a terrible thing to have a brother for an enemy. Always Ytan had been sour and clearseeing. He knew me all too well.

"When you threaten, you do not act," he remarked. "I will threaten no more, as it displeases you, my brother, but quite surely I will act if I find bold Tassida before you do. So prepare to grieve." He lithely got up and started to walk away, not even cradling his bitten arm—he let it hang and bleed. But at the forest's verge he paused. "Give my greeting to Sakeema," he mocked.

"Sakeema help you," I whispered, so softly that perhaps Ytan did not hear me. "Sakeema help us all."

" 'Ware Cragsmen farther down," Ytan added with poisoned calm. Then he left me, gone in the dusk.

Numbly I made my way back down the hard, cutting rocks of the ravine, the light rapidly failing me. Talu was waiting for me where I had left her, and she greeted me with a scornful huffing and a rolling of her eyes, as if to say, Fool.

"Hold your tongue," I grumbled at her. "Bighead."

We traveled until nightfall and past. I wanted to put distance between myself and Ytan. But riding under the thin light of a scantling moon, sending Talu stumbling through the shadows for no better reason than to get away from him, I seemed still to hear Ytan's laughter.

# Chapter Three

''Now truly I do not know what to do,'' I said to the wolf lying not far from my feet.

When we stopped at last I sat in the night like an oaf, without a fire, gnawing at the last of the seedcakes the deer people had given me. Head flattened to the ground, my companion the wolf looked back at me without moving, and I frowned in sympathy.

''You are hungry? I am sorry you do not eat seedcakes, wild brother. There has been bad hunting for you, has there not? Even the lemmings are scarce, and the mice and the voles. No pika in the rocks. We must find Sakeema. . . . But what if my heartless lout of a brother comes to Tassida meanwhile?''

Perhaps he was somewhere in the darkness near at hand, listening and taking pleasure in my unease. I had tried to leave him far behind, but it was possible that he had followed. And there I sat, speaking to a wolf as if it could help me more than already it had, and it gave no reply but to raise its head and yawn, showing bone-white teeth and a pink expanse of gullet and tongue, shadowy in the moonlight. Suddenly I felt how very much alone I was. The night hung dark, and talking to this indifferent creature made a poor substitute for talking with Kor.

Powers help me, every time I thought of my bond brother I felt as if half of me had been torn away. And if Ytan was to be believed, the other mortal whom I chiefly loved was in danger as well. A long-limbed, knife-twirling, wild-haired, bold-riding, mettlesome mystery of a warrior woman named Tassida.

"Blast," I whispered between clenched teeth. The wolf looked at me blankly.

"I feel as if I am torn in three parts, Kor and Tass and Sakeema. But I have forsaken Kor, and I am going to have to forsake Tass, too, until this quest is done. . . . The world, wolf, the whole ill-wished world is dwindling down to ruin! I cannot be thinking of one comely woman overmuch."

Not even when she was threatened with that most dishonorable of torments, the abomination called rape.

"Tassida is well able to take care of herself," I muttered.

The wolf grinned hugely.

"More able than I, perhaps, to deal with Ytan. She will take her sword to him, while I cannot. I must find Sakeema."

Far away an owl cried softly, darkly, perhaps bewailing its own hunger. My hunger was not of the body.

"I cannot go to Tass, any more than I can go back to Kor. I must find . . . our savior. Why does it feel so wrong?"

The wolf yawned again, laid down its head and went to sleep. A sensible creature. I did likewise.

It seemed a small while that I slept. Then sense of something wrong jarred me awake, and I could not tell whether it was moonset or sunrise or the end of the world, for a cold, crushing weight lay atop me, shutting off light and air.

A devourer had me in its grim embrace.

*Ai!* I fought to throw it off. Hard, seawater-chill breasts against my face, thick serpentine tail binding my legs, fish-gray folds holding the rest of me, I knew them all too well, and I knew struggling was of no use, and yet I struggled. I kicked, I strained against the weight of the boneless flesh that pinned me to the ground, my chest tightened, I could not breathe . . . I had to calm myself. My fear, my despair only let the creature's spearhead teeth bite deeper into my gut.

The very fitting emblems of Mahela's mindless greed, the devourers were. They had no heads, their maws were in their bellies, and like hers their whole will was to take, grasp, possess. The creatures of small self-will, the doves, the deer, the children, they took at a single gulp. Kings and warriors they found harder to bear away to Mahela, but they had the persistence of madwomen. Even the most valiant of warriors they could overpower in the course of a single long night. Seldom they found a king, such as Korridun, with the strength to defy them. Then they turned to an abomination worse than rape. The brutes could change shape by shooting out cold seawater, flattening their dugs, furling themselves into a sort of huge phallus. With serpent tail thrashing in air they could pin a strong victim to the ground and bore like a leech until they found their way within, where they took hold of heart and soul. Ytan was such a victim, unsouled because of his own strength, with only his body left to him, his own body and a keen mind to do evil.

I could not let that happen to me. I had vowed to Kor once that I would kill myself first—but then who would quest for the god?

By an effort of will I steadied myself, made my frantic body lie still. The cold, slimy breasts, large and hard as the melons the Herders grew, pressed against my face—no matter. If I stopped struggling and breathed shallowly and slowly, I could yet breathe. The capelike wings of the thing pinning my arms to my sides so that I could not reach my sword. No matter. When I centered myself there would be no need of the sword. The eely tail tightening around my legs, the maw sucking at my belly, strong as sea tide, working to take me in—none of it mattered, for the monster could not have me. I was bullheaded, my tribefellows had always said. I would be stubborn in defiance, more stubborn than any minion of Mahela, once well centered in self.

I was—a Red Hart? But no, not entirely, not since I had gone away. I did not braid my hair, I had eaten fish with the Seal Kindred, I had changed shape into a seal and traveled the greendeep to Mahela's realm. I wore woolens like the Herders, or furs, or whatever came to hand. Sometimes I even slept in a shirt. I was no longer at one with my tribe, and my thoughts were no longer their thoughts.

I was—a hunter? But hunters killed the creatures of Sakeema. Did I wish to kill the creatures of Sakeema any longer? Unsure, I let my thoughts speed on. I was—a warrior? But I had left my bond brother to face war alone. No proper warrior, I. A storyteller, yes—but I could sense no ending but doom to my tale. I was—was—

I could not remember my name. Chill of fear crept up my backbone.

Distantly I sensed the flow of my own warm blood. The teeth had pierced, perhaps to my innards. Sakeema, I silently begged, help me. Help the dolt who cannot remember his own name. Sakeema, please! Confound the god, no face to him, no place, no tribe, where was he?

Sakeema.

I was—one who yearned for the god. I was—seeker. I was—Darran?

The name felt strange. I thought it uncertainly. But as I held it in my mind, not sure whether to keep it or send it away, I felt the devourer falter in its worrying at me, I felt the grip of its wings weaken. My right hand shot out, reaching for Alar, the sword lying beside me in the grass.

The devourer knew what swords were for. It lifted off me in haste, and though a moment before I had been desperate, I was now full of gleeful daring, and my left hand darted upward, grasping the flange of one strong, rippling wing. The creature pulled me upright in its surge to get away. "Yah! Wait a moment, my beauty!" I implored it as Alar flashed in air, blazing, eager. "My mare likes fish, perhaps she would care to eat you!"

Alar slashed deep. But the monster gave me a buffet with its other wing and tore away from my grasp, and I do not know how badly I wounded it, for I was staring like a fool at—a second one, another devourer, only a stride away from me, just lifting off—off my comrade, the wolf!

Both devourers sped away in the night, and I did not see them go. I was gawking at the wolf. "Are you all right!" I exclaimed at it, though I scarcely thought it possible.

But the wolf got to its feet without so much as a stagger,

and sneezed strongly and rubbed its muzzle in the grass and rolled, trying to clean the slime from its fur. And I stood thinking of Korridun, of the time he had slept beside me in the night and a devourer had lain on him and one on me, and we had handbonded to help each other. And I had been nearly killed, but Korridun had gotten up without a mark on him.

I stood with blood trickling down from the welts on my belly and said to the wolf, my voice shaking, "By my body, wild brother, you must have the soul of a strong warrior! Is that how you have survived all these years? By having the will of a human and a king?"

The wolf stopped rubbing its graysheen fur against the grass and froze in a crouch, looking at me very much as if it had understood me. I saw a moon-white glint in its eyes and stepped back, half afraid that it would attack me. But the next moment it flashed away, gone in the night.

"Wild brother! Wait! Come back!" I called after it, knowing it would not. For the wolf in no sense belonged to me, not even so much as the horse did. Wild-fanged mare though she was, Talu balkily came to my call and obeyed me with ill grace when I rode her. But the wolf traveled with me or not, aided me or not, just as it chose. Nor had I ever presumed to give a name to it.

I sighed and sat down in the dark and thought about the wolf, wondering why it had looked so enraged and afraid, why it had left me so abruptly, how it had withstood the devourer. Then, as I rubbed the feel of the devourer from my face and smelled its stench still on my hands, my thoughts turned to the other, even more eerie and urgent matter: that of my name. I remembered it well enough now that the pressing need had passed: it was Dannoc. But that other name, Darran . . . it had helped me. It must in some wise be true. . . .

I put it into the part of my mind where I kept the things I wondered about—many things, and none of them were going to find me my way any sooner to the god. Or so I thought. I leaned back against the scab-barked trunk of a yellow pine and tried at least to rest, though I knew I would sleep no more that night.

At dawn I got up stiffly and looked around me for the wolf, and called for it once more, and waited a while, then turned to Talu and began readying her for travel. As I worked I talked to her for want of the wolf.

"Ytan has done us a left-handed favor, telling us of Cragsmen to be found on these lower slopes," I said to her, for sometime during the tumult of the night it had come clear to me what I must next do and where I must go. "I must seek them to parley with them."

She swung her fanged head and sourly looked at me as if to say, Fool, Most Reckless and Wrongheaded of Fools. Parleying with Cragsmen was not an undertaking for a prudent mortal. But my way seemed quite clear to me. I was no longer a Red Hart, so why had I thought Sakeema must lie in the cave of which Red Hart legend told? There were other tribes, other legends. Some I knew. The Herders said that the god had been reared by red wolves in a blackstone cave in the skirts of the thunder cones, and the wolves his foster brothers had come to take him back to that birthplace after his death. The Seal said Sakeema had gone out to sea in a gray coracle. If it were so I would never find him, but the Otter River Clan surely had such a saying also, and the Fanged Horse Folk, and—even the uncouth Cragsmen.

I would take a path toward the thunder cones and the Herders. More than likely Cragsmen would bar my way. To be true to my quest, I had to hope so. If a feeling so mixed with fear can be called hope.

"Keep your thoughts to yourself," I said in retort to Talu's sour look, and I mounted her and rode.

For a day I rode with nothing to eat but wild onion and cresses. The pathless way was rough, and often I went afoot, letting Talu trail after me through jumbled boulders and under the low boughs of aspen and spearpine. And more than once I cursed and doubted my own wisdom in coming this way. I saved many miles by attempting the wild slopes rather than backtracking to the Blackstone Path, but the maddening tangle of rocks and steep drops, trees and fallen trunks and crags looming overhead slowed me so that I cursed my own beloved mountains by all the dark attributes of Mahela.

It was just such a place the next day, as I led Talu between towering stones, that the Cragsmen surprised me.

I heard a sound as of rocks splitting and sliding down a mountainpeak in a rumble of snow—but I had made my way far below the snowpeaks. It was the sound of their laughter. And feeling fear crawl through my back and ribs and take hiding in my chest, I looked up and saw them.

Nearly a twelve of them, though any one of them would have been enough to give me pause, for Cragsmen are half again as tall as a man, even a tall man such as I, and hard as the crags, all the stone colors of skin, and stony of heart. Standing spraddle-legged atop the outcroppings all around me, they seemed huge, they loomed, their grinning mouths like ice-fanged caves in their boulder heads. What did Cragsmen eat, I wondered, that their hulking bodies seemed so hale when I felt so weak from hunger? They seemed scarcely human. Perhaps they feasted on the very peaks themselves.

I felt Alar stirring in her scabbard with her eagerness to taste their strange brownsheen blood, but I did not move my hand to meet her pommel. I felt no such eagerness to fight them.

"World brothers," I hailed them, "well met."

The one who seemed to be their leader, a slate-blue fellow with chest and head greenfurred as if by moss, ceased roaring with laughter and instead roared even more loudly with rage.

"You," he bellowed, "who have sent my comrades to Mahela, you dare to call me brother?"

Though truly, I had seen no Cragsmen in Mahela's undersea realm. The louts, they must not have been among her choice of pretty things to enslave.

"It was you who attacked," I reminded him mildly. It is wise to speak softly to Cragsmen and keep them talking as long as possible. "Men of the mountains, what know you of Sakeema?"

At once they all began again to laugh, a deafening sound. I had never been more glad to be thought a fool. Cragsmen became less dangerous when they were amused. Talu's reins in hand, I began to edge forward in the narrow space between rocks where I was trapped.

The blue Cragsman roared, and with a single swipe of his blackwood cudgel he toppled the several spearpines that stood between him and me. He spun the cudgel over my head. He could as handily have lifted me and spun me by the feet, for the club and I were of nearly the same size. "Be still!" he commanded, though there was no need—I was fairly cowering amid the boulders, like a pika cowering in the scree.

"But I must find Sakeema before it is too late," I said earnestly, trying to amuse them again. "Before Mahela swallows it all. Are there any wild sheep left on the peaks?"

"You cannot go through here," the leader growled.

"What do we care, meat-eater?" taunted another at the same time. "It is nothing to us that the sheep are gone like the wild antelope of the peaks."

"Yes," I said softly, "but surely you feel heart's hunger even to think of the white antelope of the peaks." They stared at me with faint frowns as their slow wits tried to comprehend what I was saying, and in a sort of trance created by my own words I turned and got quietly onto Talu, even though the horse could scarcely move in the strait place where I had led her. I mounted her just so that I would be able to gaze off toward the snowpeaks. "Where is Sakeema?" I asked again. "I must find him while the mountains still stand for you to tread upon."

A babble went up of a sort I was not expecting. "He is not here!" blurted a huge granite-gray Cragsman who loomed to my left.

"He's gone!" agreed another.

"The place is empty except for—"

"Silence!" thundered the slate-blue leader, furious, his shout echoing away in the quiet that at once followed. He turned on me and pointed his cudgel at my head, enraged but uncertain, shifting his great weight from foot to massive foot in annoyance or unease. "Who are you," he demanded, "that we should bandy words with you?"

It was time to show mettle. "Who is my brother Ytan," I retorted, "that you should obey him? Is it not he who sent you here to waylay me?"

"No!" bawled the granite-gray Cragsman. "We always guard this place!"

The blue one swung toward him in menace—I saw a rivalry there. "Be silent!" he bellowed at the other Cragsman, and to me he said fiercely, "Who are you?"

I had told them Ytan was my brother, so they had to know I was a son of Tyonoc. They had seen me and fought against me before. Why, then, did they ask who I was? And what was I to tell them? That my name was Dannoc, or Darran, whatever? Blast and confound them, what would be the use of telling them either?

I did not know how to answer, not with the mighty blackwood club nearly grazing my face and wonder spinning along with the fear in my mind. A guarded place, just beyond them? Of what sort? What did they mean, saying Sakeema was gone from that place? Some sign of him there, perhaps? "Sakeema," I breathed aloud in wonder or in plea, and to my astonishment the Cragsmen stepped a pace back from me. Even their slate-blue leader stepped back, and his club wavered. On the Cragsmen's hard faces came a look of doubt and awe.

"No!" I exclaimed. They thought I was taking the name of Sakeema—how could that be? Why did they not laugh? It was laughable, or it was blasphemy, and even for the sake of saving my skin I could not let it happen. "No, I mean—people of the peaks, what are the tales you tell of the coming of Sakeema?" I was pleading, eager. "Where do you say is his resting place?"

Roars of anger answered me. Anger, glaring in their faces along with a plain disappointment. They surged toward me. "Bah! Kill him," the granite-colored one shouted. Clubs swung up.

But the blue leader, who stood nearest me, turned on them furiously. "We kill him when I say!" he thundered.

"When you say! We'll be here all day, waiting till you say!"

They quarreled and tussled, taking sides, their roars and rumblings echoing off the mountainpeaks, their blows and shovings shaking the rocks—I heard the name of Sakeema shouted in tones fit to make the mountains shudder. The rivals were bludgeoning each other, some of the other

Cragsmen doing the same and the rest of them clustering around like so many gawking stones, gray, greenish, tan, rimrock red. Few of them fixed their hard eyes on me any longer. When their uproar had reached a hopeful height I sent Talu quietly forward—

A club came smashing down across my path, the slate-blue leader's glare met me, and within an eyeblink the commotion, which I had considered to be at its height, redoubled. By my mother's bones, but it must have been a precious thing they guarded! I had not thought they could come out of their quarrel so quickly to turn on me. One more breath and I would be dead—I could feel rage hot as blood in the air. But Talu, as terrified as I, reared high. Teetering on her hind legs, she somehow managed to turn in the narrow space between rocks, and at a plunging, panicky gallop she took me back the way we had come.

I was in nearly as much danger from her as I had been from the Cragsmen. I could not have stopped her if I had tried—and, mindful of wrathful enemies not far behind me, I did not try—but Talu's every wild leap threatened to throw me against a boulder, or smash my knee against one, or my head against a tree, or send us both crashing down when she snapped a leg between stones. Her hooves slipped and scrabbled on dizzying slopes—this was terrain that scarcely should have been ridden at a slow walk! I held onto her by clinging to her mane until she took a man-tall drop at a leap, but then I considered that I had had enough. Moreover, there was a thought in me that I did not wish to be carried too far from the place the Cragsmen so fervidly guarded. So I swung down by her neck and took my chances with a landing on hard rock. Then I lay, the breath knocked out of me, and watched her plunge crazily away, and took accounting of my bodily harm. Bruises, nothing worse.

Behind me, out of sight but not yet out of tongueshot, I heard the noise of the Cragsmen, who were quarreling still. I lay where I was until their uproar had quieted, that and my ragged breathing and the thumping of my heart. Talu had careered out of sight and hearing. I rose cautiously and walked away from the direction she had gone, back toward the Cragsmen but to one side of them.

It was not hard for a Red Hart hunter on foot to elude Cragsmen. I stalked softly past them, and they knew nothing of it. I dare say they thought I was yet on Talu, blundering back up the mountain. Few travelers are foolish enough to let themselves be separated from horse and gear. But being a fool, and afoot, I found the many boulders more to my liking than I had when they threatened to break my neck. They gave me good cover as I stalked, and though the Cragsmen ceased their scuffling and moved back to lines of guard once again, I eluded them easily enough. I crept between rocks until I had left them behind, and then I softly walked, looking, searching. Even though I did not know for what.

But there was no doubt in me once I saw it.

Boulders ended suddenly, spearpines thinned, sky showed. Underfoot lay a smooth, flat place made of many small stones—I noted that later, for at the time my seeing was all taken up by the crag. An odd sort of tall, jagged crag, very steep, very aspiring, loomed ahead. And in its side opened a most peculiar cave. As I drew nearer, step by slow, cautious step, I noticed that the rock wall around the entry was all networked with small lines, like cracks—they were cracks. With a shock I realized that the crag was no crag, nor the cave a cave.

Name of the god, it was a place made by the long-ago kings whose powers I scarcely understood, a place left from time lost in time.

# Chapter Four

Times so long ago, they had been forgotten even in Sakee-ma's time. Their kings and peoples, unknown even in leg-end. Even I, a storyteller, had never known of such times and such people until Tassida had told me of them. How she remembered them, I did not know, for there was much I did not know of her. But I had since seen such lodges, though much smaller, standing in Mahela's sad undersea realm.

A strange word Tassida had once told to me: *castle*. This, then, a castle? Awesome, even though silent, empty, ruined.

Gazing, scarcely breathing, I stepped within the shadow of the entry. The place, as I thought, was hollow, like a great hut. It was indeed a dwelling—though the men of those times must have been giants, I thought, to need such a lofty dwelling. Their powers that had raised this great dwelling made of the very bone of the mountain, that had cut the stones and featly fitted them together, had been lost in the many passing seasons. I could feel the weight of deep time, standing in that place. Dim light filtered down through cracks and through the distant top of a tall place, where there had once been, I supposed, a roof.

There were bones strewn about. Something had denned in there since the long-ago people had gone. An animal nearly as lost in time, perhaps a catamount? More likely many sorts of animals. Likely the small squirrels had nested between the rocks of the walls. They were all gone, the creatures, leaving only the ghost, that lived in my mind, as starkly gone as the people who had once lived in this place.

Not much trace of them, the people. Thrones and harps of wood, hangings of cloth had long since rotted into dirt, if such things had been left. I stared around, looking for something, I was not sure what. Surely something lay in this place if the Cragsmen so guarded it, so reverenced it as to leave none of their own clumsy marks there. Something had to be yet left to us of these strange, long-dead people who had sailed on the sea in great ships and built such huge lodges that they could keep fruit trees within them over the winter. People who had painted a strange magic on thin-stretched sheepskins, a potent magic they put in hinged boxes called *books*. . . . It was such magic I wanted of them, though sheepskins also would have long since rotted away. These folk had been mighty in power and knowledge. Had there been any seers among them, I wondered, any dreamwits, any visionaries? I needed a sign such as no shaman could give me.

"Where is Sakeema?" I whispered aloud to the inside of the silent dwelling of the dead.

The yellow stone in the pommel of my sword began softly to glow. Alar was alert, nearly as alive as I.

Swordlight fell on a stone fallen from the archway of the door, and I saw—no, it was nothing. Only a carving in the stone, an ornament, a trefoil. . . . Alar's light shone on bare walls, a raised platform of stone, debris, nothing more. But I felt a tremor in her, an urgency, perhaps a longing to match my own. As old as this place was, she might be as old, she, the sword. Perhaps she would show some sign to me.

Drifting, as silent as a leaf on the wind, and trying to be as yielding, as random, I wandered that dim place. There were stone steps to climb, but I felt no urging that way. I turned back toward the center of the great room, where the knee-deep pile of bones and branches lay under the open roof, and I circled it and turned back toward it again, and a third time I found myself facing it. Then I began to think.

Even Cragsmen, if they reverenced a place, would they not have cleaned it of leaf litter and bones and things that stank? Unless, perhaps, they wished to hide something under them.

"All right, Alar," I murmured, and I strode into the rubbish heap.

Dead things in there, and stench, and a squishy feeling as of wet leaves underfoot. Perhaps something worse. No sane person would have gone into that muck of his own will. "Slime of Mahela!" I protested, and nearly turned to go back. But then I recalled that I was no sane person, but a madman, Mahela's buffoon, and certainly I had not been daintily reared. Standing in the very center of the foul heap, I felt a waiting stillness in the sword, and blithely I dropped to all fours, my hands wrist-deep in filth, and began to scrabble like a badger, sending dirt and branches, bones and scats and bits of dead mouse flying. But I dug to what felt like hard, flat stone, and found nothing.

"What now?" I sourly addressed the sword. "Have you a cuckpot for me to play in, perhaps?"

Alar's jewel flared more brightly, and I saw.

Sunstuff.

Right under me, lying beneath my hands, a glint of that strange, bright, uncommonly beautiful stuff that Tassida called gold, which I had never seen except in Mahela's dwelling beneath far too much green seawater.

Not only the one small glint of it, I discovered as I rooted and scraped and shoved offal to one side. It was a large panel, perhaps as long as my arm and a little less wide than it was long, wrought into some pattern I could not yet see. Once it had been placed on the wall behind the throne, perhaps, or perhaps it had been part of the throne itself. I pulled it gently from its mucky bed and traced the bright curves with my filthy finger, gouging away the dirt.

Trefoil pattern in the corners, the same as I had just seen carved on a stone. But also, in the center of the panel, something more.

There was little enough cloth on me anywhere. I wiped my hands on my deerskin leggings, then worked at the panel again with my fingers, my fingernails, my spittle. Dirt was maddeningly slow to yield, and all I could see beneath it were bright bits of sunstuff in which I could not sense a wholeness. Sitting in some god's midden, cuckpot of sky, I had to scrub and clean my prize with my skin and my hair before I could comprehend. And then I understood nothing.

The middle of the panel bore the emblem of a tree, not a forest tree but some sort of round, tame tree covered with trefoil blossoms. And a long-necked bird of some sort was flying away from the tree, carrying a fruit in its beak. But the fruit was falling into three fragments that scattered to the mountains, the plains, and the sea.

I scarcely looked at the bird, the fruit. My gaze was caught on the tree, for the trunk and some branches of it were made up of three swords crossed in the shape of a six-pointed star, swords just such as Korridun and Tassida and I wore.

But it was overweening, I told myself, to believe that this emblem showed the very same swords. Many such swords must have been made in those forgotten days. Still, I touched the sunstuff swords curiously, tracing their shapes with my fingers. And as I did so, Alar blazed so brightly that I could scarcely see for the sword glory and the glory of the strange substance in my hands.

I looked long at the panel by Alar's warm glow, so long that I could close my eyes and yet see it, shadowed. But nowhere in it could I see Sakeema or a place where I might find him.

Finally, when I began to feel stiff with sitting amid a pile of old bones, I got up, awkwardly hefting the heavy thing I had found. "What am I to do with this?" I muttered. It was too large to take with me, even on horseback, should I ever be so fortunate as to find my horse again. Moreover, I did not want a twelve of Cragsmen pursuing me. And I had a feeling about the sunstuff panel, that people would think it beautiful, that some people would deem it a thing not merely to look at with pleasure but to have, to win, the way the Fanged Horse Folk win slaves and trophies of battle. I did not much like that way of having things, and in the end I put the sunstuff back where I had found it. I carefully covered it up again, making the stinking heap look almost as if it had never been disturbed. And when I had done so, Alar's light faded and went out.

The place seemed very dim after that. But I remembered where I had seen steps to climb, along the inside of the wall, steps in the stone. I felt my way to them and clambered up. There were lofts and ledges and the remnants of rooms above. There were yet more steps to a higher, lighter place where a lookout might once have stood, or where a king had perhaps stood to overlook his demesne. I stood there and looked, blinking into bright sunlight.

Far, I could see far, nearly as far as the hunter of my name vision. Behind me and above me, the vast snowpeaks. Far to one side, northward, the blue sweep of the tallgrass prairie, a goodly land where few folk went because north of it again lay the bleak steppes where the warring Fanged Horse Folk roamed. Straight in front of me, but far to the eastward, no more than obsidian glints in the sunlight, the thunder cones. On their flanks somewhere might be a blackstone cave where red wolves had once denned. . . . Somewhat nearer, spread out like the rich mantle of some long-ago king, my homeland, the Red Hart Demesne. I studied its treegreen folds as if one of them might hide the god. I scanned the hills to southward where the Otter River began. Nowhere, no matter how far I looked, could I see anything that might lead me to Sakeema.

But for one thing, much closer at hand. Nearly straight below my feet, a deep mountain tarn, glinting like an eye of earth.

And I felt suddenly glad, eager, and pensive, all at once, for I knew the place where I was. Below me winked the pool of vision, the uncanny tarn where Kor and I had found our swords and formed our bond of blood brotherhood. He had looked up, and seen the strange pinnacles and spires on the mountainside above us, and he had said, "Men made that."

I left the platform where princes out of the past had once

stood. I walked down the stone steps, through the dim great hall and out the gaping entry feeling lightheaded, not so much from lack of food as because I had walked out of legend.

And at the entry I found Talu standing tied by her reins to a young spearpine, as if I were the king of the place and someone had brought her and left her there to wait for me.

Like a colt I shied, and I leaped away like a startled deer into the shelter of the nearest thicket. Who had brought Talu back to me? Who could it have been but some enemy? For a friend would have found me and spoken to me.

Cragsmen? But it was not like them to be so clever. Had they known where I was, they would have come bellowing in and smashed my head into the stones of the floor. At their very wittiest they would have laughed while I stared at my horse, then flattened me. But if not Cragsmen, then who? Ytan? I would have heard his laugh half a heartbeat before my heart stopped forever, pierced by his arrow.

Moving with a hunter's silent skill, and with sweat of fear trickling down my all-too-naked ribs, I scouted around the great stone lodge in every direction upmountain—for downmountain of that place lay sheer slopes and the barren country around the tarn, and no one could have gone that way without my seeing him. Ever wider half-circles I made, until I came within sight of the backs of the sullen Cragsmen guarding the place. Nothing had disturbed them.

Who had brought Talu to me? Though still puzzled, I lost my fear. An enemy would have killed me by now, or tried to. But if it were a friend, why had he or she not stayed to greet me?

The sun was standing at halfday when I started my search, and brushing the snowpeaks when I gave it up, put away thoughts of it, untied the horse and led her off by the reins, for the mountain's ribs sloped down to the tarn too steeply for riding.

Despite whatever danger from Cragsmen, I would spend the night beside that pool of vision, I would see what it could tell me of my quest.

I let Talu drink at the tarn, then tethered her nearby for fear that Cragsmen might see her if she roamed and hunted snakes as was her wont. She would have to be as hungry as I, my Talu. I turned away from her peevish glance and went softly down to the verge of the tarn.

There I washed myself, silently, somberly, hoping it was not unseemly to cleanse myself in this place. I felt a need to be clean for those whom I hoped to petition.

I sat on the verge of the pool, waiting for nightfall, keeping a vigil, glad that I had not eaten that day. In former times it might have been necessary for me to sit and starve myself for several days, but so little had I eaten for so long that already the vigil weakness was on me.

Night came, clear and full of stars, as I had hoped. I sat and blinked at the shadow-stars floating on the surface of the deep, black pool. A wind whispered down the mountainside, out of the west, and the shadow-stars shifted, rose and drifted in air like dimly shining snow motes, took shape of—a tree like the one on the sunstuff panel? No. White starwisps still swirled, and I blinked again and saw—it was he, gloriously robed, he, the prince out of the past, regal face turned toward me as he gazed across the abyss of time.

The night we had camped here, Kor and I, we had seen two legendary warriors, they who had sailed to Mahela's realm and perhaps not been entirely bested. They whose swords we wore. And we had trembled in terror of them, and learned the comfort of handbond.

I was not very much afraid, this time. Too much had happened for me to be very much afraid. Indeed, like an ass, I was merely surprised, and before I recalled myself I blurted out loud, "Where is your comrade?"

He did not move or answer, he, Chal, if it was Chal. His eyes that looked on me so steadily seemed shadowed and saddened, his ageless face very grave. His was a somber, seeing gaze that shamed me, though I did not understand why.

"Can you hear me?" I asked more softly. "Can you speak to me?"

He did not answer. I saw a slight stirring, as if a wind had troubled the starlight folds of his robes.

"Where is Sakeema?" I begged him. "Please. For the sake of thc world's healing."

Still he stared at me without a sign or an answer, and suddenly I recognized the sorrow in his face. It was reproach.

"I am sorry," I whispered. "Though I don't know what I have done." And suddenly, though nothing had changed, I seemed to see another kingly face instead of Chal's—it was Kor! Truly, it was he, the short fur-cut hair, the simple clothing his own, and storm raged all around him, sending his sealskin cloak lashing across his face like a whip. The surface on which he stood tossed unsteadily. It was the pool of vision, and it seethed and churned like the sea in storm, rose in towering waves, opened a black maw and—took him. He sank. Only his stark face remained, filling my sight, filling the stormy, tossing surface of the sea—Kor was as vast as sea, as sky. Ocean swells were his tears, whitecaps the glimmer of his sea-deep eyes, and out of the waves he gazed at mc, looking as though I had hurt him to his heart's heart, as if I had put a knife in him and turned the blade. With a wordless shout I leaped to my feet. The vision vanished.

"No!" I shouted to the black pool, which lay as still and dark as before.

Always, since I had known him, I had sensed something fated about Kor, some shadowed, uncanny end awaiting him, some dire price he would have to pay; why, I did not know. . . . And though in the past I had felt that his doom had somehow to do with women, at this despairing time my muddled mind leaped straight to the thought I feared the most. "No, Kor cannot be dead!" I pleaded to the faceless pool. "He can't be!"

There was no answer, and for a crazed moment I felt certain that I had killed my bond brother, I, the murderer, for I had killed men once, unknowing. No amount of water could cleanse me of their blood. I would have to drown myself, as my father had once tried to drown me in this very pool. He, Tyonoc, demon-possessed, he had been a murderer too. Now I was the same, and I had killed Kor—

"No!" I roared at the night.

"Peace, my son."

I grew very still, for I knew that voice. My dead father's voice, coming to me on the breath of wind.

"Prince Chal cannot answer you."

I saw my father's shade drifting in the warm wind that summerlong blew down the landward side of the mountains, drifting nearly within my reach, had I cared to reach. His wraith, faintly aglow and greenly wavering in the night, as if seen through the darkened waters of Mahela's hell.

"She punished you," I muttered, staring at him. "The old bitch. Stinking carrion bird." Mahela had indeed taken her revenge on him and on Kor's mother, Kela, after Kor and I had escaped.

"So I am unbodied. But I am a warrior again, Dan, and

no worm.'' Tyonoc's voice came to me clear and strong, and his face wore the fierce warmth of a king. Though he roamed with the restless dead, yet in a way he was my father again as I remembered him, and like a stripling I turned to him with my trouble. I sank to my knees, facing him. ''Is Korridun well?'' I blurted.

''How would I know? But he is not numbered among the dead.'' A dark significance came into his voice. ''No more than Sakeema is.''

I cared less for Sakeema than for my bond brother, at that moment. ''Father, please,'' I begged, ''you shades, you travel like birds. Go, bring me news of Kor.''

''Plague take it, have I reared this oaf for nothing?'' My father sounded far less patient than he had of old. ''Dannoc, heed what I have said! I tell you quite surely, Sakeema is alive, somewhere! Have you forgotten your quest?''

I gave him no answer, but looked at the ground, and when I looked up again, he was gone, no more than a mote in the wind. And though I listened long, I did not hear his voice again, and I did not know if he would do as I had asked.

I turned back to the tarn. Once again the shadow-stars drifted on its chill surface. I sat and watched them with no expectation, and sometimes, very weary, I dozed. The night slowly passed.

''Where is Sakeema?'' I softly asked the pool of vision in the darkness before daybreak, but there was no answer.

# Chapter Five

Watching from the lookout at sunrise, I saw the smokes coming up from the cooking fires of my fair-haired, wandering people—it could be no other people than my kindred of the Red Hart Tribe. Like wisps of horsehair shining in the slantwise light, the smokes rose far off to the east and somewhat southward, in the region of beaver waters.

I readied Talu, mounted her and traveled to take council with my brother Tyee.

I had thought, until that sunrise, that I would travel in haste to the thunder cones and search their skirts for the blackstone cave where the Herders believed Sakeema had been taken by his foster brothers, the wolves. But perhaps Tyee knew more nearly than I where it might be. Perhaps he knew the legends of the Otter and the Fanged Horse Folk regarding the place where Sakeema lay and slept, he or one of my folk.

Better truth was, I had felt my soul yearn at the sight of those smokes.

Urgently I journeyed, sometimes late into the night under the light of the waxing moon, and every day's riding tugged at my heart.

It was perhaps the last time I would see this place, if Mahela had her way. And I seemed to know it more clearly, more sweetly, more deeply than ever before. As if always halfway into vigil I rode, every sense heightened, seeing every young unfurling leaf on each red-barked cherry tree, smelling each crescent of warm loam turned up by Talu's hooves, feeling sunlight. . . . This was my homeland, which I had roamed all my life until I had gone to Kor, and the beauty of it was like no other beauty to me, the shaggy hemlocks and the small winding streams, the meadows yellow with mallow flowers—but for all my hearkening, I rode it in silence. No birds sang at dawn. No grouse whurred away from my passing, or hawks shrilled overhead. No doves called. No coneys rustled in the laurel, or squirrels in the lindens. No deer leaped.

I did not utterly starve, for forage was somewhat easier to find in the lush upland valleys of the Red Hart Demesne that it had been in the mountains. There were groundnut and late sparrowgrass, and mushrooms like white moons in the grass. But I felt forever starved, hunger as much of soul as of body. Talu starved worse than I, kicked apart rotten logs, ate the grubs and worms. She grew thin, and I took to walking to spare her when our pace was slow, when the brush was dense.

The fifth day after I had left the pool of vision, as I struggled through one such thicket with my fanged mare at my side, something scuttled out of the cover at my feet, clucking. "Ridge chicken," I muttered, standing dumbfounded because I had not seen a living wild creature in so long. And before I could think my mouth began to water at the thought of the roasted flesh. Ridge chickens made easy hunting, so stupid that a child could walk up to them and knock them on the head. The one I had flushed had stopped at a small distance. There it stood, complaining through its beak. As if of its own accord my hand drew the stone hunting knife from its leather sheath at my belt. I let go of Talu's reins, prepared to grasp and kill.

But my heart stopped my hands. The dimwitted, rackety creature, probably it lived only because not even gluttonous Mahela wanted it, as she seemed not to want the asps and worms. But it was a creature of Sakeema even so. One of the few remaining. I could not kill it. With a fierce, joyous resolve I knew that I would never eat flesh again, and I stood rapt, watching its small eyes amid their pink wrinkles of wattle, the fussy stirrings of its dust-colored feathers—

And Talu, who had grown tired of waiting for me to dispatch the hen and give her her share, pushed past me, shouldering me out of her way and sending me sprawling into a thorn bush. She bore down on the ridge chicken in two strides, bit off its head and devoured it, bones and all. After a moment I swallowed my vexation, got up out of my thorny seat and turned away from watching.

"Well," I muttered, kicking at the loam as if I could find myself something tasty there, "better you than I. Pity we can give none to our friend the wolf."

Talu walked on with satisfied grunts thereafter, and we made good time that day.

I came to my people of the Red Hart some few days later, quietly, in the hush of dusk. When I saw the signs of their nearby encampment I left Talu in the brush and made my way afoot, skulking forward as silently as a thief, for I wanted no commotion until I had had a chance to greet Tyee. At the time of day he would be in his tent, I thought. But I was wrong.

I blinked in astonishment, for ahead of me blazed a great fire. It was hardly the season for soulfires, at the wrong end of the year, in fact, but there one burned, flames swaying higher than the heads of those gathered around it. All the tribe, even to the infants, was seated in a wide circle there. Firelight shone off the unbound, sun-colored hair of children and the yellow braids of the others, the warriors, the matrons, and the bone-white, thinning hair of the elders.

I stopped in the shadows of the nearest aspen grove, watching.

The shaman was dancing. A raven mask covered his hair and face. In a spearhead-shaped cloak of deerskin he danced, circling the blaze, and his fringes hung so long they seemed to spring from the ground, wavering like fire. To me he was a black, swaying flame of a man seen against the flames that danced and swayed much as he did. He passed his hands through the fire to show that he possessed power. He reached into the blaze, pulled out coals and held them up for his people to see. With his hands he raked out coals in plenty, like a marmot raking out a fiery burrow, and then he stood upright and walked on them with his bare feet. His head and shoulders had been thrust into the fire. I could not believe what I was seeing. This was a new shaman, a young and potent shaman, not the old graybraid I remembered. He danced again. Others should have been dancing with him, the king, the warriors, but no one did.

I scanned the tribe, seeking Tyee, but could not find him amid the crowd of braided heads in flickering firelight—perhaps he sat on the other side of the fire from me. My gaze soon turned back to the shaman. This man, whoever he was, had taken upon himself the whole burden of his people's petition. The tribe sat in utter silence, so great a silence that even at the distance I could hear the low-voiced singing of the fire.

Then I noticed the horse, nearly out of my sight in the shadows beyond the great fire, and a chill crawled into the back of my neck and found its way down my spine. Not since I was a child and the tribe beset by smallpox had a horse been sacrificed. But there it stood, firelight turning its dun flanks sunstuff-bright, a great-eyed, high-headed yearling that must have been the tribe's pride. The white feathers of the victim glimmered in its mane and tail.

As I watched, a child led the horse forward. Another brought the shaman the blackstone knife with handle of carved human bone, a knife used only for this. Then both children backed away.

The shaman struck the victim with mercy, straight and hard to the throat, and bled the colt into the fire, and himself heaved in the body—he was great in power, his must have been the strength of four men! And the signs were good, for the flames took the flesh eagerly.

Again the shaman took up the dance, circling the flames, the long fringes of his cloak and leggings fluttering and tossing like a deer lure. This was the dance that needed no music but the rhythms of life itself, quickened breathing, heart's beating, ever-faster drumming of feet. More strongly, more wildly every heartbeat he danced, breathspan by breathspan more vehement, until he was whirling like a tempest as he circled the fire, his fringed cloak flying higher than his head, higher than the flames. And then, spinning, he toppled and fell so that he lay nearly in the fire, writhing as the trance took him. And then he lay as still as if he were dead.

Very silent, very sober, some of the elders of the tribe

came and pulled him away from the fire, then placed around him many objects, of what sort I could not see at the distance and against the light of flames. Some of them they placed in his limp hands. Then every member of the tribe came forward and placed around him things of like sort, even the smallest children bringing them, even the babes, until the offerings, whatever they were, some no bigger than pebbles, others as large as a man's fist, made a mass and a circle around the body of the shaman like the circle of the tribe around the fire.

Which circle the tribe once again took, sitting in their places, utterly silent, waiting. And still I had not seen Tyee.

I stood in the aspens, watching, waiting, knowing by then where my brother was, wishing him well in his quest—though I did not yet know what quest it was. The fire burned low and ceased its soft singing, but no creature noises eased the silent passing of the night, not even the uncouth voices of frogs.

The great fire had burned down nearly to embers when at last the shaman stirred and slowly rose. He stood, a black figure against flames no longer, but a lean and shadowed man. Slowly, even more slowly than he had come to his feet, he put up his hands and lifted from his head the carved wooden black-stained raven mask with its lappet of black feathers that covered his hair. For a long moment, as he lifted it, he seemed very tall, very looming. A gasp and a whispering went up. Then he took it off, and he was just a man again.

He was my brother Tyee.

Once more the king, he looked around at his waiting people, the circle of their offerings and their selves all around him, and his look was bleak.

"I have failed," he said.

Stark silence answered him.

"I flew high," he said, "above the paths of sun and moon, above the stars, above sky into beyond. But I could not find the god. Then my strength failed me."

Silence was broken by a sullen murmur, but no one spoke out loud for all to hear. Nor did anyone speak to Tyee. His people got up and walked away from him. One of the women handed him something, a bundle of some sort, then turned away like the others. As if stunned or weary, without much talk, they all went to their tents to sleep, for it was very late.

I stood struggling to center myself, to encompass my anger at the tribe, my Red Hart people: anger because they had received his striving so churlishly. Tyee, my brother, a shaman! And a potent one. He had grown and changed much since I had seen him last. To fly above sky in search of a god—it was a thing seldom heard of, a quest worthy of a master shaman, a hero among shamans. But in those worst of times, the people had no regard for defeated valor, however courageous. They wanted only victory, and their king's word that all would be well.

Tyee stood alone, with bent head. Softly I stepped out of my cover and walked toward him.

Even in heartache he was a king, Tyee, and a warrior, and not easily to be taken unawares. His head snapped up. He swung around to face me. There he stood in the light of the remaining flames, splendid.

There he stood, cradling an infant in his arms.

I stopped where I was, at the verge of the firelight, looking at him as if I had never seen him before. He was a shaman, and now—he was a father? I had not known, I had been away from him far too long, too much had changed without my knowing. . . . He had changed. He had grown very thin, haggard, all bone, taut skin and too-hard muscle, as if he had seen much hardship. And his look as he gazed back at me smote my heart.

"Dan," he murmured, surprised, but—why did he not stride forward to greet me with joy? Something heavy in him, something more than the night's defeat. In his blue eyes, the numb, glazed look of a creature in a deadfall trap, suffering long.

"My brother!" I went to him and embraced him as best I could without disturbing the baby in his arms. I kissed him on the temple, held his head between my hands so that his eyes met mine. "My brother, what is it? What has hurt you?"

His eyes narrowed in pain, and he did not speak. The silence of the night all around us gave me the answer.

She whom I remembered would not have left him alone at such a time.

My hands dropped away from him, I stepped back, feeling my knees tremble as a weakness took hold of me. I nearly lurched into the fire. "No," I whispered. "Sakeema, no."

"Leotie is dead," Tyee told me.

My onetime lover, but his—his life's love, his lifemate.

"She died in the birthing of this little one here."

It could not be. It could not be. She was all he had in the world.

"Tyee," I said, my voice breaking, "I am sorry."

"Don't be." He spoke with stark calm. "In a way it scarcely matters. We will all be food for Mahela's maw within a twelvemonth."

*Ai*, his honesty. So it might well be, if my quest failed.

Something had cracked beneath my clumsy foot. Numbly I looked down, I looked at the objects that had ringed Tyee. All around me, small figures carved of wood, such as shamans often made for the sick. But those were of human form, and the one I had broken was in form of a deer.

I saw others. Deer, mostly. Standing harts, fawns lying in thicket or suckling at the hinds. But also birds, eagle and partridge and songbirds, hawks with spread wings. And beaver, pika, marten, squirrel. Even the carved figures of foxes. There was a fox lying curled with its brush covering its face. There was a mighty bull bison. There were tens and tens of them, the creature carvings. For months everyone in the tribe must have been making them, and they were very beautiful, some of them, especially the deer. All the animals, all my people's longings, standing mute by a dying fire.

I crouched and picked up the hart I had broken, stood erect again and tried to fit the splintered thing together, cradling it in my hands as he cradled the infant in his arms. I did not speak, but my heart cried to Sakeema for the sake of my brother, his babe, all the forlorn world.

Tyee must have seen something in my face. In the same bleak, hard-muscled way he said, "Call no longer on Sakeema, or on any god. There is no god. I have sought even to the far, dark spaces between the stars. There is no savior. There is nothing."

I think it was then, facing his grief, that the change began in me, for I did not gainsay him.

# Chapter Six

The king's tent was the largest one, with the emblem of the red hart painted on its deerskins in colors made of red ocher. I knew it of old, and urged my brother there, for he needed to sleep. He was exhausted, and without reason I felt nearly as weary. I sprawled on skins like the child I had once been and slept deeply.

In the hush of earliest daybreak the mewling of Tyee's infant daughter awoke us. He got up, cradled the baby to his chest and sat cross-legged by the small, cold firepit at the heart of the tent, rocking his body to quiet her. I sat by him.

"I have seen our father in the air," I said after a while, "and he tells me that Sakeema lives."

Dawn made me say that. But Tyree did not speak to the matter of Sakeema. Instead he said, "You have been speaking with our father? You parleyed with a spirit of the dead, and you are yet alive?"

Since I myself had been dead for a while in Mahela's realm, it did not seem so strange to me. I shrugged. With the whole world sinking down into ashes, perhaps the dead were closer to us all than they had ever been before. Or perhaps we were all closer to them.

"Why should it surprise you?" I asked him. "You, a shaman? Have you forgotten I saw you last night? You were magnificent."

"Hunh. For all the good it did." Something struggled in Tyee's face, and he turned on me suddenly, thrusting his jaw at me. "Why are you not with Korridun?"

His tone took me so aback that I did not answer him. He scolded on.

"Have you no name anymore, that you wear no braids? You hair has grown long enough and half again."

Had I no name any longer? My ways were no longer the ways of the Red Hart. Quietly I told him, "I dare say you know why my hair hangs loose."

"Are you so much beyond us?" Tyee flared. "Why not call yourself Sakeema and have it done with?"

"Your grief speaks, my brother," I said softly. "Let us not quarrel."

A quiet, for the span of several breaths.

"I am sorry, Dan." He did not look down as he once would have, feeling himself in the wrong, but met my eyes steadily, holding the baby against his shoulder. "Grief, yes, the same grief you know. Not only for Leotie."

There was a ripple of light as the doorflap raised, and a young woman slipped in. When she saw me she stood rooted with surprise. "Dannoc!"

I gave her a smile of greeting, and was glad that I remembered her name at once. Powers be praised, I had not forgotten these my people no matter how much had happened since I had seen them last. She was Karu, a proud warrior and the flower of the tribe. Many were the young men who would have put their hands in fire if it could have earned them the gaze she was giving me now. Glance I should answer, for I knew she did not offer herself lightly. . . .

I looked away, looked down at the ashes near my feet, and in a moment Karu came and took the infant from Tyee, bearing the baby away somewhere, perhaps to another woman to be fed at the breast. The doorflap dropped behind her, and there was a small silence.

"Well," said Tyee wryly, "now I know for certain that the world is coming to an end, when Dannoc refuses a virginal maiden."

And when Dannoc ate no meat, though neither of us said it. "And when the Red Hart have taken to eating fish," I retorted. I knew they had, for I had seen the offal piled outside the camp. Most likely Talu was munching the stinking bones at this moment.

"No joke, my brother. Is it not true that the world is ending?" Though he had said that it was, too often he had said it. I knew then that hope still moved in him despite all his dark thoughts, stubborn as a heartbeat, hurting him worse than his grief.

I knew how hope hurt, and kept silence.

"There are those among my counselors who think that we can live like this," Tyee said, "netting fish in the beaver ponds, eating wild carrot and biscuit root and the hearts of the bulrushes. But without the beavers to tend the ponds, without the birds to spread the berry seeds and eat the midges, without the deer, how long can it last? A turning of the seasons, perhaps two."

"Likely Mahela will not let it last even so long," I said. "She will grow greedy for the flowers, next."

Tyee looked at me as if he did not entirely understand

me, but pursued his own thoughts. "Biscuit root is good food to put by for the winter," he argued, as his counselors must have argued with him. "There is black rice, and groundnut, and cherries can be dried. Fish can be dried like meat. But without the creatures. . . . Dan, am I wrong to feel doomed? They tell me my thinking is colored by despair."

He sat hunched, his long braids swinging in front of his shoulders, the slate-blue peregrine feathers of a king tied to the ends. His braids were the color of dead grass in winter. The feathers, I saw suddenly, had grown tattered and old. It had been too long since a peregrine had lived to give new ones.

"You are one who has the heart to grieve," I said in a low voice.

Tyee sat up straight, looked at me sharply. "Dan, why are you not with Korridun?" he demanded once again. "What has happened since I saw you last? You are—more than thin and starved, like the rest of us. You look as if you have been to hell and back."

I said, "I have."

He gazed at me.

I told him, "The world is ending, as you have said. I must find Sakeema and awaken him before it is too late."

My brother stared at me for the span of several breaths without letting his face move. I could not tell what he was thinking, but although he had not stirred I felt as if he had edged away from me. "You have always been like that," he muttered finally. "All your days, speaking of Sakeema as if he lived."

I shouted, perhaps too loudly because of my own doubts, newborn, faintly stirring. "But he is alive! As alive as I am!"

"How do you know? Have you seen him? Has he touched your hand in greeting?"

There had been visions so fire-true, it was as if he had. But many people had visions. My visions would not convince Tyee. Or even me, any longer. . . . "How do you know anything is true, when you cannot see it?" I retorted. "How do you know the air you breathe?"

"I have seen the wind stir the trees. But I have seen no such stirring of Sakeema."

"How can you say that? A white lily floating on the water, not Sakeema? I see his traces everywhere." Or at least, so I always had seen my god. . . . A thing I had never told anyone, that I seemed to see Sakeema's trail wherever I went, in the mountains, the sky, the hollow of my own hand. Before my inner eye as I rode floated the face I could not remember, seen like the echo of a ghostly touch, like the faint scent of a forgotten song on the wind. I had never told anyone, not even Kor—perhaps there had been no need to tell Kor. But this was my brother Tyee.

"I have told you I have searched," Tyee said starkly. "I have sent my spirit beyond the stars, and there was no god there. Nowhere. Nothing but emptiness."

"He is here, then! Somewhere. Our father has told me that he is alive in the world somewhere."

Tyee said, "It is nothing new that you are a dreamer." A bitter love in his voice. "This quest of yours, it is nothing new. All your life, you have been seeking Sakeema."

And I realized with a small shock that he was right. I had looked for the god in my father, in Korridun, in dreams and in Mahela's realm. I could only hope that it made more sense, now, to look in a visionary pool and an empty cave. Swallowing, I nodded. "There is truth in you," I admitted.

"Truth enough to know that it is folly. You are off chasing a dream when you should be with Korridun."

That hurt so badly that for a moment I could not move

or speak. Then I shouted at Tyee, "How do you know where I should or should not be? How do you know anything if you do not dream! How do you know Leotie loved you?"

The pain on his face at the mention of her name drove me to my feet and out of the tent before either of us could say more angry words.

There was an uproar outside. Someone had heard my voice, or Karu had spread the news that I was there. As soon as I lifted the entry flap and they could see my face there was an outcry, half joy, half like the clamor of a colt taken away from its dam for weaning. And as soon as I had stepped clear of the tent the entire kindred of them, elders, warriors and children, rushed me to embrace me.

"Dannoc! You have come back to us!"

"Dan, we have missed you so! Things will be better now that you are back!"

"We will braid your hair for you again, Dannoc! *Ai*, but it is good to see you!"

And the little sunny-haired children, some of them perhaps mine, clustered around my knees and gazed up at me large-eyed, as if I were a hero stepping out of legend to see them. I swung a few of them up by each arm, and still they stared solemnly.

I tried to tell my people that I had come back to be with them only for a short while. But they were not hearing me—it is odd and marvelous, how folk will not hear that which they do not wish to hear, no matter how plainly one's mouth forms the words. And I felt weary because something lay wrong between me and Tyee. So I said no more for the time. I let them talk, and I listened. There was much to be listened to, news of births and deaths and lovers' pledgings, and journeyings in search of game. Much talk of the search for the red deer.

"Our arrows, our bows, they are useless now, for nothing stirs on land that is larger than a frog. They are quaint keepsakes, good only for show and ceremony, like the elk antlers I once wore on my head."

Antler crown that had made him a king. It was Tyee, standing beside me, his hand resting lightly on my shoulder. I turned to him. His blue eyes, clouded by the quarrel, like mine.

"Tyee, I am sorry."

"Hush," he told me softly. "We'll talk later."

Like a begging dog I wandered from cooking fire to cooking fire, and my people feasted me throughout the day. They gave me cress and amaranth, and fish, and a sort of bread made of biscuit-root meal, very good and filling, but after a while my heart felt so full of love and grief that I could scarcely eat. At every firepit I saw the small deer carved in wood, and often a man or woman sat carving another with hands now practiced at what must once have been a strange art. As if each one of them were a shaman, seeking to bring back the creatures by this magic—but no. I saw nothing in their faces but wistfulness. The shaping of the small wooden creatures was but a wanhope pastime to hunters now idle.

"Dannoc! Come, sit, eat! We have eels, here."

Which a year before would have been scorned, by me and all the others. But I ate, and the food tasted not too foul, not with my people looking on.

"Dannoc. When you left us last, you laid before us a—an undertaking. . . ." They were hesitant to speak of it. A strange quest it had seemed to them at the time, and no less strange now.

So I gave account to them, of how Kor and I had traveled to the Mountains of Doom, Mahela's undersea realm of the captive dead, which she called Tincherel, "the haven.'' She had a twisted way of seeing, Mahela. I had spoken with Tyonoc there, and failed to bring him back with me, but Kor and I had learned to know the glutton goddess, our enemy. Kor had learned to know her all too well. . . . And I told my people what my quest now was, no less uncanny than the last one. They sat silently and listened to me, and said little afterward, for none of them wished to call me fool, but neither would they speak to the urgency of our need for Sakeema. To do so would have been to admit the desperation of our plight. The world's plight. And of them all, only Tyee had that honesty.

And I asked them to tell me all they knew of Sakeema, where the Otter said he lay and slept, what the Fanged Horse Folk deemed of him. And they told me that the Otter said he had floated down the river in a spruce-root basket, and the salmon had taken him and borne him out to sea. He would come back with the salmon some day, the Otter said. It was a saying of no use to me. And what tale the Fanged Horse told of the god, my folk knew no better than I.

Nightfall neared. Embers glowed in the dusk. Tyee came up to me, his baby daughter nestled on his shoulder in a blanket of the Herders' softest wool.

''She has had her milk,'' he said, ''and now I must walk her asleep. Come with me?''

Not knowing what to say, I walked along in silence at his side. But Tyee did not lack courage to speak.

''They like you better than they do me,'' he remarked when we were out of earshot of his folk. He had been among the listening crowd, my brother Tyee. ''Better than anyone. They very nearly worship you.''

I shot a surprised look at him in the half light. His face looked calm, almost serene, and there had been no hint of self-pity in his voice. Tyee had a strong mind, as strong and hard as the lean muscle and bone of his body. At one time I had thought him a weakling, but no longer. He had earned kingship, and kingship had changed him. I did not deny what he had said, though I very much wanted to, for I would not insult him with lies.

"Even Leotie liked you better," he added in the same clean tone, "for all that she chose me."

"Tyee," I whispered, stunned, "forgive me for coming here. I will go away."

"No, stay. Come more often. You are my brother." He gave me a soft glance. Yet his voice had gone dark when he added, "None of it matters."

"But it does. Is that why you wish me to go back to Kor, then?"

"Dan, my brother, think better of me!" For the first time he sounded less than calm. "I am comforted to see you, I wish you could always be by me. What I have said, truly, none of it matters. We are dry leaves in a bitter wind. This little one will not live to learn her own name."

He stroked and patted the infant in his arms. We walked in hemlock shade. Nor, again, could I deny what he had said, for a cold doubt was growing in me whether Sakeema could be found by the way I had devised.

"I said you should be with Korridun because you belong at his side," Tyee told me. "All sense shows it. I have never seen two such comrades as you."

"Tyee, nothing less than—than the world's peril could have taken me from him." For all that I tried to match his quiet courage, my voice shook. "My heart longs for him always, even in my sleep. I ache for him as much as I do for Tassida, and I see her face in my dreams."

My brother looked at me in surprise, for Kor had been courting Tassida when Tyee had known them both. But

Tyee was a king, with a king's wit, and in a moment he nodded as if he had understood something.

I said, "Yet, as much as I long for either of them, that much I long for Sakeema. I hunger for him more than I hunger for meat. Tyee, I am pulled apart like a flower in the hands of a child. It is as if the nameless god's half-witted brother has hold of me, trying to make me be in three places at once. But all sense tells me that there is no hope for any of us unless I find Sakeema."

"By my braids, I had forgotten that old tale of the half-wit who makes all the mischief!" Tyee sounded grimly amused. "He holds us all in his hands right now, for certain. I find it far easier to believe in him at this time than in Sakeema." His voice went bleak. "Dan, as I love you—go back to Korridun."

Something stark in his voice kept me from being angry at him. "For what purpose?" I asked softly. "That we should die together? I have told him I will not give up hope while the sun yet stands in the sky."

"He may die sooner than the rest of us," said Tyee. "Pajlat has gone to take council with Izu, and they have dipped their knives in wine."

The Fanged Horse Folk and the Otter River Clan would attack Kor together, he meant. My stomach clenched at the news, though it was no more than I had already surmised. No more than I had known when I left. No more than Kor had known when he had bid me a gentle farewell.

"I would be but one more warrior at Kor's side. Better that you and the Red Hart Tribe should go to his aid, Tyee," I challenged.

He looked away from me, and we walked in silence beneath a cloud-shadowed moon. Full dark had fallen. The baby slept on my brother's shoulder.

"I will," said Tyee quietly after a long silence.

I turned my head to stare, for the Red Hart are not much in the custom of seeking out war.

"I will," he said softly but fiercely, staring back at me. "I will lead my people to Seal Hold and we will fight at Korridun's side. It will be a better way for us to die than by waiting here."

"It might not be to die. Kor's Hold is deep and strong, with springs of fresh water. And if his people have gathered seaweed you will not starve. All he needs is numbers." A fool's hope was growing in me. "Tyee, if you mean it . . . I am comforted that you will be by him."

Dark merriment got the better of him, and he laughed out loud into the night, making the infant on his shoulder stir and wail. "I do not mean it to comfort you," he declared amid laughter. "I mean it to shame you into doing the same."

"Think better, then." There was that between Kor and me which did not permit shame. "Still I must seek Sakeema."

Tyee sobered, calmed his baby daughter, squatted down in a hunter's crouch beside a beaver-felled birch, now rotting, for the beaver were gone. I sat on damp ground, facing him. Pond water lapped beyond us, wraith-white in moonlight, full of echoes of what had once been.

"Is there no doubt in you, Dan?" Tyee asked softly, in a sort of wonder, or plea.

I would not yet admit to doubt. "Is there nothing you believe in?" I asked him.

"Ay. And that is the hellish thing." He looked away from me, out over the level water that rippled in the moonlight. His voice was very low. "There is a feeling in me that whispers and niggles, insistent beyond all reason, about you and Kor. That all might yet be well if you were together."

Moonlight slanting off the pond's surface made watery shadows on his still face, like the ghosts of tears. And I seemed to feel a spear nudge its way into my heart.

"And Tassida," said Tyee in a voice barely above a breath. "That strange, scornful, wandering warrior of yours. There is a prickling in me when I think of her."

That did not smite me, for who could see Tassida and not remember her with awe? Or Kor. He had died and come to life again, and Tyee had seen it all. I found my voice.

"Tyee. If there is truth in you, tell me of Sakeema."

"The god who is dead?" he said harshly, though not to argue with me. He was done with arguing, and spoke merely the truth as he saw it.

"Tyee," I urged.

He looked at the ground, and the moonshadows flickered on his face. "Folk say the Herders have wisdom," he told me finally. The saying was a gift he gave me against his will, and I touched his hand in thanks.

In the early morning, before many folk were about to protest, I left the Red Hart yet again, bound toward the Herder village beyond the thunder cones. The last one of my people I saw was Karu, standing in the meadow mists, plucking the petals from a starflower. She gave me a single glance as I rode by, and I knew without hearing them the timeworn words that she chanted.

*Pluck me one, pluck me two.*
*Will you love me if I love you?*
*Pluck me two, pluck me three.*
*Sakeema, please come back to me.*

# Chapter Seven

It was not Talu I rode. I had left her behind to rest and fatten herself upon the fish offal my people threw daily on their midden heaps. She could not have much longer survived the journey with little on which to feed her ugly bulk but grubs and lizards and sometimes snakes. Fanged monstrosity, she had not even raised her bony head from her greedy feeding to watch me go. Scant gratitude in her, and I felt sure I had saved her life—for a time—by leaving her.

I rode a curly-haired pony, Tyee's gift. A stallion, dun of color, as were all horses I knew except Tassida's Calimir, and blue-eyed, as were the pride of my people's horses, and tough enough to travel far, even on scant forage. But like all such grass-eating ponies it was round, so that I felt as if I were sitting on an overlarge mushroom, and the long spirals of its fur made it feel soft, too soft to suit me now that I was accustomed to Talu's hard, gaunt frame. I admitted to myself that I did not miss her high, jutting withers bruising my groin. The curly-haired stallion was shorter of leg than she, and I hoped I would not miss her warlike stride.

Bound eastward, I traveled more northward than eastward for the time, heading toward the Traders' Trail, which lay on the skirts of the Red Hart Demesne. It would take me around the black barrier of the thunder cones to the dry, vast plains where the Herders gazed their six-horned sheep. It also took me to the reaches of the Steppes where the Fanged Horse raiders roamed, a circumstance that did not much please me. But Pajlat's minions were hosting somewhere westward, to the best of Tyee's knowledge, in order to attack Kor. None of them were likely to be on hand to trouble me.

The curly-haired stallion's name was Muku, "fleet as a deer," and I found him far less satisfying to talk to than Talu. He had none of her responsive scorn. He walked and loped tamely, just as I told him to, by day, then grazed hungrily through the evenings without looking at me when I spoke to him. He did not stray, or run away and refuse to be caught, or lay back his ears and glare at me, or buck, or resist the headstall, or kick idly when I came near, or do any of the annoying things that Talu did. I missed her.

Traveling at good speed, I passed out of deer meadow and beaver water and hemlock forest into the prairies: open, grassy country with much sky, shallow valleys, soft-crested hills. Once, not long ago, foxes and badgers and blue hens and burrowing squirrels had lived here, and longer ago, in Sakeema's time, the black-tailed deer, and perhaps also the gray and fallow. It was rich, pleasant land. Only because of the Fanged Horse threat did the Herders not stay there, and only because of Red Hart warriors driving them back from the edge of the Demesne did the Fanged Horse Folk not make the prairies their own. And if it were not for Pajlat's raiders the Red Hart might have come there more often. So this goodly land was roamed by everyone and no one.

I grew no less thin as I traveled, for I was living on the redberry and onion and wild carrot in the grass, saving the provision Tyee had given me, wayfarer's food—he had been generous, but it would be little enough to see me through the Steppes. And I was just as glad to build no cooking fires, for I felt exposed on the prairie, treeless but for small thorns and junipers.

Later I had to build fires, when grassland thinned into the Steppes, and use some of my hoarded water for stone-boiling, because biscuit root and dried fish cannot be choked down uncooked except with wickfish oil, and I had none. And I found no forage, not even grubs or toads or snakes under the rocks I lifted, not even grass seeds on the stems. The Traders' Trail, my first sight of it at dusk, was a rocky gully worn across a flat plateau nearly as barren as the trail itself. Short, scant grass and prickly blunderbrush grew on that high plain, and nothing else.

I ate sparingly of my supplies, and saw that they would not last me the journey, and considered that I might starve. But as it turned out, the Fanged Horse Folk did not give me time to starve.

My first day on the Traders' Trail I saw them at a great distance across the flat shadowlands. And they also saw me, for I saw the dust rise as their horses leaped into the gallop, speeding toward me. Perhaps if I had put Muku to the run at once I might have escaped them yet. And Sakeema knows every muscle of me wanted to, for even Cragsmen were less dangerous than Fanged Horse marauders. Cragsmen could sometimes be diverted by talk.

The Fanged Horse Folk made a custom of striking before parleying, and they were not known for honor or mercy. But parley with them I must, if I wished to know what their tribe said of Sakeema.

I drew Alar from her sheath and awaited them, the sword's hilt warm in my hand, her pommel stone glowing like a second sun.

They galloped near enough for me to see of them more than their dust. Six of them, their greasy black hair flopping on their shoulders as they rode, and they grinned as they saw my weapon, and let out shrill yells of mockery. They were youngsters, I saw in a sort of disgust, merest puppies. Not one of them had the withered head of an enemy hung from his riding pelt or a tassel made of an enemy's hair swinging under his horse's chin. Indeed they were mere striplings, beardless, the armbands sliding down the flat muscles of their arms, their chests hollow under strings of bison teeth. Pajlat must indeed be hosting all his choice warriors to the westward, if he had sent these cubs to be his patrol on his eastern reaches.

But youngsters though they might be, they were as dangerous as a nest of infant vipers, and I knew it well.

I waited. Under me, Muku waited uneasily.

The enemy bore those vicious weapons I most hated, long whips of heavy bisonhide, fit to take out an eye or stun a man and beat the life out of him. As they rushed toward me they taunted me with yipping laughter and raised the whips, eager to wrap a lash around me. Each pup of them would strive hard to take my head for his own, to wear at his knees, his first victim. They would vie with each other for the trophy.

I waited. Until they had come within a stride of striking I waited. Then, "World brothers," I hailed them, "where is Sakeema?"

A lash curled around my neck. I steadied Muku with my bearing and did not move, though the sword flared bright in my hand. The blow had been aimed for my face, but the youngster's hand had jerked at my words, I had seen it. The attackers swirled around me, but I did not turn. Then their dust coiled up like a squat serpent as they brought their horses to a halt in front of me.

"Where is Sakeema?" I asked again into the heartbeat of silence that followed.

They opened their mouths wide and hooted their derision. "We do not speak of Sakeema!" one of them cried, his head flung back so that he yelled up at the sky.

And another shouted at me, "You ask us of Sakeema! You, who killed our tribesmen with your bright knife!" He drew back his lash hand to attack me, but the one who had shouted at sky stopped him with a hand to his forearm.

"Where did you get that strange, long blade?" he asked, not entirely taunting, and looking back at him I saw him with an odd clarity, his small eyes narrowed and bright on me, like a ferret's sharp eyes, or a pine marten's, and his grin—or grimace—his teeth were brown, they must have been causing him some pain.

"Out of black water," I told him. "Why do you not speak of Sakeema?"

He spat. "Whoreson bastard," he said, and I did not know if he so named me or the god.

The spittle fell against Muku's curly-haired forehead, and the little horse shook it off, as he did everything, tamely, and the Fanged Horse youngsters laughed. There was no fire in Muku, only a humble obedience. Red Hart ponies are meant for walking sturdily through long journeys, standing quietly while the deer are stalked and shot, hauling the fresh, bloody meat calmly on their backs. Hot temper helps for none of these things, but only wastes strength and makes noise. Small wonder Muku had no such mettle as a fanged mare might, though if I demanded it of him he would die as he had lived: steadily, bravely.

One of the Fanged Horse cublings told me, to mock me, "Our old tales say that Sakeema will return riding a *fanged* steed."

Under the scorn in his voice I heard the wistfulness I knew well. It was because I had spoken of Sakeema that they had not yet attacked me, say what they would of me or the god. With softened voice I asked, "What else say you of Sakeema?"

"Whoreson!" the one with the aching mouth burst out, and this time I knew he spoke of the god. "We tell the tales no more. Where is the bastard oathbreaker now, when the world is dying?"

"He sleeps," I said when I should have kept silence. I spoke, and far too quickly, because my own dark doubts were muttering and fingering their whips like the enemies I faced.

"He sleeps no whit!" cried out one of them who had not yet spoken.

And the one who had cursed Sakeema said, "The stable stands empty, it always has. Yet the wise women say he is not dead."

"No more is he," I declared, speaking like a fool again when I should have kept silence. "I have been to the Mountains of Doom, and I have spoken with spirits. Sakeema is not in Mahela's realm."

Five of the six who faced me stared and murmured. But the one with the bitter mouth took no pause. He thrust his jaw toward me, and his eyes glittered marten-hard.

"Better he would be dead," he said. "For if the god is not dead or asleep, he is awake, and our betrayer."

And all my own half-formed doubts rose up and lashed my heart. If Sakeema was awake and roaming the world somewhere, why was Mahela having her way with us all? Had the god forsaken us? Was there a devourer in him?

Our betrayer—as my beloved father had betrayed me—

"No!" I roared, a madman's bellow, and kicked Muku hard, so that he leaped forward like a startled hare, blundering into the one with the hurtful mouth. Alar blazed, lifted. Before the youngster knew what was happening, I felled him with a single stroke to the throat.

Life is a twisting dance. These Fanged Horse whelps, they had gone against all their warlike dreaming and training to parley with me, and I, a treacherous outlander, had attacked them. I was their betrayer.

But the combat was now well joined, and I thought no such thoughts at the time. I saw only enemies, and I thirsted for their blood as much as my sword did. I kicked Muku again, pulling at his reins, and he almost toppled, trying to whirl and lunge at the same time. I cursed him and forced him into an unsteady charge. A whip whistled toward my face—Alar cut it off in midair, so that the severed section fell like a snake, writhing. I saw the frightened face of the not-yet-man as he struck at me with the butt, and Alar found her swift way to his heart. Fanged Horse fools, they scorned those who fought with their women at their sides, valiant and well-grown relentless women, yet did not scorn to send their half-grown children into danger! I turned Muku to face another one, aware of the beating of their whips on my back and sides, but not yet feeling pain or weakness—my wrath had taken me out of such feelings. I was crazed with battle fever.

Three more died before Muku slowly sank away under me, his knees folding as he lowered me gently to the ground.

Tough little mount, he had gamely done all I had told him as the fanged mares cut him through his thick fur, so that his neck and chest and flanks ran red with blood, his curly sand-colored hair lay flattened into an ugly fen of blood, until at last a slashing fang had found the large veins of his throat. But he had not fought back by so much as striking with his forehooves.

There he lay on the Steppes, dying, the little stallion my brother had entrusted to me. One enemy yet left to deal with. . . . Why had Sakeema let Fanged Horse Folk be in the world?

It was as Tyee had said, I decided bitterly. The god was dead. No, worse, as that aching other had recently said: the god was our betrayer.

The thought chilled me worse than the whips had. Standing beside Muku's body, my wrath running out of me like my blood, suddenly feeling all the pain of my wounds, I let Alar sag to my side. I no longer cared if I died there on the spot. If Sakeema was so cruel, it did not matter.

One more Fanged Horse stripling yet faced me.

I stared up at him stupidly, not moving, and he stared down at me from the back of his fanged mare. By all my forebears, but he was ugly, he with his low forehead and the black hair hanging down in oily strings, his sharp nose, his sharpened teeth between lips that never seemed to meet. He still carried his long whip coiled in his right hand, and his mare stamped and pawed in her eagerness to run me down. But he held her on tight rein, and he had not moved, no more than I had, though I could not comprehend the look in his too-small eyes.

"Go away," I told him thickly. "I no longer feel like killing you."

He said in his harsh Fanged Horse speech, he who had not spoken to me before, "Who are you?"

Why did they always ask that? And what, for the god's sake, was the right answer? And what did it matter? I laughed, I stood there laughing, for all my life seemed like a joke big as the world. "I am a fool," I told him, still laughing. "I am Sakeema's fool."

If he had charged me at that moment I think I would not have raised Alar to cut him down. He could have had my head for his trophy. The world is ending, I seemed to hear Tyee's sardonic voice say, Dannoc no longer eats meat or kills Fanged Horse shitbottoms. The scum.

The youngster swung his mare around and loped her away. Until he was very small on the distant Steppes I watched after him.

Finally I turned and wobbled away, afoot in a vast, arid plain.

There were fanged mares running loose. No use trying to catch one, I could tell merely by a look at their tossing heads and rolling eyes. I had no strength left to subdue one, and they wanted only to tear at the bodies of their former masters with their yellowbrown tusks, eat the sweet red meat and the sweeter guts. I staggered away and did not look back at them. All powers be willing, when they were done, and finished eating Muku as well, they would be too gorged to come looking for me to rend me and eat me in my turn. Yet they might come and stand around me, waiting like vultures until I died.

The thought enabled me to stumble a considerable distance down the Traders' Trail before I fell.

After that, all is clouded. I remember that the sunlight shimmered down far too hot, the night seemed too chill. I remember crawling on again from time to time, then giving it up and lying in the dirt. I remember thirst. I remember calling on Sakeema for succor—for I had not yet ceased to love my god, despite my dark thoughts—whispering his name with lips that would scarcely move.

Sometime, perhaps after only a day, I entered into a dream. It seemed to me that Kor was somewhere nearby, just around the hip of the mountain, but I was afraid, the Cragsmen were going to see him and slay him, I had to warn him, yet I could not shout.

*Kor!* I shouted within my mind.

No answer. Odd, he had answered me that other time. It was how we had learned mindspeak.

*Kor!*

Where was he? He had to be nearby, within tongueshot and therefore within mindspeak's range. We had never been far apart since we had met.

*Kor!*

Was he already dead? No, Sakeema was dead. No, Sakeema was Kor. I had thought that once.

*Sakeema, bond brother, answer me!*

Something—something strange. No mindspoken answer, yet I felt, I sensed—a passion I could not name. Something.

*Sakeema!*

Moving warily, somewhere near.

*Sakeema! Help me, help us all!*

Even the Fanged Horse Folk? Yes, if the world were to remain, they would have to be on it. They also were his creatures.

*Sakeema!*

I felt presence, like a mind's skin lying next to mine . . . no, more like a frightened animal, shy but curious, snuffling the air, not yet daring to show itself, to see. Some animal with speaking eyes and warm fur.

*World brother, come to me. It is all ending, I need comfort.*

Fear.

*Yes. I, also, am afraid. Kor?*

But Kor would not have been afraid to come to me. He was nowhere near. I began to weep, quietly, scarcely moving—perhaps it was only within my mind that I wept. But I remember a blur, as of tears. I remember lifting my head with great effort, trying to look around me, seeing nothing but flatness and the thunder cones in the distance. The mountains, my beloved snowpeaks, had been only in my dreams. Perhaps Sakeema had been only in my dreams, too, all this time.

*Sakeema,* I mindspoke, not in pleas any longer but in heartache. And with great clarity and tenderness someone answered me.

*Dan. Be still, I am coming.*

Voice I knew well, yet knew not at all . . . my mind spun, and vision faded into blackness.

Awakening came slowly. Aware that someone was with me, wondering who, yet I could not gather strength to open my eyes and see. Afraid, perhaps. So often I had seen the god in vision, or thought I had seen him in truth, and then heartbreak had followed.

Feel of furs under me, softening the hard ground, covering me, shielding me from chill air. Thirst, gone. Someone had given me water. Bindings—my wounds had been tended. Taste of food, bread and berries, in my mouth.

When at last I found strength, or daring, and opened my eyes, I saw only blackness. My hands jumped in alarm, my legs thrust at the ground, and I sent daggers of pain through myself even as I realized it was only the clean blackness of night. Eyes clenched shut against pain, but my gasp had brought someone to my side. Gentle hands felt my forehead, straightened the pelts that covered me.

"Kor?" I whispered.

But it was not Kor. I could feel the presence, the being of this person, and it was not the being of Kor. He was all loving courage, but in this person there was an edge like the edge of an eagle's wings in flight, and a distance, and a lonesome singing. And a bitter wound not yet healed, and a daring, a venturing, despite it. I felt it all, yet I had never been able to feel the being of any person other than Kor. . . .

I centered myself, opened my eyes again and looked. Warm glow of embers, the coals of a cooking fire, somewhere not far away. But the person bending over me was only a shadow in the night.

*Who are you?* I mindspoke.

Fear, the other person's fear, I sensed it at once, though I myself felt no fear. I fumbled a hand out from under my covering, raised it to touch or comfort or try to keep the other by me, but the shadowy one edged away.

Too weary, or weak, to persist or wonder much longer, I drifted back into sleep.

I awoke to a feeling of peace and healing. Head and upper body, I lay not on furs but in someone's lap and arms. Warm glow over my still-lidded eyes told me it was daylight, and a sunlit day. I blinked my eyes open, squinting, and a hand appeared to shield them from the rays. Dark eyes looked down at me.

Dark eyes in a proud, fine-boned, handsome face. Tendrils of light brown hair curled down, taking the shape of hawk flight, around shoulders clothed in patched doeskin. I sighed with love and relief, laying the side of my face against a small, firm breast.

It was Tassida.

# Chapter Eight

Hunger and my whip wounds had left me very weak, in need of nursing, though as always when Tassida was near I recovered far more quickly than seemed fair to expect. There was plenty of food, for (as she told me acidly) there had been quantities of it on the bodies of the Fanged Horse marauders I had killed and on their horses. Stoup's worth of oats and dried salmonberries. Glutton's share, and still Pajlat cried out that his people had not enough, and struck with his raiders to take from other folk.

"Lunkhead," she told me, not as fondly as I would have liked, "if you had but stayed at the bloody place, there would have been food, and goatskins of water, and a mount for you."

"I did not care to stay and watch the mares feed."

"They were well gorged and sluggish when I came upon

them,'' Tassida admitted, meaning that she had taken their baggage from them without danger.

''Also, there was the matter of the young brigand I had sent on his way.''

''A stripling with sharpened teeth in a dolt's mouth? I met with him and killed him.''

The turn of events struck me as wry, and I laughed, or tried to laugh, and Tassida must have thought I was laughing at her. She spoke sharply.

''He wanted to take my head to make up for yours he had missed! And I could not understand why he was alive, yet not cherishing your yellow hair. Why are you yet among the living? What happened?''

I told the tale to her, as best I was able. Briefly, for even after a day of her care I felt weak, and sitting up on my own to speak truly was an effort. But I sat and faced the evening's campfire, as is proper to the telling of tales. The last sunrays of the day still lingered when I was done.

''He could have killed me handily enough,'' I mused. ''I stood like a stump, I could not have lifted the sword. Why did he show me mercy, I wonder?'' I would never know unless I met the man in the realm of the dead.

Tassida snorted, for Fanged Horse marauders were regarded as of somewhat less worth than vipers or Cragsmen by anyone of the other tribes. ''Mercy!'' she scoffed. ''Fanged Horse Folk know nothing of mercy. The cub must have been parlous well frightened, that he would forego your pretty yellow-haired head.''

I expected small understanding of Tassida, and her scorn troubled me no more than Talu's would have. I shrugged, then grimaced at the pain that small movement gave me and lay down on my deerskin once again.

''How maidens will pursue you now,'' Tass teased me,

"with such a tale to tell, and a comely scar on your temple."

"They will be disappointed," I told her quietly, looking up at her from my bed of pelts. "I want no woman, any longer, but you."

The words shook her. I saw her eyes widen hugely in the firelight.

*Tass,* I mindspoke her. A solemn act, to mindspeak her by name. I had never done so with anyone but Kor.

"Don't!" Her hands went up to shield her head, and all her muscles hardened against that single silent word.

"Yet you answered me once," I said softly.

"No!" A violent denial. Had it truly been the god, then? The thought made my heart pound. Or was Tass so frightened that she would lie to me?

"You are afraid? It will go away." An odd quirk, that so fierce a warrior as Tassida could be so routed by the closeness of mind. But I remembered how terrified I had been of it at first. I remembered also, with a small pang, how Kor had not been afraid, but full of wonder, for all that mindspeak was as new to him as it was to me. "I, also, was afraid. We are more alike than we know, Kor has said."

"Go to sleep," Tass commanded me rudely. I smiled and did as she bade me.

The next day, though I could scarcely sit upright to ride on Calimir behind her, we traveled to the flanks of the thunder cones. Tass worried whether Pajlat's people might find the bodies of their dead patrol, or be alerted by the wandering mares, and she was afraid Fanged Horse raiders might pursue us for revenge. I felt no such fear, for the chances seemed remote. (Afterwit tells me that she wanted to take me to a certain place, and found reasons that hid her true reasons even from herself.) But certainly

I was willing enough to go where she said. In the flanks of the thunder cones, she told me, there were folds and crannies where fire could not be seen, good hiding. And they would not think we had gone there, for no one went willingly to that bleak, black, sharp-stoned land where almost nothing grew. There were passages that would make my way to the Herders shorter. I accepted all this without question, for she spoke as one who knew.

Calimir moved like flowing water under us, shining black water, for he was black but for his white belly and mane and legs, and a marvel among horses in many other ways as well. What a steed, that one. Swifter than any fanged mare yet soft in his gaits, fierce in battle yet gentle and beautiful, generous, great of nostril and eye. His small ears pricked eagerly forward, his finely shaped head nodded with his swift, smooth walk. Even sitting behind Tassida, on his rump where the jarring of a horse's gait is the worst, I rode in comfort. But I was yet weak, I had to fold my arms around Tassida's waist for support, and before halfday my head rested against her back.

"Tass, why are you here?"

The warm sun, the rhythm of the walk, had lulled us both. She answered me without edge.

"I came to the Red Hart only two days after you. They were still preparing to travel to Seal Hold. Tyee told me which way you had gone."

"You followed me? I am honored. But why?" Softly, gently, not wishing to press her. I knew that she loved me, in her way. But was there something more that she wanted of me than my love for her?

She sighed, and though she did not stiffen or bristle as was her wont, it was the span of many breaths before she spoke.

"Why do you seek Sakeema?" she said in a low voice,

and it was not a question or a reproach, but an answer I could not quite encompass. I laid my cheek against the tough muscle and bone of her shoulder blade, and thought much but asked no more.

These were my thoughts: that she had last seen Kor and me quarreling, yet did not ask how it stood between us, but seemed to know. That she, unlike many others, had not asked me why I was not at my comrade's side. That she knew I sought Sakeema, but how did she know? Had Tyee told her? Or were there things about me that she knew in her soul, as if I were a part of her?

I put the thoughts away with the other mysteries in my mind.

Edau, Val, Rawnie were the names of the thunder cones. Fire, Redheaded Warrior, Wise Woman. And Senet, Keb, Methven, Catalin Du: Elder, Earth's Ire, Spirit Flame, Black Wizard. We rode up the skirts of Catalin, and the land lay all in black ripples and shining black edges sharp as knives—indeed, skirts like this one were where my people came to gather blackstone for their knives, though I had never done so. Above it the cone loomed, not as big as a mountain, but twice as forbidding. Drifts of gritty black brickle had gathered between sheets and swells of rock like black ocean waves—this place seemed far too much like Mahela's Mountains of Doom to suit me, nor was I comforted because a few hardy plants grew in the brickle. Looking down at the cindery talus, thinking what a place like this had once done to my bare feet, I winced.

"Calimir's hooves," I murmured to Tassida, for it was much to be expected, that he should carry the two of us over such terrain.

"They are tough, and he chooses his footing with care."

She rode him at the very loose rein, letting him find his own path, and Calimir held his comely head almost to the ground, studying every step he took. After a while, as the way grew even more treacherous, Tassida swung one foot over his lowered neck and slipped lithely to the ground, leaving me perched like a child on a led pony.

"His hooves are worn evenly, and only a little," she reported, and she walked along beside the horse as the blackstone cut into her deerskin boots and the fiery sun beat down on us both. It would have been a fine, brave thing if I could have walked instead of her, but I knew I could not. Already I was bracing myself with a hand against the horse's withers just to stay upright. But I slipped off my boots of thick bisonhide and passed them down to her, and she put them on over her own, without comment.

On toward evening she pointed out a hollow blackness under a billow of shining black rock. A cave. When she stopped Calimir beside it, I blundered down without waiting for my boots and collapsed under that stone roof, in cool shadow.

It was a cave like no other I had ever seen, I found when I had rested awhile and sat up to look. It went on and on, like a mole burrow or the hollow under a curling ocean wave, and somewhere in its depths ran a trickle of water, for I could hear it. And like the stone lodge on the mountainside above the pool of vision, it was full of bones. Animals had once lived here, animals now all too bitterly gone.

Tassida had stripped Calimir of his gear, poured water in a hollow of rock for him and turned him loose to eat the tough cinderslope plants. Our bags lay stacked within the cave, along the curving wall. When the sun had set, in that brief twilight span between day's blazing heat and night's chill, I crawled out and sat at the entry of the blackstone burrow-cave, and Tass came and sat beside me. We ate oat cakes and dried berries. Tassida ate a few ends of dried meat—for the Fanged Horse Folk yet had dried meat, it seemed. How they must have hoarded. She offered me some, but I refused it. We made no fire.

Twilight darkened into night. Small clouds swam half-seen in a liquid, starlit sky. There should have been the barking of great-eared foxes beneath that sky, and the stirrings of pika and mice. There should have been owl's call or the long note of a desert wolf. Instead, there was silence. Nor had there been any bird twitter in the twilight, any flash of swallows' wings.

"Mahela's hand is heavy," I said softly, for the place, the silence, oppressed me with thoughts of her.

And as if I had summoned her, she appeared.

She was a greenish gleam, at first, far off to the westward. I thought at first of the shades of the dead, dancing in air. But Tassida gasped and leaped to her feet, hand on the pommel of her sword.

"Devourers!"

Rippling like the face of the ocean, yet flying more swiftly than hawks, they drew nearer, Mahela's twelve less one less the four Tassida had killed. I had forgotten, or willed myself to forget, how at night they glowed with the same fishy-shining, eerie gleam as seawater. And I had not known they could be ridden—indeed, I had once been overweening enough to think that I could capture one by sitting on it. Now, to my dismay, I knew better. Flying in a wedge, like cormorants or brants, the devourers swooped nearer, and on the one in the lead sat the goddess, naked and proud in her nakedness, her flesh shimmering whitely. Nor did I find myself any the less afraid of her because she was unclothed. Her hard white face, the haughty lift of her head, prevented that, and the sight of her pale breasts chilled me, for they moved no more than two rocks might have. I struggled up to stand beside Tass, drawing my sword, though I swayed on my feet.

"Is that—she?" Tass whispered to me, her own blade at the ready.

"Mahela. Yes."

The sound of Mahela's laughter floated through the sky to us, uncanny laughter, for even in that clear night it sounded as if it writhed to us like a sea snake through water. Even though she and her foul retinue flew quite close, within a stone's throw away, her voice sounded chill, distant.

"Dannoc!" she hailed me gaily. "My renegade storyteller, well met! Or is it my rascal Ytan?"

The venomous joy in that cold voice! Like a snake-dazzled bird, I could not take my eyes from her. And one of the devourers, swooping past me, struck me a glancing blow with its heavy eel-like tail, sending me sprawling. Tassida's sword Marantha flashed, and the tail lay beside me, thrashing horribly as greenish blood gouted the cinders. I edged away, though I could not yet rise, and Mahela laughed again, circling her greensheen steed so that she could watch us.

"There, Dannoc, you long for something living, and now you have it! You want the creatures back? Here are some more!" Snakes issued from her mouth as she spoke, writhing like the severed tail, falling to the ground and twisting and coiling in their agony as they hit the hard, black stones. I could see the convulsing of their pale underbellies in the night, and though I staggered to my feet I found I could not stand without leaning on my sword, half bent over, as if it were an old man's stick. Alar was angry. Her pommel jewel shone a fierce yellow, and Marantha's blazed as angrily, a clear red-purple hue like that of the healing flower of Sakeema after which she took her name. Wry, to see that hue in so deadly a weapon. The sword, as uncanny as the one who lifted her.

"Hag!" Tassida breathed between bared teeth, though I had thought Mahela was too comely, too ageless, to be called hag. "Filthy corpse-eating shitbag! Come closer, and I will cut you open!"

"Put away your sword, little daughter!" Mahela sang in reply, her voice far too glad for anyone's comfort who knew her. "My fell servants will not take you tonight."

"Indeed so, for you know I would slash them to pieces." Tassida laughed, a grim laugh nearly like Mahela's. "Where are the others of your twelve, old goddess?"

"Do not overween, upstart." Mahela's voice had gone dark. "You will be mine soon enough. You and all the others."

The dark tone of her threat did not chill me nearly as much as her laughter, for Mahela did not often need to threaten—she merely took what she wanted, with boredom or joy. I straightened, finding some of my strength. Eyes on the goddess, Tassida muttered at me aside, "Dannoc, be of some use! Where is your bow?"

Atop our bags of provision, it was, within the shadow of the cave. Tassida had brought it to me from the place where I had dropped it along the Traders' Trail. I tottered toward the cave, crawled into it, hoping Mahela would think I was fleeing. She must have, for I heard her laugh again.

"Old coward," Tassida taunted. "You call me upstart? Is there anything in your belly but snakes? Come closer, show me this much-vaunted power of yours."

"There will be time enough for that, little daughter." Mahela's laughter had faded, she sounded merely bored, she turned her head away as if to give her foul steed the signal to leave. Within the shadow of the cave, I had strung my bow and was frantically seeking an arrow. Mahela was not a creature of Sakeema, that I should hesitate to kill her, but more like a demon, she herself the demon of death. All powers, let Tass keep her just a moment more—

"Why do you call me daughter?"

In Tass's voice, not so much challenge as a desperate plea. Mahela's head came around in a wordless answer, and in her still, hard face no laughter showed any longer. The devourer she rode grew as still as her face, seeming almost to hover on air, and I took aim. This one time I would not risk the mercy bolt to the neck. This one time, thinking of the world's dying throes, I aimed for the heart.

"Sakeema guide it," I whispered, and I loosed the arrow.

It sped through stillness and the night and buried itself to the feathers in her breast.

Oddly, neither Tass nor I shouted in triumph. We stared, and the only cry was Mahela's, and she cried horribly in pain, making me feel as much the monster as she. A birdlike scream as she toppled from her mount—she was a bird. Changing as she fell, her wings beating the air, she was a cormorant the size of a hart, feathers as black and greenly shining as her hair had been, and with her strong, bone-colored beak she tugged the arrow from her breast and let it drop. Her white-ringed eyes glared at us. Then, heavily, with her wedge of devourers following her, she flew away westward. I blinked, watching the flight of that great cormorant in the night, feeling a vague stirring as of something not remembered, something I had once seen.

Tass stood with Marantha dangling from her lowered hand, swordlight fading. I sheathed Alar and went to her, staggering as I walked.

"It was a good shot, Dan," she whispered, staring off

the way Mahela had gone. "Yon beldam should have been dead."

"Yet she is no demon," I said shakily. "She was hurt. The blood, dark on her breast, and she cried out—"

"She should have been dead," Tass insisted.

"She is the goddess," I said, hearing in my own words an echo of other words: She is far stronger. She always wins.

"She must be," said Tass. "I am trembling."

I put my arms around her, for all the good it would do. I was no steadier than she, and she was quivering like an aspen leaf.

"Tass," I queried gently, "who is your mother?"

She shook her head and buried her face against my shoulder, not answering. That did not surprise me, for she had scarcely ever answered any of my questions about herself. What touched me was that she refused me with so little fire. Her fist, lying clenched against my chest, a hard knot—I smoothed it with my right hand until it eased, felt fingers touch fingers as her hand turned to meet mine—

An unaccountable tide of strength surged through me, and a feeling I could not name.

I knew that strength. It was handbond, yet not the same as handbond with Kor. Not touch of comrade, friend, bond brother, but—something other. Strength not of four heroes, but better, strength of—I could not name it, or the passion, the exaltation I felt. Not even the name of love encompassed it. Though love pulsed in me, warm and strong in me.

Tass had stopped shaking. For a moment, I think, we had both stopped breathing. "Sakeema," she murmured in awe, "what is it?"

"Don't be frightened," I whispered to her, keeping the

handbond, and I kissed her on her temple. Her face turned upward, and her seeking mouth found mine.

Hands softly slipped apart, quested elsewhere—we no longer needed handbond. Together we were very strong. Somewhere in the darkness lay a devourer's severed tail, dead or dying serpents. We paid them no heed, we laid aside our swords and paid no heed to dying, we defied the world's dying. We placed pelts within the shelter of the cave, soft brown furs, all that we had left of the creatures of Sakeema, and we lay on them and made, maybe, a new life, attempted it in the old, old way and yet all was new, all was Tass, Tass, and I would never again lie with any other. My mouth pressed against the side of her face and I whispered her name, felt her hands and her loins answer me, and I was strong, deft, I was mountainpeak and she was sky, and—how she welcomed me. . . .

Her tough young body lay all night close to mine, and I could scarcely sleep for love of her.

# Chapter Nine

We stayed two more days at the blackstone cave, though it could no longer be said that I needed to regain strength. But Tass seemed to like the place, for all that the thunder cones stood bleak and black-smoking beneath a stark sky, and after the first night I looked around me with new eyes, for she had turned it into a place for me to love. In the springtime, she told me, tiny sunset-purple flowers, the most frail and winsome of flowers, no more than a finger tall, sprang out of the cinders in great numbers so that they lay like a red-purple mist all over the slopes, then were gone again within a few days.

Then she fell silent, as if to wonder, would she ever see them again . . . would they ever be, again?

On the third day, early, before heat and nearly before light, we filled all our waterskins and set out to travel to the Herders, riding Calimir by turns.

Picking our way between the thunder cones Methven and Catalin Du, wearing our boots to tatters on the sharp stones, wrapping our feet with my buckskin leggings and wearing them to rags as well, all in the fierce heat of midsummer—it seemed a long, hard journey and yet far too short, for I was alone with Tass, her comrade during the day's toil, her lover in the cool and pleasant nights. Food and water were nearly gone at the last, and we sustained each other with touch and glance when we stumbled, when our tongues and lips swelled and the sun blistered us. And in six days we came through the blackstone lands to the red-earth plains where the Herders roamed with their goats and donkeys and their brown sheep. Then we both rode Calimir, and came swiftly to the place where they had dug their dwellings.

I did not understand, at first, when I saw the smokes issuing from the ground in the evening shadows of Methven, the Spirit Flame. I thought that they were perhaps his tiny children, nestling there at his feet, that someday black rock would spread over that place as well, or a new cone rise. For I had seen the brushwood huts of the wandering Herders often enough, the traders and those who followed the flocks, but never this place where they came to die, where they had dug their red clay and made their pit homes. The smokes came up from their cooking fires, of course, and but for a few children keeping watch over the small herds close at hand there was no one in sight above ground.

"Smarter than us," Tass said wearily. "They keep out of the heat when they can."

She was riding in front of me. I looked at her, sweat streaking her lean face and the lovelocks curling and clinging with damp, and I felt the sweat of her back against my chest, and smelled the scent of her skin, and in that moment I knew more of loving than I had known since the day I was born. Finally, love lay under my sun-scorched hand, and the world was ending. . . . Before I could give her more than the glance, one of the far-off children spied us and lifted a shout. Small spotted dogs began to bark, and folk swarmed out of the pits, blinking and squinting as they peered at us. We must have been but looming shadows in sunset light to them at first. Then Tassida lifted a hand in greeting, and the glad cry went up.

"Tassida! The wanderer has returned!"

"It's the wayfarer, the wandering wolf!"

"Welcome, Tassida! What news?"

"It is Tassida! And who is that with her?"

Silence fell, and there were whisperings. Then old gray-bearded Ayol stepped forward with the ceremonial blanket of many colors circling his shoulders, to give us king's greeting, and I got down off Calimir to face him levelly. His look was stern, for he and I had quarreled the last time we had met.

"You both wear those strange, bright weapons now," he said. "Do you come in peace?"

He did not lack for bluntness, Ayol! Tassida huffed. But before she could answer hotly, I spoke. "I come to take council with you, Ayol. And if you will forget the rantings of a certain mad fool, I will be grateful to you."

"And I come to cut off your beard, Ayol," Tassida said, very much on her mettle. "With a hundred warriors at my back. Do you not see them? Where in this merry hell is the water?"

Ayol gave her a dour look, for he had known her years longer than I and perhaps was as accustomed to the rough side of her tongue. "Come within," he said briefly, and turning his back on us he stumped off to his pit.

I very nearly blundered into the fire, following him. The

entry was the smoke hole, and the fire stood just below it, under the slant of the notched pole that I descended. First I choked in the smoke, then baked my belly, then nearly charred my foot. But it was well worth it, to enter into the shady coolness of that place after the sunblazing heat above. Here in the ground would be complete shelter from icy winter winds as well. Small wonder that the Herders were called wise.

"Sit," Ayol said curtly.

A year before, perhaps, I would have taken offense at his tone. But it seemed of small importance to me anymore how folk spoke to me. I sat where I was, on the cool floor of dirt or clay. This place strongly reminded me of Kor, of the prison pit where he had first befriended me, and I felt a hot ache of longing at the thought. To send it away, I peered around me, my eyes slowly seeing more of what was in that dim dwelling. An old woman working with a finger loom, not looking at me. Hanks of wool hanging overhead. Clay pots and bowls in plenty, larger and better than any that had ever come westward along the Traders' Trail. Something baking in the coals of the cooking fire—

And then, as I looked near the fire, my throat tightened and tears stung my eyes worse than the smoke.

For there, standing on the stones that ringed the fire, there were the creatures in their many, clay creatures, small, frail, very much like the wooden ones my folk of the Red Hart had taken to carving. Silent, great-eyed, lifeless, they faced me, red clay in the red glow of the fire. There were antelope and prairie falcons and bison, skylarks and songbirds, deer, gophers, badgers and ferrets. There were great-eared foxes. There were even figures of wildcats and wolves, though the meat-eaters could not have been much beloved by these sheep-herding folk. Yet there they stood, the yellow clay cats and red wolves, in plenty.

There was a small sound, and, blinking, I looked up at Ayol. He squatted before me, offering a goatskin of water, and he must have seen my burning eyes, for his voice, when he spoke to me, had turned very gentle.

"Drink water, Dannoc. I think I cannot give you what you more truly want."

"Water is a good gift," I whispered, and I drank deeply. The old woman left her finger weaving, climbed up the pole and out the entry. Ayol sat across the fire from me, and his weathered old hands, as if of themselves, sought out a lump of clay from the pot by his side. He began to shape another creature, an owl, all the while speaking in a soft old voice, as if he did not much care whether I listened to him or not, his yellow eyes half lidded.

"My folk say, some of them, that we can live, for we have never been hunters. We have the goats for milk and leather, the sheep for mutton and wool. We plant beans and corn. But I cannot believe that anything can ever again be well without the wild creatures, the creatures of Sakeema."

With a scraping of her weary feet Tassida came down the entry pole, avoiding the fire more gracefully than I had managed, taking the waterskin from me without ceremony, gulping at it. "The well water is brown," she accused Ayol after she was done. Or perhaps she said it merely to explain why she had not drunk there when she had watered Calimir and turned him loose to graze with the donkeys. Her inner fire made everything she said sound contentious. But Ayol only looked up mildly at her, pale old eyes amid soft folds of skin.

"The well is low," he said, his voice even and steady and throaty through phlegm. "There is not enough water for us to pour on the beans, the corn, and they are dying. The ewes dropped mostly dead lambs this year, and the goats have not freshened with milk. All who are older than I, and many who are younger, died in the winter past. This winter, if all does not end before winter, we will eat the corn and beans that should be saved for seed, and the ewes that should be saved for breeding, or we will starve."

Tassida sat down silently by my side.

"Small use in keeping them for the morrow," Ayol remarked, "when all the signs say there will be no morrow. I am surprised the Fanged Horse Folk have not been here ere this, to kill us all while bellowing that they have not enough."

"They are hosting to the westward," I told him, "to attack the Seal Kindred." Pain pierced my heart like a lance, as always when I thought of Kor. And Ayol gave me a surprised look, peering at me through the wavering smoke above the fire.

"Then why are you not with Korridun? I know you are not a coward." A fool, maybe, his tone said, but not a coward. Or perhaps I only heard the thought, Fool, in him. And suddenly, in the presence of this gruff old man, all my doubt burst from me.

"May all the powers help me, I am not sure any longer!" I stood up, needing to pace, though there was not room enough for pacing and my head nearly brushed the beams of the earthen ceiling. "I left him to go seeking Sakeema. Just find the god, I thought, give him a hearty shake, and all our troubles would well-come-hell be over. Sakeema would save us when nothing else could. Sakeema, the god who has died. . . ." The bitterness in my own voice startled me, and I sank to a cross-legged seat on the clay floor again, glad of the dimness that somewhat shielded my face.

"A worthy quest,"Ayol said, his voice as dry as the plains but without mockery.

"I could not have left Kor for any lesser cause. But now it seems to me that I have left him for no cause at all! And the quest feels as awk and awry as the world. . . . Ayol, does Sakeema yet live, think you? For if he does, how can he be letting these things happen?"

"These are weighty questions," Ayol said, and he slowly set down his owl of clay beside the fire, took more clay and started another. We all three of us sat in silence. The old woman, perhaps Ayol's pledgemate, came down the pole carrying strips of dried mutton, poured water in a clay basin, put the meat in it to soften and went out again. Meat, in our honor, when the world was ending.

"Questions without answers," Tassida said at last, a hard edge in her voice—despair?

"Ayol," I urged, "my brother Tyee has told me that the elders of the Herders are wise."

"I am the eldest now, and I am not so very wise. I know only the ordinary things of Sakeema: that he was good, and loved peace, and all the creatures loved him, that he made marvelous new creatures out of clay and by the power of his hands. The many-colored wolves of wonder he made. When he died, or went away, my people say, the wolves carried him away across the great plain, into the sunrise."

I had thought that the wolves had taken him back to the blackstone cave where he had been suckled. Hearing what Ayol said, I grew somber, for I had seen that plain spreading away from the skirts of the thunder cones, and it looked as vast as the sea. "How am I ever to find him?" I asked.

"I do not know. Is Sakeema to be found in such a bodily sense? My inwit tells me not. But you are a dreamwit, Dannoc, and I am not. You must decide."

The old woman came back with mint leaves for us to chew, and she kneeled near the fire, scraping coals aside, pulling bread of some sort out of them. In order to show respect for the king, she had not spoken, but suddenly she turned her face toward me and said, "When I was a child, it was a saying of the elders that he who sought Sakeema must seek the tree that grows in the sea."

Ayol stared at her in astonishment, we all stared at her, and she became abashed. "Eat," she muttered, thrusting bread and strips of meat at us.

"Not yet, Yola. First tell us more of this thing you have remembered," Ayol said.

The old woman shrugged. "It is nothing. It was a way for them to say, do not attempt the fool's task. There are no trees that grow in the sea."

"But there are," I told her. "I have seen them, hanging heavy with red fruit. I have seen the captive tree that grows by Mahela's throne, the round blue fruits bending its branches. But Sakeema was not there."

"It was pomegranate, in the song," Yola said. "If it was the same tree."

We all stared, and Ayol said drily, "I had forgotten there is yet one here more elder than I. One who pays attention to foolish things. What is a pomegranate, Yola?"

"I do not know."

Ayol sighed. "What song, then, my sister?" he asked with pointed patience.

I should have known when I heard her name that she was his sister. The Herders gave lifelong names to their newborn babes, and sometimes named them much alike.

"Just a chant we sang as children, for the treading out of the corn."

"Say it," I begged.

So in her whispery old-woman's voice, with hesitation, she recited it:

*Three in one and one in three,*
*The pomegranate on the tree.*
*And what lies in the heart of it*
*No mortal eye can see.*
*Return to us, Sakeema,*
*In sunset days we beg thee.*

Sunset days. Had they felt the world ending, even then?

"We were allowed to make small birds of the corn hulls, as an offering," old Yola added in a voice like the voice of a spirit speaking on the wind. And with a flat, hardened look on his weathered face, Ayol set down the clay bird he had been fashioning in his hand.

We all sat in silence. And with my mind on the tree in the sea, I did not think of the sunstuff panel I had seen.

Some moments later Yola again offered the strips of meat she had prepared, and Tass took some gladly, but I refused, explaining, so as not to give offense, that since I had started my quest I could no longer eat the flesh of any creature of Sakeema.

"It is only mutton!" Tass grumbled at me.

"That is meat, of a sort, which you hold in your hand," Ayol added.

I looked down at the bread, astonished. The flavor was unfamiliar to me, some sort of root, I had thought.

"Grasshoppers," Ayol explained. "In hard times we catch them in trenches by the tens of hundreds, then grind them up to cook them."

In silent bewilderment I ate the grasshopper bread. Meat that was not meat. God who was and was not. Sakeema was asleep in a cave somewhere, he was in the sunrise, in the sunset, in the sea, in a tree whose name was strange to me. Where was I to search for him, if he was everywhere? Or nowhere. Dead. . . . I pushed away the bread. I could not eat.

"Though it is not likely to help," Ayol said to me, "let me tell you the Herders' tale of Sakeema."

We all gazed into the low flames, as was customary for the telling of tales. When he had centered himself, Ayol began.

"Sakeema was born, so my people say, in one of the serpent holes, the long, low caves, in the midst of the blackstone barrens, somewhere in the skirts of the thunder cones."

"So was I, most likely," Tassida interrupted the tale, "yet no one calls me savior."

I gaped at her, for it was unlike her to speak of herself, and this was a greatly strange way of doing so, and a strange saying. But Ayol only glanced at her in mild annoyance.

"It has been many years, Tassida, since we of the Herders decided that you would not make a likely god for us."

She laughed out loud in perverse delight, laughed so long and so merrily that even Ayol broke his dignity with a grin that showed his brown teeth and the wide gaps in them. And I smiled broadly, savoring the jest, for indeed Tass could scarcely have been less like Sakeema. For all that I would love her until I died, I could not gainsay that her courage, though great, was all outward. Within, she was as needful as an abandoned child, and her needfulness, or the need to shield it, made her arrogant, willful, mettlesome.

"And were you suckled by wolves, as the Herders say Sakeema was?" I asked her, half jesting, when she had quieted somewhat. But she grew suddenly as still as stone, looking hard at me.

"Yes," she told me levelly, "I was."

I gaped anew, but Ayol seemed far less astonished. "Red wolves," he said in his phlegm-thickened voice. "The large-eared, thin-furred red wolves of the plains and barren hotlands, and it might have been the very last pair."

"When they died, I was bereft." Tass had lifted her chin, and her dark eyes dared me to pity her, or disbelieve her, or do anything but silently listen to her. "I lived wild among the rocks until the Herders found me and tamed me."

"No more than half tamed," Ayol admitted with regret. "We did our best."

"I hate Sakeema, Dan," Tass blazed suddenly.

Though I had sometimes of late thought the same, coming from her this was a shock. "In the mighty name," I exclaimed, "why?"

"All the tales of him reproach me. He was everything that I am not: gentle, peaceful, loving, and a man. I sometimes feel that I was made by a demon, left in that cave only to be a mockery of him, just as your brother Ytan is a mockery of you."

My head swirled as if I had been fasting and had gone into a visionary trance. All seems plain to see in a tale, but in life it is not so. I was in a riddle place, a confusion, the hold of Mahela's sunstuff ship, the innards of the dark stone lodge where I had seen a tree of sunstuff, three crossed swords. I was lost, my own name in doubt, a riddle, and somewhere close at hand Sakeema was hiding from me, I could nearly see his face . . . I blinked, and it was gone. The face before me was Tassida's, startling in its beauty. She, as much of a riddle as my name or Sakeema.

I blurted, "You—you do not know your human mother."

"I do not know her, or any human father, or any name that either of them might have given me."

Her name, Tassida, "the horseback rider"—she must have taken it for herself. I gazed back at her, the proud bearing of her head at once defying me and imploring me, and I fiercely wished that she would let me mindspeak her, for I had begun to have a faint sense of the Tass within, of how to love her, and no spoken words could be as soft, as gentle, as that silent touch of mind . . . and in front of gruff old Ayol, yet . . .

Nevertheless, I tried it aloud, softly, gently, and let Ayol listen all he liked and watch with his pale yellow eyes. "The cave . . . where you were born . . . it is the one where we—"

"Where we stayed. Yes." The hush in her voice told me that she had heard my hidden message, of love, of acceptance.

But still I did not know which way I would ride when it came time for me to leave this place.

# Chapter Ten

When sunset had lengthened the shadow of Spirit Flame so that it shaded the Herder village, Tass and I went outside to wander. All the Herders were out and about now, and we exchanged greetings with many of them, but none of them knew any more than we did of Sakeema—indeed, many of them angrily did not wish to speak of him. When twilight was deepening and stars were springing forth like frost flowers in the eastern sky, when the sudden nighttime coolness lay on the land, Tass and I walked apart from the others and talked until long after dark.

She told me of her many travels. Telling me of her beginnings seemed to have tapped a wellspring of talk in her. She told me how far she had ventured, searching for the tribe, the parents she did not know: far to the north into the unknown mountains without names, far southward to where the coastline was no longer rock but flattened sand, far eastward onto the plains that seemed never to end. Northward and southward, she had found nothing. Eastward, nothing but the ruins of great stone villages that must once have been ten tens of times larger than ours.

"The fortress above the pool of vision," she told me, "I think must have been an outpost."

Those words were strange to me, *fortress, outpost.* She had learned them in vision, as she had learned other things she had taught us of, Kor and me, things long forgotten. Swords, sailing ships, castles, crowns, thrones, kingdoms, jewels. Tass made a poet and minstrel and visionary such as none other in the dying world.

"What did you see in the pool of vision," I asked her, since she was in a mood to talk, "the day you brought forth your sword?" But she fell silent. We walked on across the level land in a long silence.

"Ask me anything else, Dan," she replied at last, far more tamely than was her wont.

We spoke of Ytan, of his threats, a peril far smaller than the other perils that faced us, threats nearly laughable compared to threat of world's end. And we spoke of Kor. Long and softly we spoke of Kor, turning and turning him in our minds, as if he were a part that had to be pieced together with the two of us, a shard made to fit into the pattern of our lives somehow. But we could not comprehend Kor, or the pattern, for we scarcely understood ourselves. The longer we talked, the stranger everything seemed. Love, our love for each other, for Kor, should have been simple, but there was something uncanny. . . . And there was the feeling I could not name, the passion that had filled me when Tassida's fingers had touched mine in handbond, a feeling so awesome that I was afraid to touch her hand again. Since we had talked I knew more of Tass than ever before, yet I seemed to know less. Indeed I scarcely knew her at all, and I scarcely knew myself anymore, and I did not know how to pursue my quest.

And though I felt an unreasoning hope just being with Tass, there was small hope for me in her words. The world, so vast—I had known that a solitary rider was small and the world so vast, yet I had not truly known. Tassida had searched most of her life and found nothing. To the north, nothing, to the south, nothing but wilderness, to the east, nothing but empty plains and ruins. To the west, world's end, or edge, and Kor, and Mahela's greendeep. How, then, could I expect to find the god?

Tassida and I talked quietly and wandered a great circle on the level plain until we came back to the Herder pit village again. Except for the soft movements of livestock, all was silent. The Herders had long since gone to their beds. We found our pelts, heaped with Calimir's gear where Tass had piled it, and lay on the open ground under the stars, and defied death in the leisurely ways, pleasuring each other for a long time. Later, still naked and pressed closely together, we eased into warm, sweet sleep.

It was the last such sleep we were to know for a long time.

In the lifting darkness just before dawn a sound like thunder started in the earth, jarring us out of slumber, a moving thunder within earth itself, like a stampede of a hundred hundred great bison running swiftly nearer, and the ground shook as the earth-storm passed under us. Then more, again, waves and tides of the ground thunder, like ocean swell breaking again and again, so that I could not tell the coming from the going of them, and the ground shook constantly. I tried to stand up, Tass and I clinging together tried to stand up, but every time we tried we were knocked down before we had more than struggled to our knees, and all around us rose the screams of the Herders from their houses below the ground, screams that we could hear even above the earth's roaring.

"Powers, they are being killed!" Tass exclaimed, her fingers digging into my shoulder, her voice near enough to my ear so that I could hear her above the uproar, could hear the sobbing in her throat. "They cannot get out. Ayol. . . ."

We could not even stand up to help them.

And with a thundering louder than any clamor of storm or ocean surf, with a hollow bellowing more fearsome than any tens of hundreds of bison trampling, with a jolt that sent us thudding hard to the ground, as if earth had twitched her hide to throw us off like so many flies, with a vehement roar Methven the Spirit Flame sent up a mighty spurt of red fire and a black shadowy hurling of stones. And to the northward I saw the wrathful blaze of Catalin Du, less fearsome only because farther away. And to the southward, Keb raised a tower of flame in the same way, and Senet—I could see no farther, but for all I knew every thunder cone was shuddering forth bloody blazing rock, earth's innards gone mad. A choking stench filled the air, and overhead the sky was utterly black.

All seemed dim and heavy after that, and slow, as if done under water. Tass and I did unaccountable things. We could not stand up for the earth's shaking, so we sat and pulled on clothing, I my lappet, she her tunic and trousers of wool, as if it would matter whether we were naked once we were dead. A slow flow of red fire was edging down Methven's shoulders, like a courtier's bright cape, and at last the tremors had calmed, but still we could not stand upright because of the stinging smoke. We crawled across ground cracked and pitted, roof timbers jutting out of an awful silence, no weeping of mothers, no wailing of children, it was all too deadly for that. In the bloody glow we could see a few Herders pulling themselves out of half-collapsed dwellings, then lying on the ground. Crawling past them, Tassida found the hole she wanted and went down it headfirst, like a rockchuck, and instead of helping her I lay and waited numbly. A while later she came up dragging Ayol by his shirt. The old Herder still lived, though I did not see how he could do so much longer, for his breath rattled and bubbled in his broken chest as he breathed. Yola lay dead below.

"Something—terrible—is happening," Ayol wheezed when he caught sight of me, and I sat up and solemnly agreed with him.

"Yes, it is terrible."

"No!" His smoke-bleared eyes flashed with annoyance, red in the glare of Spirit Flame. "Not—here. Somewhere. Something terrible."

"Hush," Tassida told him, her hand lying lightly on his injured chest, and he quieted under her touch and seemed to breathe more easily.

"Will the fire flow come here?" I asked her. "Must we move him?"

"I don't know," she said.

The wooden weariness in her voice awakened what small courage was left in me. Keeping my head low and coughing in the stinking smoke, I blundered off until I found another pit not utterly destroyed, heaved up the timbers and clambered down to bring the folk up from underneath. Some of them yet lived, and there was a child who seemed hardly to be hurt at all, only stunned. I laid them down and found another dwelling. Haste, haste, my mind was crying out for haste now, lest folk smother because I had been such a slowcome. I labored until the sweat ran down my body as the streams of fire ran down Methven, wrestling bodies and sometimes living Herders from every pit in that place, and not until full daylight had come did I look up long enough to notice that the smoke had spread and thinned somewhat, making a thin gray blanket fit to lay over a corpse. Dawn sun on it turned the whole sky to a blood-colored haze.

And Herders were walking about, some of them whole, some of them wounded but strong enough to walk, tending those who were wounded worse than they. And at a distance I saw Ayol sitting up to drink the water Tassida offered him.

I lurched over and sat, or slumped, beside him. "What terrible thing?" I asked him as if we had only just spoken of it.

"I do not know." His voice was far stronger—how could he still be alive, at his age, with his chest crushed in? Yet be seemed almost well again. "I do not know. But the thunder cones do not send forth fire unless dire events are afoot. Methven has not done so since Sakeema died."

"Sakeema," I muttered bitterly. The god's name meant little to me any longer.

Suddenly knowing that I was exhausted, I lay back where I was, my eyes closed against the stinging smoke. Gray ash was falling out of the air, settling on my face. I lay that way, drowsing but too weary to truly sleep, until I seemed to hear a voice coming to me on the thick and foul-smelling air.

"Dannoc."

Spent, I ignored it.

"Dannoc! Sakeema help us all, what is the use of this lummox?"

Startled, I opened my reddened eyes and looked. At some distance to the westward of me a greenshade shimmered in air, drifting amid the gray smoke and ash and the red glow off the thunder cone's fiery slopes.

"My father!" I cried, scrambling to my feet, for once I had hearkened to it I knew that voice to my bones.

Ayol, blanket-wrapped and sitting at my feet, glowered up at me as if I were a madman. "He's lightheaded," I heard Tassida say to the old man, and then to me, "Dan—"

"Do you not see him?" I exclaimed without looking around at her. "My sire! Hush, he speaks!"

"Pajlat and his minions have come to Seal Hold," Tyonoc was telling me, his voice hollow and toneless on the wind. "Izu and the Otter River Clan have thrown in their lot with him, and the Cragsmen have come down from the crags to avenge their slain comrades. Korridun and his Kindred will face hard battle. Only Tyee goes to aid him, he and his warriors, and they have not yet topped the Blue Bear Pass."

Though there had been no edge of reproach in his voice, in his words I heard nothing but most bitter reproach that I was not at Korridun's side. Bitter reproach, and cause for bitter fear. Dry-mouthed, I asked, "What means this fire out of the thunder cones?"

"First blows, perhaps, or first blood. I do not know."

Such a cold fear lay heavy on me, crushing me like a devourer, that I could scarcely speak. At last I whispered, "The seven black peaks do not roar and flame every time men strike blows."

"It may be that a king has died."

And suddenly instead of my father's spirit it seemed to me that in the swirling of the smoke I saw Kor's face, the quiet quirk of his mouth that was as close as he most often came to a smile, his sober, dark eyes looking on me with love. But his dark hair was damp and matted with blood, and blood ran down the smooth shell-tan skin of his face.

I must have staggered, for in a stride Tassida was at my

side, shoving a none-too-gentle hand under my elbow. "Dan," she demanded, "what in Sakeema's name is going on? You are talking to air."

"Kor," I breathed, and I could make no more sense than that, for mountainpeaks were splitting asunder inside me, the sky had slipped upside down, earth cracking apart under my feet, all was falling to pieces, and in a single uncanny moment, with a feeling as if my own sword had found its way to my heart, I knew to my center of being the true meaning of despair. For I had a choice that was no choice, to pursue the quest that had once seemed so right, or to go to Kor—and I knew I would go to Kor, let the world writhe and die as it must. Let Sakeema sleep on, or laugh, the betrayer, for I would never find him. Let Mahela laugh as she surely would. Who had called me Darran, "the seeker"? I would seek no longer. I would go and die with my bond brother—if he was not dead already. Fool that I was, I should never have left his side.

"Kor is not here!" Tass snapped, and I flung off her hand.

"Do you think I do not know that?" I shouted at her as if it had somehow been her fault. "By my great, stupid body, what am I doing here? I must go to him! Small thanks to me if he is not already slain!"

"Go sleep," Tass ordered. "You are raving."

Nothing in the sky but ashes and gloom. My father's spirit was gone, and it seemed that Tass could not see it even had it stayed. And in a sense I was, indeed, raving, for I was in a frenzy to be off, with small sense and no patience left in me to explain to her that I was—what? Giving up, turning back, failing yet once again, yes. And likely I would fail to come to Kor in time to be of any good to him, for in all the lands of the six tribes I could not have come much farther from him than I was that dawn. Wrongheaded, thrice-accursed wantwit that I was.

"Where is that horse?" I demanded, blundering off in the direction of the herds, coughing in the smoke that still hung pungent in the air. Tass brushed past me and planted herself in front of me, straddle-legged, fists on her hips and elbows jutting.

"Calimir goes nowhere without me," she told me frostily.

"Get your gear, then! Quickly!"

"Are you moon-mad? I am needed here! And so is your great, stupid body. Is there no honor left in you, that you would leave the Herders in such a pass and not offer to stay and help?"

Such was the tug on me that not even Tassida's passion swayed me. The blaze in her eyes only shifted my own gaze into the past. "I left my bond brother lying under the lash of Mahela's storm, once," I murmured. "I saw him lying beaten on a shore and turned away. No, there is little honor left in me."

Tassida gave me a glare of wholehearted, uncomprehending fury. "You can well-come-hell walk," she said.

There must have been some honor left in me after all, for I did not consider stealing her horse or taking it by force. Instead, I thought fervidly. My long legs, dangling over a Herder's donkey, would veritably drag on the ground. Were there no other horses?

"Perhaps the fanged mares are yet wandering near where I slew their masters," I said. "I will go that way." Though it was likely to be a fool's journey. No affection held those mares to their masters, to keep them near the bare-picked bones. But who better than I to undertake a fool's task?

Blindly I turned and started off north and eastward, on

my way toward the Traders' Trail, which would take me around the skirts of the thunder cones. But Tassida sprang in front of me again, heat in her face and her voice.

"Dan, I do not understand! One moment it was all Sakeema, Sakeema, Sakeema—"

"Curse Sakeema!" I exploded. "Curse him to Mahela's hell, if he is not dead already. He is a traitor, and he took me away from Kor." I tried to shove past her.

It is not to be wondered at, that she thought I had gone mad. I was nearly naked, without food or water, and setting off just as I was toward the sere, deathly Steppes.

She was too angry to remonstrate with me any longer. She seized me.

I threw off her grip. With deft, battle-trained hands and body she came at me again, and again I threw her off, not without struggling, for she was skilled. But I was as skilled, and too large and strong for her. A third time she attacked me, and this time I kept hold of her wrists rather than thrusting her away. It cooled my fury and gave me pause that she was grappling with me, however harmlessly. I had fought with Kor once, less harmlessly, and I wished never again to combat with one I loved.

Tass and I stood staring at each other. She was panting with wrath or emotion—I noted the rise and fall of her small, firm breasts under her shirt.

"Come with me, Tass," I softly requested her.

"How can I, with folk lying hurt here?" Sharp weapon-edge in her tone, as always when she felt her shield slipping. "Stay a few days, and I will come. Perhaps."

"I cannot stay another breathspan."

"Then go, and be damned. But at least have the decency to first say your farewells to Ayol."

So I let go of her and did so to calm her, if only a little. And, as she had known he would, old Ayol serenely directed me to find food and water in the ruined dwellings, and to take a dead Herder's clothing and boots, for the man would no longer be needing them.

Thus it was that I set out dressed in woolens, trousers instead of my ruined leggings, and even a woolen tunic to protect me from the fierce sun and nighttime chill. Truly the world is ending, I could hear Tyee say. Dannoc is wearing a shirt. Woolens, yet. Well, it was a fitting thing, to wear clothing that did not require the killing of an animal to make it, and I had told Ayol so.

My boots, the largest ones I could find, were yet too small, for the Herders are a small folk. Before I had reached the edge of their village, I stopped and slit open the fronts of them. Then I girded Alar more tightly to my waist, shouldered my bow and bag of provision and set out at the trot.

"Dannoc!"

Only for that voice would I have stopped, even for the moment. Tassida came and stood before me, a haunted look in her eyes, but she did not speak. "Say it!" I demanded.

"I do not understand—how you can just leave."

"I have to go to Kor. You will not come with me."

She seemed not to have heard. "After what we have shared," she murmured, "I had thought we would always be together."

I puffed my lips in exasperation. "Since I have known you," I said, "and since you have known that I love you, how many times have you left me with small ceremony? For reasons of your own?"

"We ought—I could not help it. We ought to be together. Everything has changed, now. Do you not feel it?"

Everything had indeed changed, my world had slipped into ruins around my witless head, and I did not dare to feel anything except peril in regard to her. Hers was the one plea that could have kept me from Kor's side.

"We will be together again," I said, trying to speak gently, for it was not Tassida's wont to humble herself as she was doing, pleading with me. "You will find your way back to me again, as you have always done before."

Her dark brows drew together. "In Mahela's hell!" she snapped, and she turned and strode angrily away. I set off at speed on my journey, not looking back at her.

# Chapter Eleven

Through what was left of the day I traveled in utmost haste, at trot and brief walk and trot again, and on past dusk into nightfall, through the smother of smoke that blotted out the stars and moon that might have guided me through the night, and only for that reason, because I could not see to travel, did I stop to eat, and after I had eaten I could not rest, but stood up and paced and circled where I was. Sometime past halfnight a sharp, cold wind came up and blew the smoke away, and then I could see, though not to run for fear of laming myself against a stone, and I walked on again.

Kor. . . . Tass. . . . But Tass was in no danger except the world's danger, which was on all of us. With an effort of will I pushed the thought of her aside. Even the brief moment of thinking of her—behind me—and Kor—ahead—had made me feel as if I were being torn asunder.

At first light I began to run, and I ran on through the blazing day with only brief pauses to walk or drink, and still I had not drawn abreast of Catalin Du! By Mahela's stinking bowels, but it was a vast, doomed world to one afoot and in haste. Even had I been mounted, it was all too vast, the distance all too far that I had come from my bond brother.

That night, when full dark came, I had to rest or I would have fallen. But with first light I was up again and stumbling onward like a crazed thing, like a lemming, toward the sea. A murky sunrise the color of old blood lay over the immense eastward plain. Smoke had spread that way, lying over the world like a blanket over a corpse, making even sunlight seem dim, leaving a wincing smell and a bitter taste in the air.

Before me, the treeless roughlands of the Steppes. Behind me, small with distance but yet there, no matter how I strove to leave him behind, Methven, red tattered cape turning to dull black on his shoulders. Beside me, seeming never to change shape or move, Catalin Du, his red cloak darkening in like wise. Overhead, a vast sky that could give me no joy. I, very small, running raggedly beneath it.

I began to dream of Kor that day, seeing his face instead of what was before me, or I could not have gone on. Kor, tending the murderous madman in the prison pit. Showing me the ways of mercy. Kor, dying in torment for my sake—I blinked, shaking my head, to drive that memory away, seeing instead his sunrise smile after my tears or some uncanny power had brought him back to life. Kor, my bond brother, questing to Mahela's undersea realm with me. And the beaten despair in both of us as we had crawled naked back onto the shore. . . .

Vision shifted. As plainly as if it stood before me, I was seeing something new and unknown to me.

A sandy shoreline. Endless sky, endless water, ocean surf seething at my feet. And flying landward, low over the waves, two great ernes—I gasped in glad surprise, for I had never seen such eagles before except in the realm of the dead. A white-tailed sea eagle and one of pure white, its wings flashing bright as swords against a storm-dark sky. And the white eagle flew wearily, heavily, heaving at some burden that dangled from its hooked beak. The other flew close to its side, slowing its wingbeats to match its comrade's laboring speed.

They swooped down, or nearly fell down, and with a thump they both landed in the sand, just out of reach of the waves. The dangling burden was a round, bright fruit still on the stem, a fruit as blue as highmountain sky. It had rolled into the sand, and tiny grains of sand clung to its glistening rind. But I was not looking at the fruit, for the eagles at the touch of the land's edge had turned to two goodly men, and I was gazing on them in happiness and longing, for I knew them. They were Chal and Vallart.

He who had been the white-tailed erne was Vallart, and he was sitting up, then staggering to his feet. But Chal, who had been the burdened eagle of entire white—Chal was lying still, with lidded eyes, and the strange fruit had rolled away from him to nestle in the sand by his side. Then I saw how horribly he had been hurt. It was no mere tale, that he had been put to torment in Mahela's realm.

Vallart went to him, sat in the sand by his head, and softly gathered him up, head and shoulders, into his lap and arms. Then with a tremulous effort Chal opened his eyes.

"We've done it," he murmured, looking up into his comrade's face. "We've bested her."

Vallart nodded, swallowing, seeming scarcely able to speak. "Hush," he said finally. "Rest. You must grow strong again. I must go find you food, some covering—"

"No. Stay with me. Please. . . ." Chal's voice dwindled away into a gasping breath. His eyes closed again.

"Chal." Vallart shook him slightly, but Chal did not stir. "Chal! My lord, my comrade, you must live!" Vallart's voice broke on the words, and he held his friend and king hard, close, fiercely, as if holding him could keep him. But Chal lay still. I saw his face grow smooth as pain left him. He had ceased to breathe.

For a moment Vallart did not move. He sat as rigid as a mountain, still clutching at Chal, his body nearly as hard as mountain stone. Stunned with sorrow, I thought, not yet knowing the passions clashing inside him, the sense of duty, the anger and rebellious hope. . . . His head snapped up. Then with a yell of despair or defiance, a heart-torn roar that seemed to echo through generations of mortal dying to reach me, he turned and snatched up the sky-blue fruit in his hand.

He held it over Chal's wounded and unmoving chest. His fingers ripped into the bright rind, tore the fruit wide open, flung it asunder. Inside, blazing white, it was all light, so shining I could scarcely see—stones, dropping out of it, one of sun yellow, one as red as Chal's blood. And naked in Vallart's hand glowed another stone, or jewel, of such a vivid, perfect hue, nameless as the nameless god, never seen but in the flower that had perished with Sakeema's passing, the amaranth. Jewel of an impossible color made all of sunset light, dazzling me with its brightness so that I could scarcely look at it—Vallart laid it on Chal's chest, pressing it into place with the warmth of his hand, and I saw that he was shaking.

The stone flared so that its light blazed, amaranthine, even through Vallart's hand, and he cried out but did not move. Then came a gentler glow—

And Chal stirred and started softly to breathe, and I saw his wounds closing even as I looked. I had seen such a healing once before. And Vallart was weeping, his shoulders shaking, his chest heaving, weeping as I had wept, that time I had held Korridun's body in my arms, first dead, then living and healed. . . . Vallart's tears were falling on his comrade's face, and when Chal opened his eyes in bewilderment, Vallart gathered him up and embraced him.

"What. . . ." Chal struggled to sit up, his own tears filling his eyes. "My god, Vallart, I was dead and now I am alive. What price have you paid? What have you sacrificed?"

The jewel of amaranthine hue had fallen to the sand with the other two, the one sun yellow, the one red as blood. Shakily Vallart lifted it—his palm bore a raw, red wound. The stone blazed darkly in his burned hand, and Chal stared.

"No," he breathed.

"I had to." Vallart could scarcely speak for weeping.

"No! Better you had let me die than sunder it."

"I could not let you die."

"You would rather let the world go down to death?" Chal sounded not so much wrathful as utterly dismayed. "All our striving has come to naught. All goodliness of creation will come to naught."

"Chal, do not reproach me, please!" Vallart covered his face with his hands—the fingers still glistened, moist from ripping the rind of the fruit, dewed as if with its tears. Then he let drop his hands and faced Chal starkly, heedless of his own weeping. "My lord and king, my friend, my comrade, even though the world should die I yet had to be with you."

In the vision, it suddenly seemed to me that Chal's face was Kor's calm, kingly face, and that Vallart's impassioned face was mine. Even though the world should die, I yet had to heed my heart.

And Chal, or Kor, reached out to embrace his comrade, saying, "All will yet be well, somehow. What seems so right to you must yet somehow be well." But the words faltered, and the beloved face was bleak.

Kor's face, bleak and grim. . . .

Why was I stupidly standing in a desert on the wrong side of a black cinder cone? Why was I not with him? What had seemed right to me had been wrong, wrong, wrong, or what now seemed right would be wrong, I did not know which, I knew only that I must be with him, and I felt a doom riding on my shoulders along with my heavy bags of provision, the burden I bore to stay alive. I began to run again, strengthened by desperation, the sun blazing down, my sword slapping at my leg.

Run and walk again, walk and trot, walk and trot, through the day. . . . Mind hazy with weariness and longing, I thought of my strange vision in a drifting way, without much comprehension. Only when I saw the sunset spreading in the western sky did one shard of understanding come to me, came like the point of a knife, for I had not much wanted to think of Tassida.

The amaranthine stone that had healed Chal now glowed in the pommel of her sword. I had seen the fierce blaze of that jewel, and I felt certain of it.

Tass. . . . She was like the sword, an edge that cut and a touch that healed. The thought slowed my steps to a faltering walk, as if something tugged me to turn and stagger back to her. Instead, I stumbled to my knees, then thudded to the hard, rocky ground, and I lay there until the nighttime chill roused me with my own shivering. Then I groaned and got up and went on.

At dawn I saw that Catalin Du was beginning to fall behind me at last.

Hasten, hasten. . . . My sense of urgency had not abated. My feet, rubbed raw and bleeding from the borrowed, ill-fitting boots, moved as fast as I could drag them. I leaned forward so that I reeled along, half falling with every frantic step. It was the only way I could go on except for crawling. And I believe I crawled sometimes, also. I do not remember clearly. The three or four days after I passed Catalin Du and turned westward are a blur. I knew only that I had to go to Kor, and that if no mount were waiting for me along the Traders' Trail I would fail him.

No mount awaited me.

No living creature met my sight across the flat Steppes in any direction when I reached the place where the bleached bones of my former enemies lay. Perhaps the mares had run back to their herdmates, to the westward hosting. More likely they had gone feral and were feeding on asps in some of the dry, steep-sided streambeds that gouged the high plain. Hidden from my sight in such a scar, they might be not even very far away, but I was exhausted, in no condition to track them or wander the Steppes in search of them. I had come the distance from the Herder village in less than a tenday, as fast as a horse and rider would have done it at middling speed, and to no avail.

I lay down, or fell down, on the hard ground by the skeletal bodies and went to sleep. Or swooned.

Perhaps a day passed, for it was daylight again when I

awoke. Perhaps not. I was in no fit fettle to reckon. I sat up and drank water. One goatskin of water was left to me, and one bag of dried berries, cheese and grasshopper bread. My burden of food and water had lightened all the way to the place where I sat, or perhaps I might not have been able to make it so far. But even so lightly laden, even had I left the things and walked away without them, I could not go on. I was emptied, like the flattened waterskins I had hurled aside. I was spent.

Numbly I sat staring westward, not even hoping any longer for a horse, not hoping for anything, not even that someone might come this way and find me. No one would be stirring on this trade trail in these ominous end-time days full of the rumor of war. I sat and stared, not knowing what it was that I looked for. It might have been the better part of a day I sat that way, and in time, as seemed to happen to me more easily with every passing day, my awareness faded into vision, as if I had been fasting and keeping a vigil.

I saw sky first, and wind blowing the high clouds into long strands and wisps like horsehair, like the scant tail of a fanged mare. Then I saw two men fronting the wind, their hair blown back from their foreheads, their eyes narrowed and the bones keen in their faces, so that they made me think of eagles. Indeed they had been eagles, at least once, for I knew them. They were Chal and Vallart, the rich and heavy cloaks of kings whipping about their shoulders. Older, yet I would not have known it except that whiteness lay like frost on their hair. And they were splendid, they in their broidered robes, the sunstuff glinting at their necks and chests and sleeves. Chal wore a circlet of sunstuff on his head—a crown. So that was a crown such as kings had worn in those long-gone times. I had only heard of crowns from Tassida—I had never before seen one. Chal had the look of a king followers would die for, glorious, but Vallart stood no less glorious.

"The cycle speeds downward toward doom," Chal said softly, staring off into the distance somewhere.

Silence. I could see the wild sky and snowpeaks behind the two of them, and a low wall of stone that seemed to encircle them. Somewhere there was a low rumbling sound.

"Feel the earth quiver, even here," said Chal, and then I began to understand, for I stood with them, and I could see the thunder cones in the far distance, eastward, all seven of them flinging blood-red flame and black rock skyward. And I knew the place where I stood, it was the tower on the mountainside above the—the—I could not think of the deep tarn's name except to call it a strange name, Sableenaleb, "dark eye of earth." And with a shock I realized that I was seeing through Vallart's eyes and mind, that I knew the things he knew and felt the things he felt, that somewhere on the far plains to the eastward kingdoms were warring in a fateful war, and kings, friends and sons of old friends, were dying in anguish by the lance and sword—

Frightened, I wrenched myself away, but not before I had felt the stone platform shake under his feet.

"We had better go down," Chal said.

They descended the narrow stone steps in a numb silence, and I went with them, or my spirit did, hanging back so as not to come too close again. Very much at one with them, I felt, too much at one with them—but that was an old, useless fear, the terror of being lost and drowned. I ignored it.

No folk were about in the great hall. Perhaps they had all fled somewhere. Tremors were causing the hangings to swing—long, beautifully wrought hangings in some rich cloth, they showed Chal and Vallart sailing away in a high-headed ship, and Chal confronting Mahela and being imprisoned, and Vallart coming after him to rescue him. Then they showed the rescue of the mystic fruit, and the flight, and the sundering of the fruit into its three colors. The banners hung three on each side of the throne—a modest throne, as I knew from having seen Mahela's—and the panel of sunstuff, which I had seen before, hung on the stone wall above and behind it. I stared, for now I knew the bird thieving the fruit from the tree. It was a cormorant. It was Mahela. She must have thieved the tree itself, in some distant time past, for I had seen it in its pot by her throne.

Head bowed, Vallart settled himself on the step at the foot of the throne, and Chal sat beside him.

"I must return to the Mountains of Doom," Vallart said to his hands. "In time, there will be another pomegranate of our god on the tree. I must bring it hither. Round, perfect and whole."

Chal was gazing at him quizzically, and Vallart must have felt the look, for he raised his eyes. But they were narrowed in pain.

"I am old and due to die soon in any event," he said to Chal. "I cannot expect to go there and live another time, I know that. And it is not dying that troubles me. It is the thought of leaving you."

"No need," said Chal quietly. "I will go with you."

"No! I must go alone."

"I seem to recall," said Chal with a sort of tender amusement, "that I once thought I would go alone."

"Chal, do not dispute with me! Old friend. . . ." Vallart's hand came up to meet Chal's hand, and his voice faltered. "Myself I can sacrifice. But if you were wounded . . . the same thing would happen all over again."

"Nor could I bear it if you were hurt." Chal's grip tightened on his comrade's hand, but his voice was steady. "Therefore it follows, Vallart, that we must both be dead to start with."

Vallart's eyes widened, met his king's. Gazing levelly at each other, the two of them came to some wordless agreement. Then the stone walls around them shook again, the hangings swung wildly, the wooden door splintered and the arch of the doorway cracked. With a crash the trefoil stone at its peak fell down to the floor below.

"Let us go," said Chal, getting up as if it were no more than to walk a small distance to a neighboring lodge. "*Ai,* my poor old bones, they ache with the damp."

"The swords," Vallart blurted, far less calmly. "What are we to do with the swords?"

"Leave them for the three who may yet come."

Marantha, Tassida's sword, hung on the wall behind the throne, the gem in her pommel blazing. Vallart went to her in haste and made as if to grasp her by the hilt, but with a swift, fierce movement she cut at his hand. He jumped back, swearing.

"Bitch!"

"It is of no use to speak to her in that way," said Chal mildly. "Address her courteously."

"You get her, then."

"We both forged her. We must both go to her."

And they did so, standing before her like humble petitioners, each with a hand outstretched, coaxing her by name, "Marantha." And the sword came softly down off the wall and nestled in their hands.

Then Chal and Vallart made their way out under the ruined archway and down the rumbling mountainside to the pool they called Sableenaleb.

They presented Marantha gently to the dark water. She

left their hands of her own will, slipped into the tarn as if into a sheath, point and blade, then vanished. Chal wore Zaneb at his waist, and Vallart wore Alar, each weapon housed in a scabbard of *bronze*—Vallart's mind had joined with mine again, or I would not have remembered the strange words Tassida had once told me. No matter. I withdrew a little and watched as they unbuckled their swords. The stones, red and yellow, were blazing. For a moment the heroes stood holding the weapons in silent farewell, and then Zaneb and Alar sprang from their scabbards and followed Marantha. Without a ripple the pool of vision closed over the three of them.

Chal and Vallart looked at each other for the span of several breaths. Then they dropped the empty scabbards to the shore and turned away. Up the mountainside they strode, past the shaking towers of their outpost castle, onward, westward, toward the sea. The wild wind still blew, bringing smoke, spreading it like a corpse-cover over the world. Before long the king and the afterling disappeared from my sight, gone into shadows, like the swords.

I wanted to follow them, I wanted to be with them, but earth was shaking under me, my whole body was being roughly shaken—

"Dannoc! You pigheaded fool, wake up!"

I blinked and looked up. It was a dark figure seen against a swirl of sunlit smoke or cloud, a head crowned in light. I could not see the face.

"Sakeema," I whispered. But I had forgotten, the god was dead, or a villain. Less painful to blame Sakeema than to blame myself for failing to find him.

"Confound it, don't 'Sakeema' me." She sounded disgusted and more than a little annoyed. I knew that voice.

"Tass!" I scrambled up, wincing as my sore feet found the ground. "What are you doing here?"

For a moment she seemed quite speechless, and I thought I saw dew in her eyes, a tremor as of aspen leaves about her lips. Then her fists bunched, and I believed she was going to strike me. Tottering as I was, she could have knocked me over easily.

"Balls of Mahela!" she shouted at last. "Would you come and get on the horse, you who were so frantic to be on your way?"

Calimir stood close at hand. She vaulted onto him, took my hand and heaved me up behind her, none too gently. Then with a leap we were off westward, the lovelocks of her wild hair lashing my face in the wind of our passing.

## Chapter Twelve

South and westward. That way lay water. We were not so desperate that we chose to use the Fanged Horse Folk's wells or ride into their encampments. We would ride to the Demesne, cross the mountains by the Blackstone Path, perhaps join forces with Tyee. But that would be days, tens of days hence. Even the upland forests of my fair-haired Red Hart people, days hence. Calimir carried us swiftly across billowing, treeless grassland, and I let my head rest for a moment against Tassida's back.

"What of the Herders?" I asked after perhaps half a day had passed.

"They seemed not as badly off as I had thought." Her voice came back to me muffled, indistinct. "Many dead, and everyone grieving. But those who lived seemed not too badly hurt."

"Because you were there," I muttered into her shirt, a vague understanding sharpening into words in me.

"I left after four days," Tassida said, not hearing me, "and you had so outstripped me that it took me four more, at speed, to find you." Awe tinged her voice. "You frighten me, Dannoc."

"Because you were there," I said more loudly, not replying to her fear. "It was because you were there with them that the Herders seemed not too badly hurt. Because you had touched them. You are a healer, Tass."

She stiffened, and the sudden tightening of her legs sent Calimir leaping forward. "Dan, stop talking like a half-wit!" she said harshly.

"There is healing in your touch, there always has been!" I insisted, intent on the new knowledge. "I am a fool not to have seen it before. Kor and I, however we were hurt, we always healed far more rapidly than seemed likely when you were near."

"You are indeed a fool! It is because—because you—" She broke off the thought and suddenly burst out in anger, "I, who am always filled with bitterness and vexation, a healer? I, who have not even nurture enough in me to laugh at you, as I ought?"

"The jewel in your pommel, in Marantha," I told her earnestly, "it is the stone that healed Chal after he came back from Mahela's realm. Just as you healed Kor and me."

She pulled Calimir to a sliding stop, jerked him to a halt so roughly that he flung up his head and half reared in protest, and I was nearly unseated from my undignified place on his rump. I grabbed at Tass to keep from falling, and knew at once that was a mistake—her every muscle was sword-hard, stone-hard, under her ragged tunic. Perhaps she had wanted me to fall.

"No more," she said softly, with a catamount's perilous, padding softness in her voice, "no more of this, if you wish Calimir to carry you any farther."

Therefore, since I had no desire to go afoot again, I did not tell her that already my feet were half healed.

We went on that day past nightfall, until I was too weary to speak to Tass or badger her in any way, as she well knew. When at last we stopped I lay down without eating and slept a sleep like that of the dead.

Within five days we were back to the hemlock forests of the Demesne. There was no lying together for us during that journeying, no soft touch of fingers and lips, no lovemaking. Whether because she felt an urgency like mine, or to silence me or vent her incessant anger on me, Tassida kept up a merciless pace. At night we both stumbled to the ground and slept lumpishly, without a fire. We gnawed food on the move by day. After reaching the forests, within two days more we had ridden to the region of beaver waters.

There we paused to do a quarterday's worth of fishing, starting before sundown and fishing on through the twilight, for we were nearly out of food. I fished with bow and arrow, Tass with her stone knife lashed to a trimmed sapling by way of spear. But all our patient standing won us only two gudgeon of middling size. We saw no pike or bass or any other fish but those two and a few fry.

"Even the fish are scarce, now," said Tass in a hushed voice.

I went in after the fry, trying to use my woolen shirt for a net, and caught none. We gathered swamp onion and bulrush stem instead, made our fire and steamed our two fish, peeled the bulrush for the pith. Far too silent, the night around us, I noticed now that I was not too weary to care. The pond creatures should have spoken to us in small lappings and ripplings, but the water lay still as death. I did not wish to speak of it, for it was heartache even to think of the sounds that should have been, sleepy conversing of wood ducks in their nests amid the reeds, bat twitter overhead, heron crake and beaver splash. But now even the whispering and buzzing of insects was nearly gone.

"No chanting of summerbugs," I said softly to Tass.

She merely looked at me and nodded, for there was nothing more to say. Her lean, boyish face, sad and angry, eerily beautiful in the firelight.

"Tass," I told her, softly, gravely, leaning toward her, "there are only the three swords."

I had once thought that there were more, there had to be more, though in fact I did not know fully what the swords were for or what they meant, except that they slew devourers. Perhaps Tass knew even less than I, but she knew without telling, we all did, that the swords were uncanny. I saw her stiffen, saw her eyes narrow as she looked back at me.

"Yours. And mine. And Kor's." I touched the pommel of my own sword, Alar, fingering the yellow stone. "Tass, it is as you once said: For some reason we do not know, we belong together, we three."

Abruptly she took a green stick and scraped the coals away from our supper. She lifted the fish from its wrapping of lily leaves. "Eat," she commanded.

Nor am I known to be a sluggard where food is concerned. But I sat and stared at her, my portion untouched. "Tass. Speak to what I have said." She was not meeting my eyes, and it annoyed me.

"How can I?" she flared. "How can you know what you have just told me?"

So I related the tales to her while I atc, related my

dreams to her, or my visions, as best I could. There was a dim sense in me of a pattern, a wholeness, if I could but grasp it. Though what, indeed, could it matter? The world was dying, and I had failed in my quest to save it. Still, I told the tales.

Tass sat uncomfortably while I spoke, staring into our small fire. She sat in like wise when I was done, and said nothing.

"The blue fruit, the pomegranate," I added after long silence, for I was not sure I had made myself clear. "I saw in the sunstuff picture, the one that still lies in the stone lodge above the pool of vision, how Mahela took it away. Though I deem she took the whole tree, for I saw it myself."

"Perhaps, Mahela," Tassida said harshly to the fire. "Perhaps, the same tree."

"What is the use of thinking otherwise?" I protested. "Say it is the same tree, the same fruit, the pomegranate of the god. I think Chal quested to the Mountains of Doom to get it back."

"You say it was Vallart who sundered the fruit. Yet the sunstuff panel shows it dropping from Mahela's beak."

I puffed my lips impatiently, for the fault was Mahela's, and legends were often pictured so, to show the first cause. And she knew it as well as I. "Tass," I chided.

Still she would not look at me. "Blue rind, white light, three puissant stones, or jewels," she murmured, more to herself than to me. "Might it be the stones that lend life to the swords themselves?"

Alar stirred softly in her leather sheath by my side, and I stroked her. The yellow stone glowed beneath my hand.

"Nor could Chal and Vallart have worn the swords as their weapons," Tass went on as if I had answered her, "unless Alar and Zaneb themselves had willed it."

"Very true," I agreed. "But Marantha kept to a place by herself, on the wall, and threatened when Vallart came near her."

I was half teasing, half trying to help her see how much like the sword she was, how she fit the pattern. But at last she looked up at me, a dark look. "So perhaps it is not as you say," she challenged, "that we three, Kor and you and I, belong together."

"Tass," I complained in exasperation. She knew it well enough, she had been the first to sense it! She had pledged her word to stay with us forever, but then in our quarrel we had frightened her away.

Her glance fell to the fire again. "Three stones from the same mystic fruit," she muttered. "Dan, I always knew that you two, you and Kor, were—fated, somehow, something from the god. But I cannot think as well of myself."

I reached across to where she sat, lifted her fine-boned chin in three fingers of my right hand so that her eyes met mine. "Stay with us," I requested her softly, "if only because I love you."

The amaranthine stone at her belt glowed warm. But her dark eyes flashed in fright, she pulled away from the touch of my hand, and I knew I had pressed too hard, too fast. She stumbled to her feet, fear taking away her usual feral grace. "I—I do not know," she stammered. "I must think." She started away into the darkness.

"Tassida!" I leaped up and strode after her, catching her by the arm, catching her gaze with my gaze again. "Promise me at least this, that you will yet be with me when I awaken in the morning." For I knew her. She was not one to tarry in her leave-taking, Tass. Like a hummingbird frightened from the flower, she could be gone in an eyeblink. More than once I had awakened or turned around from some task or dream to find her gone like a bright leaf blown away by the wind.

"Promise," I urged her.

"Slime of Mahela, Dan," she flared, "what do you deem I am? Do you think I would leave you afoot here, when you must come to Kor with all haste?"

That had to suffice, for she jerked her arm free from my hand and left me. Like the wild thing she was, she stalked off to wander in the night.

I fed more wood to the small campfire, threw the fish offal into the brush, peevishly took Tassida's bedpelt as well as my own and lay down to stare at the flames until sleep came to me.

It was long in coming, as I knew it would be. Always during those days the world's doom lay heavy on me, and I ached and yearned for Tassida's touch, the warmth of her lithe body next to mine. Ardently I wanted to follow her into the night. I wanted her comfort, her love—but I knew I did not dare to woo her by so much as my silent presence. Her old, old fear had hold of her, and she would flee.

I slept at last, but my slumber was full of formless darkness and uneasy, shadowy dreams.

Something huge and dark was moving somewhere close at hand, moving nearer . . . black storm of war? Black storm of Mahela's making, shot through with greenish lightning and the corpse-sheen of devourers? Heavy, hideous, cold and crushing on the chest, devourers. Crashing sound, thunder cones shuddering forth black rock and red fire. Stone thunder, storm thunder growing nearer, something vast and fearsome was moving in the forest—

I awoke with a start and sprang at once to a warrior's crouch. Something was indeed crashing about in the underbrush at a small distance, some large, shadowy creature. A devourer? It reeked of—death. . . . I heard a rending sound, a hollow thudding, a rippling or fluttering as of great fish-gray fleshy wings in the wind—

Or large nostrils, fluttering with a strong breath. Weary and desolate as I felt, the drollness of it struck me all the deeper, and I laughed aloud, uproariously. I laughed until I was bent and breathless. It was monstrous, certainly, and hideous, and devouring fish offal with a ghastly stench. It was my fanged mare, Talu.

Intent on munching fishbones, seeking to lick every last morsel of fish juice and fish innards from the laurel leaves and the forest floor, she sourly let me approach her and did not threaten me. Evidently she was not in heat. I caught her by her straggling forelock and felt for her ribs, the gaunt line of her spine jutting from her back. She seemed not much thinner than she had ever been, and she swiped at me lazily with her fangs in greeting.

"Did my people feed you well until they left, Talu?" I rubbed the coarse hair of her forehead even though I knew she was not fond of patting, it was so good to meet a living creature in those dying times. "*Ai,* Talu, have you seen Tassida tonight?"

And even as I said the words I knew with a taut, chilled feeling how happenstance that seemed like all good fortune might turn out to be all ill. Tassida had not said that she would cleave to me or come with me to Kor. She had merely said that she would not leave me stranded, afoot. Now that I had Talu, Tass's promise did not bind her. I stiffened myself against a panicky urge to go searching for her at once.

"No need," I whispered to the horse to calm myself. "She loves me, I know it well enough. The love draws her to me."

And frightened her, and drove her away. But I would not say that.

I fed Talu the cold ends of our fish supper, and as she gulped them I hobbled her with the rawhide laces of my wretched boots so that she would not stray before morning. She was a sour thing, Talu, as likely to kick me as come to me when I wanted her, especially since she had been roaming free for a while. I had to make sure I could catch her. As soon as she had bolted her bits of fish she laid back her ears and started away from me, then squealed in vexation when she found she could not go far, swung down her head and lashed out with her hind hooves. I dodged away in time, and smiled, for the mare's ill temper made me think of Tassida, and Tass would not have thanked me had she known it.

I found my way back to bed, hearing Calimir browsing at the birch branches somewhere not far away—that sound comforted me somewhat. Tass had not yet left me.

At dawn, when I awoke, she was sitting by the cold ashes of the fire.

"Yon uncouth mare has eaten our breakfast," she grumbled.

"I fed it to her," I admitted. "I had to bait her with something, or she would not have stood still for the hobbling." I got up and stood awkwardly, feeling absurdly sorry that Tass must go hungry, absurdly anxious to feed her or please her somehow. There was no time to spear and cook more fish. "Let me get—there ought to be groundnut hereabouts. Wait, and I will dig you some."

Tass eyed me strangely. "Never mind, Dan. There will be berries. Come, let us ride."

Nor did she tell me any word of what she had thought in the night.

I had no riding pelt nor any proper headstall, only my bootlaces knotted together into a single rein and looped through Talu's mouth. Tass held her by the nose and forelock while I vaulted onto her—the prospect that faced me seemed to restore Tassida's good humor, and she smiled through the morning, riding along quietly on gentle Calimir, eating wild black cherries by the handful off the slender red-barked trees. There were no cherries for me. Talu was so fractious that I could do nothing with her but hang on by my hands and heels, my crotch jarring against her parlous sharp spine, as I tried to urge her in the right direction. Sometimes I succeeded, so that Calimir cantered along merrily after Talu and me, and more often I failed, so that Calimir stood at ease and Tassida ate cherries while my mare and I serpentined through the thorn thickets.

It was during one such unplanned and unwilling foray that I spied a wisp of smoke and heard the whicker of a pony, the barking of a tan hound. Then I hailed Tass, wildly waving, and sent Talu forward in spite of her most fervid balking and swerving. There was a Red Hart encampment not far away.

Only a few tents, I saw as we drew near, less than twelve. And around them, only the old and infirm, some nursing mothers and the children. They came warily to their feet as I rode in on rebellious Talu, then cheered wanly when I succeeded in stopping her. The striplings yet too young to go to war came running in from the far fringes of camp, where they had been prowling and sulking and looking off westward. They were few, and very young. Tyee must have taken near-children with him, and even the elders who could yet ride the distance and shoot an arrow. I saw Tyee's baby daughter being held by a one-armed old woman, but of course Karu was not there. She was with her fellow warriors.

And I sat stupidly on my fanged mare, gaping at those who were left behind. "Tass," I murmured as she rode up beside me, "so few." And so starkly in peril.

"Steady," said Tass quietly. She slid down from Calimir, then came and grasped Talu by the nose and forelock, as if I had been waiting for her, as if I needed her help with the mare—I needed her help indeed, but not for that. Her eyes met mine with understanding. The strength in her, when she was needed—how could she not know herself for a healer? I got off Talu and hobbled her, and quelled my heartache as I did so, then strode to greet my people, and they crowded around me, and I lifted Tyee's daughter, the little sunnyhead, high in the air while the other children climbed my back and legs as if I were a tree.

Too few of the little ones, their hair flying feathersoft. And soon Mahela intended to take them all.

Tass and I stayed with my people only for the midday meal, for we were in haste, and small need to explain to them why. They fed us biscuit root and berries, for it was the height of the berrying season, and as we ate they packed us provision to take along. A child ran and netted fry for Talu to eat raw. A hobbling old man spread a riding pelt on her back, strapped it on, brought a bisonhide headstall for me to put on her—he would not risk her fangs, for he had better sense than I. Some of the striplings, hunting about in Tyee's bundles, found me brown buckskin leggings and a pair of boots large enough to nearly fit me. I put the things on gratefully, for wool chafed the insides of my thighs where they pressed against Talu's bony ribs.

"Gentle journey, Dannoc."

Young, piping voices. Old, quavering voices, nearly as high as those of the children. A baby's wail. Farewells echoed after me as I rode away.

"Be wicked, Dannoc! Slay ten tens of Pajlat's minions for me!" That was one of the nursing mothers, a fierce and canny fighter who doubtless wished she were at the fray.

"Make haste, Dannoc, give Pajlat our greeting!" Laughter at that, quickly stilled.

"And tell Korridun we remember him. We of the Red Hart do not forget our friends."

If Kor yet lived. Ache in me again, to think that he might have died believing that I had forgotten him—no. It was an unworthy thought.

"Courage, Dannoc! Tell Tyee, courage! It is not so bad a thing to die. Only mountains last forever."

Words, all the fumbling words that could not quite say what was meant.

"Dannoc." It was a small girl-child, perhaps one of my own, her gaze deep as sky. "Come back, then, after it is over."

I rode away with set jaw. By whatever god yet lived, I would have courage for my people's sake.

"Come back, Sakeema, we love you," said Tass softly by my side, her voice half hushed, half mocking.

We rode in silence, for the most part. I managed better with Talu since I had proper gear, and I galloped and loped her wherever the terrain would allow, to take some of the sourness out of her. Calimir cantered along willingly, feeling lightened no doubt since my body no longer burdened his hips. By dark we were in the foothills and following the Blackstone Path.

At dawn, awakening, I found Tassida carefully dividing our food between my bag of deerskin and hers of woven linden. Then I stood up, my mouth suddenly too dry to speak, and went to her, knowing but not wanting to know what this might mean.

"I will take a circuit southward, to the pool of vision," she told me without looking up from her doling out of biscuit-root bread. "I wish to see with my own eyes this sunstuff panel that shows the tree, the pomegranate."

"Tass," I protested, "why? I have told you everything there is to tell of it."

She scowled at me in annoyance. "Do you never think you might not have seen all?"

I swallowed and tried again. "Tass. Please. We need to come together, with all haste, to Seal Hold."

"Do you not yet know Calimir's speed?" She stood up, taking her bag of provision to the gelding who already stood in his gear and waiting. "Go to Kor. Be on your way with good heart. Go at the best pace of that ramshackle mare of yours. I will rejoin you before you have topped the pass."

She was boasting. But I took no offense, for it was a thing she had never said before, that she would leave and come back to me.

"Tass," I said slowly, "I trust your promise." Even though she had broken it once before—but there had been reason. Even Vallart had failed Chal, reaching the strand at land's end on the way to the Mountains of Doom. Tass also had reached the limits of her friendship one day, but like Vallart following Chal she had followed me.

Something in my voice had touched her. Loading provision on Calimir, fumbling with rawhide thongs, her hands slowed and stopped. Her eyes met mine.

"I trust you. But all my heart is crying out that we ought not to be apart," I told her. "There is doom in the air."

"That is why I must venture this thing!" she blazed at me. "If there is a chance that I can comprehend the secret—"

"Comprehending be damned!" I burst out, though I should have known better, for shouting never did any good, with Tassida. "Reason is Sakeema's whore. It was reasoning that took me away from Kor, and now she wants to take you away from me. . . . Tassida, what lies between us is beyond understanding. Do you not feel it?"

"Beyond your understanding, maybe," she shot back, and she tied the last knot. But the touch of my hand stopped her before she vaulted onto Calimir.

"Tass," I whispered, "do you not feel it?" That strange, nameless passion. . . .

She did, I knew she did. But she was afraid, and running away, as always. Nor could I scorn her. I had felt that fear.

And she surprised me. She turned fully to face me.

"I feel—" She swallowed, but her eyes met mine and did not waver. "I feel my love for you, Dan. I must go my own way, but I will come back to you. Truly."

I could not move, not even to kiss her, or I would have wept, and I had to let her go. What she had just said—it was courage surpassing bravery, coming from her. My gaze clung to her, but my body I managed to still. Only after she was mounted did my hands lift, trembling, toward her, for against all reason I felt I was forever losing her.

She met my stare for a moment longer, lifted a hand that shook as badly as mind, and cantered away. A stride, two, three—

I had to let her go, I had to let her be free, I told myself, but no amount of thinking it could help me. Against all my will, the mindcry was wrung from me, went winging after her. *Tass*!

Her body jerked as if it had been caught in a noose. Calimir slid to a rearing halt.

"Do not do that!" Tass sounded frightened and furious.

Tassida, my love, my Tass. . . .

She rode away, and I stood and watched her go.

# Chapter Thirteen

After Tassida left, the days that followed, the mere sight of a farewell-summer flower was enough to tighten my throat with unshed tears.

Mine was a peculiar sort of despair, a tender torment. As I traveled my senses were heightened to everything, so that even my skin seemed to feel beauty like the touch of a flensing knife of sharpest blackstone. I saw flowercups where I had never noticed flowers before, on herbs so tiny and humble that I did not know the names of them. I saw every lichen growing on every stone, their delicate finger-tip branches reaching, their many subtle colors, white-green and gray-green, puce and pink and muted orange. I saw marvelous colors in the stones themselves, specks and dazzles of sun yellow and sunset purple, hairsbreadth ser-pentines of black. I saw mosses—odd, that I had never noticed before how many sorts of mosses there were, the airy brown seed stalks of some of them, the dense spiral patterns others made. I felt their pricklesoft touch, and the sunlit touch of yellowing aspen leaves, and the tingling scrape of pine boughs. I smelled resin, I smelled leaf mold in sunlight, I felt every breeze, every shaft of sunlight, I heard the wash of wind, I saw every rainshadow, every hue and slant of light in the sky.

How could it yet be so beautiful, without Sakeema?

For he was gone, like the creatures and their sounds, gone or a blackguard, and I had turned my back on him, and I hated him for what was happening, the dying within me as well as outside of me. What was the use any longer of dreams, of my foolish notions and my stubborn, aching heart? What was the use of beauty with no creature alive in it but the fanged mare moving between my legs?

And Talu was weakening even before we reached the mountains.

Tassida was right, blast her. Talu's speed could not match Calimir's—but only because the gelding ate his fill every night of grass and browse, while for Talu there had been nothing but toads and grubs since we had left the region of beaver waters. Pitiful food for this hulking creature who had been reared on the leavings of bison kills. Small wonder that her speed soon slowed.

"For Kor's sake, Talu," I whispered to her as I kicked her into a trot that soon lagged. "For Kor's sake," kicking her again, sending her struggling up the steep, twisting slopes of the Blackstone Path. I bit my lip and whispered the words for my own comfort as much as for hers. Indeed, only for Kor's sake could I have driven her so—even a failing horse was faster than a man on foot in this terrain. The way led all steeply upslope. We had scaled the foothills and reached the mountains' knees.

I spoke to my wayward lover as if she were there.

"Tassida, may Sakeema someday forgive you for this." Then I remembered with a pang how we were all betrayed by Sakeema. "May I someday forgive you," I muttered.

Tass . . . for moments at a time I could sustain a brittle hope that she would rejoin me as she had promised, sustain it for perhaps a quarterday before it shattered into despair. I knew that there was love of me in her—but I knew also her fear of it. She had been furious with fear when she had left me. No matter, or it should not have mattered, for she would come back to me in time, as she had always done before, back to us, to Kor and me—but there might not be time. Time for the three of us, time for the world.

"Mahela might take it all into her maw before you are ready, Tass," I grumbled as if she could hear me.

Lying wakeful at night, hoping that Talu could paw out a snake or two to eat, I watched the stars as if they might blacken and die in the sky. Riding each day, I anxiously regarded the larches and lindens and the dusty blooms of latesummer flowers as if they also might wither away before my eyes.

I had not seen any devourers of late, nor had my folk, for so they had told me. Nor did I expect to see the demon servants of Mahela. Like Pajlat and his minions, like the ungrateful Otter River Clan, they would be warring on Kor at Seal Hold.

"For Kor's sake, Talu!" I urged her faster. Days past, I would have galloped a willing pony up these slopes. Talu could only lunge a few strides, then trot.

For Kor's sake. . . . Though what I expected to do for him I was not sure, except comfort him with the touch of my hand and die at his side. Was he yet alive? He had to be. I could not believe otherwise. I would have felt my heart die if he had been dead.

Talu was laboring, as always. Perhaps there would be asps for her in the rocks of the scree slopes, only a day or two ahead . . . but time, there was no time for her to rest and regain her strength. I stopped her a moment, slid off her and ran beside her up the steepening path, ran until my chest ached with panting, and she trailed me at a reluctant trot, her head hanging. There was not even zest enough in her, anymore, for her to threaten me with her fangs.

After a while I walked wearily in front of her.

Coming to Kor, after all, no faster than a foot-pace. . . . Shadows lengthened, my head hung like the mare's and I could not speed my steps for despair. Talu and I plodded through the dusk, and from time to time, hunter and warrior that I was trained to be, I raised my head to look about me, though truly I had small thought for any danger less than the world's death. The Cragsmen were all off warring at Pajlat's side, and Ytan with them, or so I expected—

Flicker of movement on the trail ahead, just around a turn. A brown form, standing.

It was a deer.

Red Hart born as I was, I had my bow in my hand and the arrow nocked to the string before it had more than raised its great, questing ears. A fool's thought had once been mine, that I would no longer kill the creatures of Sakeema, but that had been in a less desperate time. Before me stood meat, to save my mount's life in most dire need—

The deer's great eyes met mine. For a heartbeat longer it would stand, gazing at me, before it leaped away. An easy target—

I could not shoot.

I could not kill the great-eyed creature, not even for Talu's sake so that she could take me to Kor.

I was not thinking of the deer people, though afterwit tells me it was surely one of them—only a human will could have kept it from the devourers so long. But in the falling darkness I could not see the human gaze of those wide eyes. I knew only that it was warm, beautiful, alive, and my pigheaded heart would not let me kill it, even though I very much wanted to. Slay it, and save Talu, Kor, the world—at the price of a single deer. . . .

It did not leap away until I had lowered the bow, blinded by tears so that I did not see it go except as a watery blur. Then I turned and flung my arms around Talu's lanky neck, pressed my face against the coarse hair of her mane and sobbed. She could have buried her fangs in my kidneys and had me for her feasting. But she let her head droop until it rested against me instead, and all I could do for her was weep.

That night, though I knew I should lie down and rest, I could do nothing but pace beneath the waning moon. In widening loops and circles around my campsite I roamed, until at last my wandering took me to a rib of the mountain where I could see out over the pine spires and look at the night and the sky. The still, starlit and moonlit sky, stars thick as frost flowers, hovering like moths just above the treetops, night so beautiful it almost angered me—still, I craved comfort. I lingered there, trying to steady myself, trying to ease myself by breathing deeply of the night—

Waft of smoke on the air. And I had made no fire.

My head came up like that of a questing stag, and I ventured farther out on the rocky spur I could not fully see—where did it end? I did not want to find myself treading on air. Then within the span of a step, quite plainly, I could see the edge of it against fireglow. I lay down for caution's sake and peered over the lip of the stone. In a fold of the mountain's flank below me burned a small campfire, and by it, staring into the flames, sat she whom I loved. She, the bearer of the amaranthine jewel.

Tass. A great wave of relief washed through me, leaving me limp and quivering. Even at the distance I knew her, even though her back was turned partly toward me, without seeing sword or horse I knew her merely by her slender shoulders and the firelight on the tawny lovelocks of her hair.

She sat within tongueshot. I could have hailed her across the night. But no one who has been reared a Red Hart shouts without a second thought—it is our nature to move in silence. And I wanted to go to Tass with a lover's silent tenderness, step close to her before I softly said her name. I came to my knees, ready to creep back and find my way down to her.

And before I could move farther I saw aspen boughs stir beyond her fire, saw myself step before her with a lover's silent tenderness, saw my ardent smile and the firelight shining on my fair, unbound hair.

"Dan!" Tass cried gladly, rising to meet me.

It was Ytan.

His buckskin leggings, lappet, boots, much like mine in wan moonlight and dim, flickering firelight. He had unbraided his hair so that it hung loose like mine. The cutthroat, he must have been spying on me—he even wore a long leather scabbard like mine, as if for a sword. There were small differences—the marks braiding had put in his hair, the rims of his ears beneath it, not notched like mine. But it was unlikely, in the starlit night, that Tass would notice them, or notice the wooden haft of his stone knife riding in the long sheath.

''Have you come no farther than this?'' Tass was saying. ''I thought you would be a day's hard riding farther on at least, perhaps two.''

By way of reply he reached out, drew her forcefully to him and kissed her. Nor did she resist.

A shout would have alerted him as well as her. But indeed, I was not thinking so clearly. It seemed to me that already I saw her at the point of his knife of jagged flint, mutilated, and the anguish in my heart and mind welled up and cried out to her while my mouth was still dry and frozen with horror. The mindcry was no more than a single word, her name.

*Tass!*

Instantly she stiffened, flung back her head and hurled herself away from him with a suddenness that caught him utterly by surprise, or she would not have been able to escape him. His fingers furrowed her arms, clutching at her to keep her, but to no avail. Tass was strong when she was enraged. She pulled away and stepped back to give herself room for her fury.

''No! You—you brigand, stay out of my mind! It is like—no better than devourers, than Pajlat's raiders—''

He fully intended to rape her body, not her mind. ''Tass,'' I shouted aloud, ''beware! It is Ytan!''

She gasped, and Marantha's hilt leaped to her hand. Ytan was coming at her with his hunting knife drawn. I had alerted him, too, as I had not wanted to do, calling aloud, and he had the advantage over Tass, knowing himself to be her enemy before she could fully comprehend it of him. But he had not reckoned with Marantha's quickness. The sword flared, a storm-white burst that blinded him, and struck, and only his lifted knife saved him—the stone blade broke off to the hilt in his hand. The next blow would slay him—

He did not await it, but leaped away and fled downslope, speedily gone between the trees, and Tass did not pursue him, for she was badly shaken. Even at the distance I could see that she could barely stand. Though I could not understand how it had happened, she seemed to be hurt.

"Steady, Tass," I called to her. "I am coming." Her pale face had so filled me with fear for her that I swung myself over the lip of the outcropping where I stood, not able to see what lay below, searching blindly for a hold with my feet.

"No whit!" she shouted back to me, her voice harsh and trembling. Then I heard her sobbing. Shakily she whistled for Calimir, and still clinging to the sheer rock, I heard the hollow sound of hooves.

"No!" I yelled wildly. "Tass, stay! For Kor's sake—"

She did not know that Talu was ailing, did not know that I would walk to Kor without her. I heard the reckless speed of Calimir's hoofbeats as he bore her away.

I very nearly let myself drop, for I was so struck down by despair that there seemed to be no strength in my arms. I who had wept for the sake of a horse and a deer, now I was in despair too deep for weeping. Tass . . . she had given me no time to try to calm her, to talk with her, tell her about Talu, anything. And Kor—I had failed him yet again, I would come to him very much the laggard without Calimir.

Nevertheless, I had to come to him, if only to die where he had died.

Face against the rock, I clung until the thought had hardened in me. Then slowly I inched and heaved my way back onto the top of the crag.

Roundabout, I made my way down to Tass's fire, though I knew well enough that she was gone and far out of my reach. She was quick, she had left nothing that she might come back for. I stood for a while where she had stood, then kicked dirt to kill the fire and struck off across the wooded slopes, not much caring whether Ytan might be on the hunt for me or not. It was dawn before I found my way back to my own campsite, where Talu stood awaiting me dully, her head drooping, not even making a pretense of running away from me, as she had always felt she must do when it came time for her to be caught and ridden.

I strapped my gear onto her, but that day I walked. All day I trudged upslope, letting her trail along behind me at an easy pace, and my angry pride made me keep my head up, watching for Ytan, but I did not see him.

When we came to a slope of scree I kicked the stones loose myself, heedless of whether I might be stung, until I had found a nest of adders for my horse to eat. I found her more as we made our way farther upslope, and she found some for herself, and I began to hope a little for her.

I walked through the dusk, out of a sense of duty to Kor, but I knew that all my walking had not brought me even a quarter of the distance of a good day's journey on horseback. Talu and I had not yet reached even the region of spruces below the tree line.

The walking had numbed my sorrow somewhat. And I was spent. Come Ytan or come world's end, I had to rest, for I had not slept at all the night before. When dusk had darkened into nightfall, I unstrapped my bags and the riding pelt from Talu, lay down where I was, in the middle of the trail, and slept the slumber of the dead.

Nor did Ytan come. For when I awoke, shortly after

daybreak, I found the wolf standing over me, guarding my sleep.

I sat up and blinked at it, surprised by the surge of joy that went through me so that I blinked back tears more than sleep. "Wild brother," I whispered to it, "welcome. I had thought you would long since be starved and gone to Mahela's hell, like the others."

I wanted to reach out and caress it, embrace it, even, I was so glad. But I knew well from times gone by that it would not let me touch even the tips of its fur, it would dart away. So I hugged my own shoulders instead, to still my hands. Thin beneath its dense graysheen fur, perhaps, but not overly thin, the wolf sat and panted at me.

"*Ai*, I am hungry." Suddenly I found that I was ravenous, and I rooted frantically in my baggage. There were a few shriveled crowberries left. I ate them, then picked the sugar resin off the bark of certain of the pines, as I had done for days past.

"I am going to have to eat potherbs and moss and lichens again," I said to the wolf. "What have you been eating, wild brother? Have you learned to graze, like the deer, to eat the sour berries in the highmountain meadows?"

Or were the mice and lemmings and voles, which I had thought gone, not all gone after all? The wolf could not answer. It merely grinned toothily at me.

"It cheers my heart to see you," I told it.

Talu carried me part of the way that day, but no faster than I could have walked myself, and after halfday I gave up riding and walked. The wolf trotted along beside me. Talu lagged behind, and all my pity and sorrow and anger came back whenever I turned to look at her.

"Not Tass's fault," I muttered, though there was anger in me at Tassida also. But chiefly at Ytan, for driving her away. And, the viper, for what he had meant to do to her. What he might yet mean to do to her, if he caught her unawares.

"If you scent Ytan on the wind," I instructed the wolf grimly, "tell me, my friend. I intend to kill him and feed him to my mare."

# Chapter Fourteen

By the time we reached the twisted spruces that grew below the tree line, I could climb the steep trail afoot faster than Talu could manage it any longer. So I took the gear off her, shouldering what I thought I would need the worst, flinging the rest to the ground, and I told her to go hunt snakes in the scree. If she could stay in one place and find food, she yet might live—for a while. Then I strode on, urgently, underneath a mountain sky that mocked my urgency with its clear blue beauty.

Far into the night I walked, and I made my way through the stunted spruces to the thin-aired, treeless highmountain meadow beyond. I could no more than stumble when at last I lay down and slept, with the wolf by me to guard my sleep.

And the halfnight later, just as daybreak was waking me, Talu plodded up the trail, stumbling as badly as I had, gave a huge sigh and stopped where I lay, her head hanging over me. With a groan for her sake I sat up and rubbed her forehead, nor did she trouble herself to scorn the caress.

"Talu," I begged her, "spare yourself. Stay, rest."

She swung her head and butted me with her outlandish nose, knocking me backward against a boulder. Limply I sat there and picked the flakes of lichen off it to eat. The wolf, I saw, was gnawing tiny black berries off a low shrub with leaves as jagged as a blackstone knife, and as red, in the early highmountain autumn, as a knife wet with blood. I tottered to my feet and picked some of the berries for myself—the things were so small and tart and seedy that years gone by I would not have thought them worth the effort. But I ate all I could find, then made my way up the trail toward the Blue Bear Pass, stooping to pick more wherever I found them by the wayside.

And even slow and dallying over berries as I was, I soon left Talu far behind. She had grown very weak.

That night, again, she caught up to me on toward dawn, waking me from sleep with the thudding of her hooves as she blundered up to me. There had been no rest for her, after all, even less than there was for me. But the next day at last I topped the pass, and I knew that I would soon leave her behind in truth, for on the downward far side I would make my best speed.

Looking for a moment back the way I had come, I saw nothing but meadow and rock and eversnow. The mare stood nowhere in sight. "Talu," I whispered nevertheless, as if she were there, "farewell," though I knew she would not fare well, she would die and I would not be with her to ease her dying. She might be dying at the moment I thought it, and I was not with her. I would not have thought that she wanted me with her, ill-tempered mare that she was, yet she had followed. . . . With an aching feeling in my chest I turned westward, toward the sea, toward Kor, and I started to run. The wolf loped beside me.

I ran wildly, heedlessly, and Ytan attacked me at the first turning of the trail.

He was waiting atop the crags that rose to either side of the narrow way, and he caught me utterly unawares. Even as he stood and drew his bow I did not see him. But my friend the wolf must have seen him or scented him a heart-beat before he let the arrow fly, and it dodged into my legs as I ran, tripping me so that I fell hard and headlong, scudding down the rocky path on my chest, and the bolt flew over me. I had not seen it or Ytan, and I wanted to curse the wolf for its clumsiness—within my mind I was cursing it fervently, but I was knocked too breathless to speak. And then I heard Ytan laughing.

I must have made an oafish sight, and Ytan had always taken every chance to laugh at me, even before the devourer had possessed him. He gave forth great yelps of laughter. A moment before, knocked nearly senseless, I would have said I could not move, but when I heard that laughter I moved forthwith, filled with rage and a reckless despair that made me forget all caution. Talu was dead or dying, Kor dead or in mortal danger, Tassida had deserted me, my god also—or I had deserted him—the entire dryland world cowered under Mahela's heavy hand, and what was one meddling demon-thrall of a brother that he should thwart me or give me pause? I would kill him and leave his body for my mare, should she muster strength to come that way. I would feed his head to the wolf. With a roar like that of a wounded Cragsman I was on my feet, letting baggage and bow fall to the stony ground, charging him—Alar flew to my hand, the yellow stone on her pommel blazing with my wrath, blazing the color of thunderbolts. Heedless of the arrow in Ytan's hand, heedless of my own starved, uncertain strength or the steep and treacherous rock under my feet, I charged him, lunging like a bear up the crag where he stood.

Astonished or unnerved, he stood as rigid as the granite peaks, staring, and did not set arrow to bowstring and shoot me as he could have done. In another moment it was too late for that, I was nearly on him. He dropped bow and bolts—they rattled down the sheer flank of the crag—and snatched up a lance, a man-long pole of spear-pine with a sharp flint tip. He could not have chosen a better weapon. As long as he held it leveled at me, I could not come near enough to him to open him up with the sword, rage though I might.

"Bowels of Sakeema!" I cursed. "Bloody, stinking balls of Sakeema!" For in my anger at my god I no longer forebore to curse by Sakeema's name. I struck mighty blows at Ytan's spear, broke off the knifelike tip, hacked at the shaft to no avail—it was of springy, well-cured pine and would not splinter for me. Ytan thrust, his teeth set in a mirthless grin, a warrior's grin, like the snarl of a spotted wild dog. His jagged, broken spear-head was yet plentifully sharp enough to tear my innards out—I gave way, and he stepped forward and thrust again. He was driving me back toward the shoulder of the crag. One more backward step, and I would be toppling, and at his mercy when I landed. He would be able to put an arrow into me at his leisure. And his grin broadened, for he knew it.

The wolf leaped at him from the side.

It had been climbing toward a higher vantage, I think, to attack him from above and bear him down with the force of its leap and his weight, as it had done before. But seeing me in danger of being dead within the next few heartbeats, it leaped from the side and somewhat below him, growling like distant thunder, jaws agape and seeking for a grip on his arm or thigh, white teeth gleaming—

He dodged and met the wolf's throat with his booted foot, sending it over the edge of the crag with a single hard kick. I heard a sound as if a branch had snapped, and a deep-chested shriek, and then silence.

I leaped in my turn. The lance had wavered, and even had it not I think no lance could have stopped me any longer, for I was insane with anger and sorrow. Ytan's spearpoint left a red trail on my belly—I struck the weapon aside and rushed him. He gasped and tried to put the length of the spear shaft between us again, scrambling back and circling the narrow clearing atop the crag, and all the time my sword hunted him, hungry for his blood. And I was bellowing and roaring a cry of rage without words, for there were no words to tell the wrongs he had done me, the griefs I would avenge. The matter of the wolf was only his most recent evil. He had looked on Tassida with leering eyes and plotted to dishonor her. He had helped to kill my mother, he had schemed with my father to kill me, he had tried himself to kill me more times than I had fingers on one hand—

He could not escape me for all his dodging and circling. Alar pursued him like a vengeful eagle. Nor was there any quick way off the crag, that he could flee me. His death was at hand, and I could tell he knew it, for his face was pale, he panted, he had ceased to show his teeth in a warrior's grin. He tried to parry my blows with the shaft of his spear—Alar cut him lightly in the shoulder, the head. She was like a wildcat that day, cruel, taunting her prey. Or I was . . . was I cruel? I would not after all take long about killing him. Backing away from me, Ytan stumbled, fell hard to the stone on which we stood, and his hacked and ruined spear clattered away from him. Out of his belt he snatched a short knife of flint, a pitiful weapon, not even as fearsome as the blackstone one Tass had broken for him. In a final act of defiance he raised it, and I stood over him, sword lifted to strike the death blow. Alar hovered in air like a hawk stooping—

I could not kill him.

He was my brother, my shadowed double.

He was evil, and in a twisted way more dear to me than self. Had I not turned my back on Sakeema?

All my bloodthirst and my vengeful wrath left me in a moment, so that I stood weak and shaking and as pale as Ytan, and Alar bore my shaking arm down with her weight, hung heavy at my side, her light gone out. Ytan was . . . courageous in evil. Ytan was . . . a creature of Sakeema? What I saw before me was only shell, for Mahela's fell servant held in thrall what was more truly Ytan . . . but it did not matter. He could not be merely killed. He had somehow to be redeemed. I had somehow to be redeemed.

"Ytan," I whispered. "My brother."

And seeing what had happened, he grinned again, baring his teeth in a killer's snarl. Then he rose lightly to his feet and raised his stone knife to stab me. I stood planted like a tree, in a trance of disbelief, though I knew he was demon-possessed and deadly—but for a moment I had thought of him only as my brother, and all my love for him was in my voice, and I could not believe he was coming at me to kill me—and even then I could not lift my sword against him. Nor did I move to flee him until it should have been too late, until the knife was plunging at my heart—

A clashing, thundering sound, and a roaring, and with what must have been the last of her strength Talu came lurching and scrabbling across the rocks, charging Ytan.

He jerked round to face her, so that his knife missed my chest and merely grazed my shoulder. In the next heartbeat Talu was rearing over him, striking with her deadly forehooves, ready to bury her fangs in his back. Downward swing of her heavy head—fangs struck just below his shoulder blades, and Ytan howled in agony. But he was no laggard in battle, Ytan. With his puny stone blade he sliced the mare's throat open to the bone, and Talu thudded to the stone. Staggering, blood streaming, Ytan fled over the lip of the crag and out of my sight, and I let him go, standing very still and staring at the mutilated body of my ill-tempered fanged mare.

She had let her head rest against me, a few days before, and had not harmed me. Was it for affection, or merely because she was starved and weary? Had she attacked Ytan to save me, or to feed her own hunger? Had she loved me at all, in her own way? Did it matter? I had loved her, for all that she was wild as a wolf. . . .

The wolf.

Talu was dead. Later I would mourn her, but I could not help her. Hastily, half climbing, half sliding down the crag, I went to look for the one who might yet be living.

The wolf lay at the foot of the rock, whining and shivering, with one foreleg bent at an odd angle. "Broken," I said aloud.

It looked back at me with dark eyes narrowed in pain.

"We must tend it, wild brother." It was hard for me to think, dismayed as I was by the events of the day, so I thought aloud. "No sticks, up here above the tree line . . . my arrows, yes, we will use them." I went and found them, chose four, and I walked back. But the wolf growled at me as I approached.

"I know it hurts, wild brother." I sat and took the blackstone tips off the arrows, cutting the sinew bindings with my hunting knife. Then I pulled the rawhide lacings from my boots—they would do to tie the sticks with. "But if we can splint it, you will be able to hobble on it until it is healed, you might yet live. There is plenty of meat for you up above.'' My throat tightened at that, but it was fitting that Talu's flesh should feed the wolf, as her death had been warlike and fitting for a fanged mare. ''Steady, now.''

I reached to straighten the injured foreleg. But before I could touch it the wolf snarled at me most savagely and snapped in clear warning. Letting my hands stop where they were, I gave it a level look, meeting its troubled eyes. More fear than fierceness in those eyes.

''Little brother,'' I said evenly, ''Sakeema knows I am a stubborn dolt, and Mahela knows likewise, and it is of no use for you to argue with your teeth. You helped me when I needed you worst, and I will help you, even if you rend me for it. So much has gone wrong. . . .'' I shook my head in a sort of muted vehemence, determined to save the wolf at whatever risk. It was the only comrade my journey had left to me. Perhaps the only wild creature left in the dryland world.

Again I moved my hands toward it, toward the injured limb, and the wolf snarled mightily, and snapped, and shrank away from me as far as it could move, but did not tear me open as it threatened to do. For the first time my fingers touched the graysheen fur—

Swirl as of wind-driven haze before my eyes, so that I blinked, wondering briefly if Ytan had hurt me more than I knew . . . and then all sensible thoughts left me. For under my hand lay Tassida, crouching as the wolf had crouched, naked and trembling and injured, with her wolf-skin riding pelt huddled around her shoulders.

''Tass!''

''Dan,'' she said to me in a voice scarcely louder than a whisper, ''I am so ashamed.''

"Tass," I repeated stupidly. It should not have astonished me so. Birc had turned to a deer, and I myself had been a seal for a season in order to swim with Kor to Mahela's undersea realm, so why then should Tass not be a wolf? But seeing her there before me, so suddenly, so eerily, when all hope of ever seeing her again had nearly left me—it stunned me. And what was she saying, something of shame?

"I saw how Talu was failing, I knew you needed Calimir, and he was not far away, he is never far away from me. Yet I am so frightened—I couldn't—make the change—"

"Hush," I said, my mind still laboring. She had been with me, then, all the time? With me when Kor and I had quarreled, when we had mended the quarrel, when I had quested away from him? With me these past despairing days as I made my slow way back to him? She had guarded my sleep, fought to help me, broken her foreleg—no, arm. . . . "Talk later, Tass. You're hurt."

"I have never been far from you," she said as if in answer to my thoughts, "since the day I met you, except for the season when you and Kor ventured to the Mountains of Doom. There I could not follow."

It was the chill mountaintop air on her bare skin, I thought, or hoped, that made her tremble. I ran and brought the deerskin I used for sleeping on and laid it over her. She still shook. She shivered and moaned as I eased her to a less cramped position on the stony ground, and she shivered and bit hard on the pebble I gave her, though she did not cry out, as I pulled her arm straight and splinted it with doubled arrows, bound them tight. All the time I longed to gather her to me and embrace her, stroke her scarred skin, warm and soothe her, and I knew I could not, I would only cause her pain and, maybe, fear . . .

and I had to make my eyes slide over the sight of her small, comely breasts.

"Did Ytan hurt you?" I asked when I was done with her arm. "I mean, that night at your campfire. You looked ready to fall, I was sure you were wounded. But I see no marks on you."

"No. He did not hurt me in any way you could see."

She was still trembling, she must yet be cold. Trying to collect my wayward wits, I glanced around me. "Nothing to build a fire with," I muttered.

"You—you yourself are the fire, Dan."

This was fair speech indeed, from my Tass. "Will it burn you too badly," I inquired tenderly, "if I hold you? I want—I hate to see you shaking."

With a quiet gesture she welcomed me, and very gently I took up her head and shoulders into my arms, sitting by her and beneath her and warming her against my chest. I sat that way, with her lying half in my arms, the wolf pelt and the deerskin wrapped around the rest of her, I sat as if time did not matter, even world's end did not matter anymore, for I was with Tass. And in time her trembling stopped, her body softened against mine, her breathing grew deep and steady, her head lay at ease in the crook of my elbow.

"Is the pain gone?" I murmured to her.

"Very nearly," she said. And then, in the silent twilight, her face half turned away from me, half hidden by the dusk, she told me the tale of herself, Tass to the center of her being, as if by making sense of herself she could make sense of the world's doom. And in so doing she told me why she had been afraid since the day she met me.

# Chapter Fifteen

From her very earliest years she had visions.

"I felt that I was very old," she told me, speaking into the cloth of my shirt. "Even when I was half grown I felt it, that I had lived long, long, that I had seen kingdoms rise and die, men fight their way around the cycles of time, the shapes of the islands and mountains change."

Being reared by the red wolves on the bleak skirts of the thunder cones, she knew no other humans while she was growing, her thoughts were utterly her own, her visions were all she had of human truth, she had to trust them and remember them. Therefore, even before her wolf parents died and she joined the human tribe, she knew more than most grown warriors of self-will, but little enough of human love.

Her mother wolf had died at hunters' moon, had raised her muzzle to the swollen orange moon and sung, then laid it down and died. And as if by agreement, her father wolf died in the same way at the next full moon, the witches' moon. Then the halfgrown wolf girl who had no name was bereft, for she had nothing left. She stayed with her father's body, and starved—though she did not weep, for she did not yet know of the ways of weeping—and when the body began to bloat and smell, she took the pelt to keep, for she could not let him go. She huddled under the raw skin to sleep, and when she awoke, she was a wolf.

"I was a child, yet I was indeed old. My red pelt went gray with age."

"You yourself are the seer you have sought," I said softly.

"Yet there is no wisdom in me at all. I feel as if—as if the older I grow, the less I know. I weep, I stamp my feet in fits of anger, I am no better than a scantling, an idiot, I know nothing."

"We're two fools together, then." And holding her against my chest, I did not feel that I could have asked for anything better except that the world should be well.

"How old were you," I asked her, "when your—when the wolves died?"

"How should I know? Young enough, in body."

"Did you starve?" My belly pinched me. Hunger was always much on my mind, those days.

"Not in body. Dan, you know me. I have always fended for myself well enough. But I starved—I felt too much alone. I had never known the touch of humans, of my own kind. I feared them, and yet—there were not even any other wolves to be with me. I wore the skin of the very last."

So alone did she feel that one day, seeing a few of the Herders searching for a lost ewe among the black rocks of the cinder slopes, she went human and sat, naked as she was, with a wolf pelt scarcely covering her, and let them find her.

"Was it something you decided, the change, or something that just happened?"

"Half of each. If I had willed it, I could have stayed a wolf. But human form calls to human form, it is a struggle to resist it, and sometimes. . . . I could never let you touch me when I was in wolf form, Dan, because of the love. It would have overpowered me utterly."

I could not speak. She went on with the tale.

It had not taken her long to learn to love the Herders. They were good to her, perhaps the best tribe she could have gone to, for they were peaceable folk, forbearing with her wolfish ways, gentle in their attempts to tame her, patient as they taught her the human ways and the human speech, so strange to her. But they did not understand her, and even after she had learned the wonder of words, had become a storyteller and an adept with words, even after she had taken to herself human clothing and human customs she felt alone. Lonesome within herself, more so than ever, for was she not among humans like herself, yet not like herself at all?

What was she? Who was her mother? What was her tribe?

Her days, her dreams, were full of visions. In vision she saw the beautiful, many-colored horses of the vast plains years before she saw them in fact. And often she envisioned herself riding such a horse, galloping with the wind, and she took her name from that dream, calling herself Tassida, "horseback rider." And a wolf's wanderlust was in her, or the wanderlust of one in search of belonging, so that before she was well grown she went off by herself, alone and on foot, carrying her wolf pelt with her.

"I was young," she said softly, then paused, thinking of what she wanted to tell me, gathering courage to tell me. And though her arm must have pained her, she shifted her body so that I could see her face, or so that she could look on mine in highmountain moonlight.

"I was young, or my body was young, I had dreams unlike the ones I have told you of," she said, gazing at me steadily—she was the storyteller, I the fire. "Night dreams that I remembered with shame and unease in the daytime, for I was a scrawny stick of a girl, scarcely grown, and I felt awkward, unworthy of anyone's passion. But I dreamed them even so, the dreams that made me go warm in my groin. A tall, beautiful man would come to me, and kiss me tenderly, and caress my breasts, and take me, and in the dreams it seemed to me that the whole world was made anew, fresh with birdsong and dew and—and beautiful creatures I had never seen. And the man, Dan—it was you."

My breath stopped.

"I knew you the first time I saw you," she said, "even though they had cut off your yellow braids."

"But why—why—*ai*, Tass." I could scarcely speak. "Why did you give no sign? I would have loved you, even then."

"The devourer had come to me first."

The monster had come to her during such a dream and tried to take her in the manner of a man. Its cold gray wings had beaten her face, bruised her breasts and forced her legs apart. And though she had centered herself and resisted, and survived, she had been terrified to dream such dreams any longer. Fear had turned something askew in her. She found the wild horses on the far plains, and she found an orphan foal to be her own, and she tended it and loved it and called it Calimir, "peace." But when the colt grew to be a stallion and started to think of the mares, she took a knife and gelded him.

For some few years she rode the vast plains on him, with her wolf pelt as her riding skin, wandering, in search of her tribe, she told herself. And perhaps in search of something more—for she had people, the Herders, who loved her, and still she felt the stranger among them, so of what use might another tribe be? She came back briefly to the Herders on her shining black-and-white gelding, and found that homecoming was more lonesome than wayfaring, and left again to roam the steppes, the seacoast, the mountains to southward and northward—everywhere but the Red Hart Demesne, where she would have been most likely to find the yellow-braided lover she had envisioned in the night.

She searched, yet was afraid to find. . . . But a fate that had seemed very harsh at the time had driven me out of the Demesne, across the mountains in the murderous winter, to the sea. And in those snowcovered mountains, that same winter, she had seen a stranger and felt a shock and a strange leap of heart and a feeling without a name, for it was the man from her uneasy dreams.

"Bare-chested even in the icy cold," she told me softly, "and riding at the hard gallop, confronting the wind like an eagle, the yellow braids flying back over his shoulders and a wild, keen look in his eyes. I was afraid, but I knew I was no longer a stick of a girl. I made Calimir stand in his path, stopping him, and I looked at him. He slid down from his mount, and I knew he sensed something as well, for he seemed to know I was a maiden even though I was dressed as a youth. Or, afterwit tells me, perhaps he did not care. . . . I left Calimir and walked to meet him, shaking with fright and awe, I felt fated, I looked into his eyes—and he seized me and pushed me down in the snow, bared his member and tried to rape me."

I turned my face away from her, turned it against the rock, sick at heart—it had been the winter when I had crossed the mountains, fleeing from my treacherous father, maddened and full of rage, the winter of which I could remember nothing. Tass sat up with difficulty to face me, placing her one good hand gently on my shoulder.

"It was Ytan," she said. "How can you think it of yourself, that you would do such a thing? Ytan must have been pursuing you. It was he."

I looked at her, wretched still, afraid she said it merely to spare me. But her gaze steadily met mine.

"It was Ytan," she repeated. "There was no wound on his chest. He carried a bow and baggage. His horse was dark."

It was true. Relief surged through me, leaving me so weak that I could scarcely hold her when she came back into my arms again.

"But the day I rode into the Seal village and saw you standing there," Tass explained, "I thought it was you."

"Blood of Sakeema," I murmured, "it is a wonder you did not take a knife to me."

"Why do you think I did not attack Ytan to kill, that day on the mountain, instead of merely slashing at him and fleeing? For all I knew, he was you. Why do you think I did not accuse you, or, failing that, ride away? I felt that same wild leap of the heart, I was as helpless as Birc was in the highmountain meadow when the white hind took him in thrall. I skulked near you like a wolf, but I could not leave you. I loved you, even then."

"I am honored," I whispered, my fingers smoothing the dusky tendrils of her hair. "It was hard for you."

Since she had to believe it of me, that I was a savage,

she had believed all men were such savages, even Kor. And she knew Kor, also, on first seeing him, and was half afraid of him—though not as frightened as she was of me—for she had dreamed often of him, also, in her days of wandering the plains, though not in the same way. She would dream first of a darkened, stormy sky over a great expanse like the tallgrass prairie—but no, waves not of deepgreen grass but of greendeep water, the ocean, stretching dusky blue-gray-purple to forever, all the colors of abalone. . . . Yet when she looked into that stormdark sea there was a great stillness, a wisdom, a love deep and boundless as the sea . . . it was not sea. It was Kor, his salt-washed sea-colored eye, vast as the eye of sky, and he was as immense as the nameless god. When she could see his face, it looked at her out of the face of the greendeep, the vast face of ocean, and he neither threatened her nor turned away, but gazed at her out of restless water, out of the dark sheen of billow and whitecap, with still eyes that seemed to see her soul. Small wonder she was nearly as wary of him as she was of me.

"Once I have seen him like that," I told her in a low voice, "in the pool of vision."

"What else have you seen there?"

"Chal and Vallart."

She nodded and said quietly, "I saw you and Kor."

That was much later, the night she pulled her sword from that tarn. But ever since that first day at Seal Hold she had known—something. Something nameless and uncanny, so that in spite of her fear she had followed us, first as a youth, our afterling, later as a maiden, herself, our comrade. And I judged now that I knew why Kor and I had so quickly healed after hotwind wildfire had scorched us. Her touch. Tass, our healer.

But dreamwit though she was, she had not known that

truth of herself. An oddling, mettlesome, alone even when she was with friends, and bitter, full of spleen, she could not deem so well of herself as to think she could do good. In no way could she know of the nameless power within her, secret even from self, as fearsome as love. Nor could she feel healing happening. Her hands touched and found hurts less severe than she had expected, that was all she knew. Even after the power of her touch brought Kor back from the dead, we did not know her as the healer. My tears had fallen on his lifeless body cradled in my arms, and Tass had touched once, and seen the healing, and fled in terror.

"And I hated myself," she said in a low voice.

"But why? No need for shame, Tass. You had good cause for fear."

"Ytan, you mean? But I had just seen him fleeing, and I saw who he was, and that he was not you. And then I went to find you, and you were holding Kor and weeping as if you would die. . . . What a coward I was. If I had come to you even a little sooner, I could have saved you both. What am I saying? You should never have been put to torment. Kor had told me what was likely to happen—I should never have left your side."

"If you had been with us, you would have been bound as helpless as we were. Tass, let it go. What you did for us, even unknowing, was—the greatest gift. Life itself."

"I still think it was at least in part power of your passion, your tears, that brought him back to us. He dawned back to life like a dayspring. I had never seen such a thing, nor have I since."

I held her, cradled her as I had once cradled Kor's hurt body, wishing there were indeed power in me to heal her as she had healed him.

Again and again she had healed Kor or me. In a meadow

amid yellow pines, where I lay dying of the wound given to me by a devourer. Lying sleeping like a fool, she had thought, and I smiled to remember how roughly she had awakened me. And on a beach near the Greenstones, when Mahela took Kor and me in her stormy fist and flung us back to land—I might have been a sylkie yet had Tass not given me back to self with her touch. Kor and I had awakened to her scowling, vehement care. Tass, song of our love, name of our love, always leaving us and then returning to our lives like the refrain of a song. She was never enough with us, so we thought, but in fact she followed us as the sun follows the wayfarer, warm, or drew closer to us as the wolf, our shadow—always staying back a little from the fire.

"Your passion," she said softly, "your force of passion, you never credit yourself enough with that power, Dan. One night you went moon-mad, you howled with lust, and from miles away I came to you against my will."

"As a wolf."

"Yes, and called into heat by your howl. . . . I almost let you touch me that night, but I kept my secret. It was a way for me to be with you without the struggle, the fear. . . . Once you nearly guessed. I thought surely the devourer had discovered me to you."

A human in wolf form, I had thought, someone in thrall. I had not thought of Tassida, I had not credited her with such devotion. "Was it you who brought Talu back to me," I asked her, "at the castle above Sableenaleb?"

"Yes."

She had caught the runaway mare and brought her to me despite the Cragsmen. She had followed me to the Red Hart encampment and on my journey to the Herders. When I had needed her, she had been nearby, she had come to me at once.

"But—why not stay and give me greeting?"

"The fear," she explained, or tried to explain, her words halting. "It did not go away. Even though I knew—I understood—you were not Ytan. You were Dan, you would welcome me, I could belong to you, as I had never belonged anywhere. You would—love me with all your great heart. You are my tribe, you and Kor, a tribe of three. But still—I was afraid. Am afraid. There is still in me a nightmare that all that seems fair will turn out to be—otherwise."

How I knew that fear. My own father had turned to a demon. "I could never betray you," I whispered. "Nor would Kor."

"No. I think not even the devourers could make either of you betray anyone you loved. But I—I have let myself love you, Dan, and if I ever lose you . . . if you are killed . . . I will have to grieve for you as you grieved for Kor, I will die."

And utterly I understood her, and clung more closely to her. "Loving is fearsome," I said huskily.

"Yes. Fearsome as life itself."

Twilight had long since deepened into night. The waning moon went down, and we could no longer clearly see each other's faces. Voices dwindled into silence, and in that silence I heard the clink of hooves on stone. A horse shape, dark in the night. . . . The gelding Calimir stood beside us, with Tassida's bags and sword and clothing strapped to his back. As Tass had said, he had been trailing us at no great distance all the time. I could have been to Kor within a few days. . . . The thought wrenched at me, but did not make me angry at Tassida.

She slept, and I held her, keeping very still for fear of hurting her.

So silent, the night. Empty. None of the good creature

sounds anymore. Only the hollow-sounding wash of wind up the mountainslopes, wind in the distant fir spires, coming off the yet more distant sea. And the softer waft of Tassida's breathing. And then, distant, as if carried on the breath of wind, very spiritous, very low, a chant. Words, chanted in an eerie mode, pitched at intervals I had never heard. Uncanny as the voice was, at first I thought it was the shades of the dead singing on the wind, and my arms tightened around Tass. But then I felt the slight movement of her chest, her throat and mouth. It was she, Tass, singing in her sleep in a spiritous voice, like a child destined to be a shaman.

Over and over she sang the chant, her eyes never opening from sleep, sang the song out of the past so softly that only my ears could hear it.

*Two there were who came before*
*To brave the deep for three:*
*The rider who flees,*
*The seeker who yearns,*
*And he who is king by the sea.*

*Two there were who came before*
*To forge the swords for three:*
*The warrior who heals,*
*The hunter who dreams,*
*And he who is master of mercy,*
*He who has captured the heart of hell,*
*He who is king by the sea.*

* * *

After a while I dozed, still holding her in my arms for warmth, and I scarcely stirred the whole night, even when sleeping, for fear of hurting her.

At dawn, when we awoke, Tass knew nothing of the song she had sung in her sleep, and when I recited it to her—I could not manage the weird intervals, but I remembered the words—her face went tight and her lips trembled with fear, though she did not move or protest or try to stop me.

"I have never heard it before," she whispered when I was done.

"What does it mean, Tass?"

"I don't know. How should I know?" There was none of her former spleen in her denial.

"You are the seer," I reminded her gently.

"Not so, Dan," she retorted. "You are the visionary. The hunter who dreams. You tell me what it means. I am only the rider who flees."

"Horseback rider," her name meant. And Kor was Korridun, "king by the sea." The two who came before and forged the swords were Chal and Vallart. And I wordlessly gazed at Tass, for my courage was not the equal of hers, and I could not say any of this.

"What does it mean?" I murmured finally, though more to myself than to her. "What are we to do? Tass, are you strong enough to come to Kor with me?"

I hated to ask it of her. The riding would be agony for her, the jarring of her broken arm a constant agony, even on smooth-gaited Calimir. Even lying where she was, she would feel weak and sick fot a few days, until the shock of the injury had passed. Still, I knew that if she willed it, she would undertake the journey, and finish it white-faced and proud, without having uttered a plaint.

I looked at her for an answer, and saw that her dark eyes had gone wide, were staring past me, at—

"A bird," I whispered, dumbfounded.

Perching at no great distance, in the bare lower branches

of a fir, a small, dark bird with pointed wings, perhaps a swallow or a storm petrel. I could not tell which, for it was but a dark shape against the dawn sky. But I think perhaps it was the petrel, for I thought of the sea when I saw it.

"Well," I said softly to Tass, "it is an omen of hope for us, if only one such small creature lives."

She said as if she scarcely heard me, "I cannot go."

I looked at her, and saw in her eyes again the sheen of fear. The old, bone-deep fear.

"Why?" I protested, meaning why again, still, that outworn fear? But she took my query otherwise.

"Because I am not a total fool!" she retorted with some of her usual mettle. "I would be in a faint before half the day had passed."

Nor would I urge her or question her further. Any such urging or questioning would only have driven her farther from me. As gently as I was able I laid her down out of my lap, and then I got up, very stiff with lying so still and holding her, lying against the chill rock, and I went to Calimir and began to take his gear off him. And the small, dark bird still perched in the dead branches of the fir.

"What are you doing?" Tass demanded. "Take the horse and go."

I shook my head. She had never let Calimir be loaned away from her, I knew that. And how could I leave her, hurt as she was? Her face was pale, her broken arm swollen and bruised the color of stormclouds.

"There is food," she insisted. "Look." She gestured toward one of the bags. Within it I found dried berries, biscuit root, groundnut and pine seeds. Not answering Tass, I sat down and gave her biscuit root and berries to eat. She had to be ravenous, after traveling for days as a wolf with no meat. I myself gulped at the food. But she lay still and watched me.

"Take Calimir and go," she commanded when I was done. "To Kor. Forthwith."

"I cannot."

"Dannoc," she said sharply, "don't be a blockhead. I have food, and Marantha by me." She caressed the sword, which I had laid by her side. "Arm or no arm, I can take care of myself."

"Ytan has arrows and bow," I reminded her. "He need not come near your sword to kill you. I do not know how badly he is hurt. What if he comes back?"

"He will want to come near enough to ravish me," she retorted. Then, intensely, "Dan, what is the use of such talk? We must risk it!"

She was quite certain. But I was not nearly so certain.

"Tass," I requested once again, very softly, "come with me."

"I cannot! I know what I can do and what I cannot do."

"Tass," I said in a low voice, telling her what I had not wanted to say, "we must both come to Kor, or it is of no use. Unless the three of us are once again together, it will be of no use. All the old, true songs speak of three. The fruit, sundered into three. The swords. . . ."

I could scarcely explain, for my mind shrank from what I was saying. It was a new thought, and as fearsome as Mahela's doom, and a thought worthy of a consummate fool. Tassida's brows drew together as she heard me faltering. "What is this thing you are telling me?" she demanded.

"The pomegranate of the god, ripped apart. The three stones, sundered from each other . . ." Perhaps for all time, though I would not say that. Despair, edging its way into my words. Tass must have heard, or heard something of my uncertain, unspoken thoughts, and her face grew very still.

"You cannot wait until I am well enough to ride," she told me softly. "Dan, how can you say it will be of no use if you can go to your bond brother and be by his side?"

"But if I leave you here without a mount, there is no hope."

" 'Horseback rider' though I may be, I can walk, as you have walked. I have not broken my leg!" Fire in her voice, blazing into a yet more burning ardor. "Dan, you should have been with him yesterday, a tenday, a season ago! Please, trust in me and go!"

How could I trust her, when I had seen the fear still lurking in her eyes? Brooding, as the dark bird brooded in the shadow of the fir. . . . Yet I had to trust her. It was for her own sake that she pleaded, as much as for Kor's and mine. But still I could not have left her if a thought had not come to me.

"If I set Calimir loose when I come to Seal Hold, will he find his way back to you? Will you come to us then?"

"Of course! He is wise, and I have found some small courage. I give you my word. Go, quickly, Dan!"

Still I hesitated, wishing I could believe her. So often and often she had fled from us before.

She saw my doubt and did not seem to blame me for it. "Dan!" she begged.

"What can you swear by," I asked her slowly, "that I will believe you?"

"On our swords," she said at once.

I felt Alar stir in the scabbard at the words. I drew her out, laid her on the stone by Marantha, and of their own will the two blades crossed. Jewels glowed, their colors blending to make the color of sundown. At the juncture of the blades a pure white light shone out, white fire like that within the fruit Vallart had torn open with his hands. I stared, dazzled, but without a moment's pause, before I could stop her, Tassida placed her hand there, palm down, so that the light glowed blood red through her bone and flesh. She gave a small cry of pain, but did not pull away, and she turned her eyes to mine.

"I will come to you and Kor in greatest haste," she told me fiercely. "I swear it. May these swords smite me if I do not. Dan, go!"

"Are you all right?" I whispered.

She lifted her hand and laid it against the side of my face. Swordlight faded, Alar slipped back into my scabbard. Tassida's hand was warm, unhurt.

I lingered only to kiss her, then vaulted onto the gelding. The dark bird spread its knife-pointed wings and flew away before me, toward the sea, toward Seal Hold. And Calimir took me at reckless speed down the Blackstone Path toward Kor's Holding.

# Chapter Sixteen

Nothing, I knew, could ever truly save time, or make it up, or turn it back. But Calimir bore me so swiftly toward Kor that it almost seemed as if the steed could make up for all the lost time, and my heart filled with gratitude for his help, this marvel among horses, Calimir the swift, the surefooted, the beautiful. He fed himself by browsing upon low branches at the trot, the canter, without breaking stride, snapping off the leafy twigs quickly with his teeth and carrying them in his mouth until he had eaten them. We traveled dusk and dawn, bright day and moonlight, and his smooth stride never slowed.

Within five days we had reached the region of cataracts and waterfalls, the many waters tumbling off the mountains toward the sea, and I felt breathless as I had not been breathless in the thin air above the tree line, thinking of Kor, seeming to sense his—whereness—ahead, if I did not too badly delude myself with hope that he was yet alive. . . .

There came the turning of the trail from which one could see the headland, albeit from the distance of nearly half a day's journey. Too far away to discern any folk, but merely the low shapes of the lodges, their timbers bleached and weathered and mossfurred nearly the gray-green color of the rock itself, and only someone who knew the place well would notice them. I slowed Calimir only a little to look—and then I pulled him to a sudden halt, staring.

A darkness like a black fist gripped Seal Hold. The lodges, gone—unless my eyes deceived me, for in that murk it was hard to see truly. The cloud, whatever it was, whether smoke or brume, sea spume or a black storm of Mahela's sending, curled around and over the place, shadowing it like a doom. Within that shadow I saw only odd glints, like sparks. Lightning? Or the greenish shimmer of devourers?

I sent Calimir off at a speed that threatened to kill us both on the steep downward slopes.

*Kor*, I mindcalled suddenly, though I had never attempted it at such an absurd distance before, *Kor, my brother, I am coming.*

A heartbeat of silence, during which I wished myself dead because he was dead, the sea king was dead—

Then far away I felt his mind hearkening, scarcely daring to believe what it had heard.

*I am coming, Kor! For what one laggard is worth.*

*Dan!*

It was all in that single word, relief and joy nearly drowned in a desperation black as the storm pressing down on Seal Hold, and bitterness, and love. That unquenchable love of his—I could have wept, but because I knew he would feel weeping in me I bit on my forefinger instead, and lay flat on Calimir's neck, letting his long white mane whip my face as I whispered and hissed him to yet greater speed.

*Dan, where are you?*

*Coming. Perhaps a quarterday away. Kor, are you fighting?*

I sensed a tumult, perhaps laughter, perhaps anger or despair. Or equal parts of all three. No time for me to be afraid anymore, of feeling what he felt, of losing myself in loving him. What good had selfhood ever done me? Of what use was my name—whatever it might be?

*Is there anything left in the world but fighting, Dan? We have been fighting since dark of the moon.*

And it was nearly dark of the moon again. Kor had been fighting since the dawn the thunder concs had sent me hastening back toward him.

Coming nearer, I could catch sight of the headland from time to time through the dark fir-spires that grew on the slopes below me. I could see movements within the murk, men and horses, Fanged Horse raiders, most likely. In the cloud I glimpsed the rippling flank of a devourer. Then lightning flared, glinting greenly off many blackstone knives.

It was blessing far more than I deserved, that my bond brother was yet alive.

*Attend to the fighting, then, Kor*. I was afraid he would be heedless, mindspeaking me, that my greeting would make him careless, that he would be killed before I could come to him. *Be wary. I'll say no more a while now.*

*No! Dan!* Panic in him. *Be with me. Please!*

Something was wrong. Even more wrong than I knew. Mahela's hand, perhaps, heavy on him, her poison chilling his heart.

*Are you in thrall?*

*No. Just talk to me, brother, please. No questions.*

There was nothing I could say to cheer him or give him courage. No god riding with me, no savior, no worthy wisdom to comfort him, no solace, only a wanhope fool's notion of three jewels. I thought wildly, with Calimir's strong gallop pulsing under me, and found no hope but that Tass might come to us or else that we might die together. But I could not say those things until I had seen his face.

*It is hard for me to find anything sensible to say*, I mindspoke at last, *when I am plummeting down past the waterfalls like a swallow. Were there any swallows left*. For I deemed that the thing I had seen on the morning Tassida refused to come with me had been no proper swallow, or storm petrel either. But even Mahela could not be more than one place at a time. If she was ahead, beleaguering Kor, she was no longer with Tassida.

*Swallows had wings*, Kor remarked with some small amusement, *and you, I take it, yet have none.*

*No. Therefore the rocks loom parlous hard of aspect.*

We found such slight things to say from time to time. Between times, I would hold onto Calimir's mane and let my mind be with Kor, so that my bond brother could feel my presence. And though I was unaware of him, Calimir sped on. At intervals I would withdraw back into myself enough to look around me.

*I have come beneath the cloud now.*

The dark tendrils of it coiling like snakes of Mahela around me, and the black corpse-cover of it overhead blotting out the sun. Mutter of thunder ahead, and the sullen flaring of lightning. I felt a weight pulling down my heart, as manifest as the weight of a sodden cloak of wool would have been on my shoulders.

*Be canny, then*, Kor told me. *Enemies are everywhere.*

I slowed Calimir and turned him aside from the trail, letting him pick a steep path through the thickly-growing firs and spruces to the upper reaches of the headland. Devourers circled overhead as if waiting for spoils, and in the thunder din I began to hear other clamorings and roarings, the roars of Cragsmen, the shouts of warriors doing battle. More warriors than had ever hosted together in generations, since the wartimes before Sakeema's peace. Then I saw—small wonder that the lodges had been leveled. Pajlat's people and Izu's Otter River Clan and a full twelve of Cragsmen were all mobbing the headland. Kor's Holding had been turned to a hell.

And intent only on coming to him, I leaped Calimir into it.

Squeal and screech of Fanged Horse war mares clashing against curly-haired, blue-eyed ponies—yes, my people were there, though I did not see Tyee, I was not looking for Tyee, I had to find Kor. And I had forgotten there ever was a time when I had stood with lowered weapon before a dangerous foe. My sword was out, uplifted and shining in my hand. I pressed recklessly toward the midst of the battle, where I sensed Kor, and I heard the excited shouts of the Red Hart warriors as they saw me, but I did not look at them. Dark, narrow-eyed Otter River fighters all around me, on foot—I kicked them out of the way, Calimir reared and scattered them. Alar took the head off a hulking blue-green Cragsman I myself had scarcely noticed—his club thudded to the ground beside me. A lash curled around my left arm—I caught hold of the ugly thing and pulled the man off his horse, then sent Calimir leaping onward, for there was a knot of the Fanged Horse brigands ahead, Pajlat himself among them.

And facing them, alone but for his mount, Kor.

Half mad with fear for him, I charged. And just as I

reached his side, Calimir took a spear full in the chest, lunged forward beneath me a few strides, then fell.

*Ai*, Calimir, horse without an equal, my haste had killed him! Tassida's steed lay killed, and how was she to come to us? Briefly, crazily, I thought of the battle I had once envisioned, in which I was a young warrior, disgraced for letting his horse be slain under him. This, then, should be the time when Sakeema would ride into the combat on his mighty-antlered stag, stilling the spears and arrows with the power of his hands. But he did not.

And I was standing on the ground in the midst of a hellstorm of battle, next to the legs of Kor's yellow-dun fanged mare, and Kor was looking down on me with his well-beloved face gone gray as death. *I can't help you*, he mindspoke me faintly, and he swayed as Pajlak's lash embraced his back.

Help me! Blood brown on his tunic, blood clotted and matted on his temples, in his hair, he looked as if he had been fighting forever, and he thought of helping me. He was all goodness—the scum, how could they attack him so unfairly! Anger for his sake welled up in me and burst out in a shout, a yell of rage, as the stone in Alar's hilt flared with a blaze fit to dim the lightning in the black tempest overhead. I heard frightened curses all around me, and Pajlat and his men threw up their hands to shield their eyes from that glare. Pajlat was out of my reach, Mahela take him, I could not kill him yet—but already Alar had hewed her way through the closest one of his minions. I swung myself onto the fanged mare as the body fell off, turned the startled horse around and killed the next man. One more, then Pajlat—but my captured steed struggled against me, and in the next moment the Fanged Horse king had fled with what remained of his retinue pounding after him, down to their encampment along the sandy beach south of the headland.

Cheers rose behind me, but Kor did not cheer. "Dan," he said hoarsely, "come with me."

We rode back through the battle. The Otter were in confusion without their Fanged Horse allies, ready to break and scatter, and the Cragsmen were sullenly falling back. Kor had sheathed his sword, and he paid no heed to any of this. He sent his mare, Sora, at a lope up the headland into the forest, and by the stiff, swaying way he rode I knew that he was weary enough to fall, that only pride kept him upright. Or perhaps he was weakened and in pain, wounded.

"Kor, you ass, slow down!" I was trying to catch up with him, but the foul bitch of a fanged mare under me fought me at every stride, and Kor was riding recklessly fast. He took a sudden dodge toward the seat and sent Sora skittering down a shaly drop to a shingle beach between jutting points of rock. Then he started northward again, and I saw the blood trickling from his lower lip where he had bitten it.

"Kor, stop," I begged, "before you fall!"

He stopped Sora so suddenly that he nearly pitched off her, saving himself only by bracing his hands against her withers, and at last I was able to ride up beside him. His sea-colored eyes were on me. "You are so thin, Dan," he said to me, "it wrenches my heart. You have starved."

"And you are hurt," I said, staring at him. Wounded and going off, like a hurt hawk seeking a solitary place to heal—or die. . . . He honored me by allowing me to be with him.

"Help me down," he whispered.

I slid off my useless mount and let the mare plunge away. Standing on the gravel and sand of the beach, I reached up toward him, but he stopped my hands by lifting his.

*Scared*, he mindspoke, the single word, too spent to murmur it aloud, and as if mindspeak had opened a wellspring between us I suddenly felt the flow of his pain and terror, so stark that they stunned me for a moment. How had he borne it, all the seasons of feeling my passions and hurts as well as his own?

"Handbond," I told him.

Right hands met, gripped, sword scar to sword scar, and I felt the familiar warm surge, strength and courage as of four heroes, and I blinked back tears—it had been too long since I had last touched him, since I had handbonded him. Odd, that for all his need, the grip should comfort and center me as much as it did him.

"If you had not thought to me when you did, I would have fallen," he said in a rush, finding strength to speak. "If you had not come to me when you did—"

"Hush," I told him, and lifted my hands to him again, and this time he let me grasp him under the shoulders. "Steady. . . ."

I tried to ease him off the horse. But as his far leg slid over he gave a terrible groan and clutched at me—he could not stand, he nearly swooned. His knees gave way under him as his feet felt for the ground. I laid him down as gently as I could and kneeled beside him.

"All powers be thanked that you are here, Dan," he breathed. "Seal Hold—full of eyes watching for weakness. . . ."

I was tugging at his clothing, trying to find the wound. There was so much blood on him, blood of enemies I had thought, that I could not tell what ailed him. "Where?" I demanded. "Where are you hurt?"

He gestured. "Spear thrust. The same bastard Otter who took Calimir."

I tore open his trousers and felt pain stab me in the gut so that I could not move or speak or even weep. Kor was looking up into my face, and I think I had gone white with anguish for him.

"Tell me," he said softly.

And since my dry mouth, my lips and tongue, would not obey me to form speech, I mindspoke him. Gentler that way, if such a terrible thing can in any way be said gently. *It took your manhood*, I told him, and I made my hands move to peel back the stiffened, bloodsoaked cloth from the wound. His member came away with the cloth and dropped onto the beach where he lay.

There was a small, stunned silence, and then he spoke. "No great loss," he said bitterly. "Little use I ever made of it."

This, then, was the fell fate I had always sensed for him—or part of it. . . . A mischance dreadful enough; why did I not feel doom was done with him?

"Kor. . . ." I murmured, aching for his sake, not knowing what to say, how to help him—there was no help for what had happened to him. "I am . . . sorry. . . ." I was all awkwardness, and my horror would not let me move my gaze from his bloody cock lying on the pebbles and sand. "What—what should I do with it?" I blurted, and he stared at me a moment, then suddenly barked with laughter, a hard laughter that made him moan as he drew breath, so that I laid a hand on his chest to stop him.

"Let Mahela have it, Dannoc!" He laughed anew, but more softly. "Fling it in the sea, and let the old hag have it. She wanted it badly enough before."

So I took it in the palm of my right hand and went and

gave it to the waves. When I came back, Kor was still softly laughing, a sound with heartbreak in it.

"Truly, it doesn't matter, Dan." He sobered suddenly, weak and panting with the pain of his wound. "Most likely . . . we will all be dead ere long."

So he knew. Or perhaps his despair spoke, but I knew how I had let Calimir be killed and doomed us. Therefore his despair had an equal in mine.

"I take it . . . you have not found Sakeema?"

I met his eyes, too wretched to be angry with him. "Sakeema is dead," I said, "or a traitor."

"It must . . . be true. If anyone . . . could have found him, it would have been you, Dan."

I found water in the skin slung from his sealskin riding pelt, washed his wound and bound it with strips cut from his sleeve. He did not cry out—he seemed nearly indifferent to the pain. When I was done, I pulled his clothing back into place as best I could, then took the sealskin off his horse and covered his legs with it. Then I sat beside him, cross-legged, pillowing his head on my knee, and I took his right hand in handbond again. Westward, beneath black fingers of cloud, the sun was swimming blood-red at sea's edge. Without moving, Kor and I watched it until it sank. Sundown turned to twilight, a gloom scarcely to be called twilight, as dense as nightfall.

I felt numb, no pain in me, but at some time I had started quietly weeping, so that my eyes sent salt rain down on Kor's hand I held clasped in mine. After a while he noticed, and shifted his head slightly to look up at me, and gifted me with one of his rare smiles. "Heal me with your tears?" he said wistfully.

How I wished I could. "It wasn't me. That was Tassida."

His brows went up in inquiry, his eyes grew keen. "It was Tassida? Why do you say that?"

"She is the healer, Kor, not I." Too weary, and distraught, and starved, as he had said, to tell him much more.

"Well," he murmured, mostly in jest, "may Tass come to me, then."

"She is up at the Blue Bear Pass with a broken arm . . . ." She, the healer who could not heal herself. "And I have let Calimir be killed. How is she to come to us in time?"

"She is better off out of this hell," he said gently. He did not understand, for he did not know about the three sundered stones, and I was in no fit fettle to tell the tale. I vehemently shook my head.

"Unless Tassida somehow comes to us, to make us three," I told him starkly, "we might as well die now, and be done with it."

Kor accepted that at my word. "We will send for her," he said.

It was a simple thing to do, so forthright that I felt more than ever the fool for not having thought of it. My weeping ceased, and a sudden, frail hope tugged at my heart, lifting my head. With Kor lying so sorely wounded, it could not cheer me much, but my hand tightened on his. He spoke no more, but lay quietly, resting against me, handbonding as much for my strengthening as for his.

The night was full of noise, hollow noise with no life in it, surf's roar beneath the tempest, wind's keening, thunder groan. So I did not notice the splashings of seals hauling out of the sea onto the beach, seals in their half a hundred. In the gloom I saw their dark, recurved shapes moving against the faint greenish glow of the sea, and I straightened, blinked and looked again, stiffened, let go the handbond and reached for my sword. Kor struggled to sit up. But before he drew Zaneb, the seals had clambered up to us, and we saw what they were, and smiled.

"Welcome, my cousins," Kor said softly. "But it is not your wont to be so tame! Is something amiss with you, as it is with us?"

One of them touched his face with its whiskered nose and changed within an eyeblink. There on the beach lay a sylkie, a man of the sea, one of Kor's distant kindred, his pale, hairless skin faintly glistening in the night as he came to a crouch on his long feet. He met Kor's gaze levelly, his eyes dark pools of shadow in his strange, fair face, and one slender, loose-jointed hand stretched out toward us in a gesture we could not understand, so wry was the slant of it.

*Dan, what does he want?*

*I cannot tell.*

Others had crowded around Kor and their leader, touching them, touching each other, so that a ripple of change spread through the cluster of them like a swell through the sea until they all faced us in their human forms: tall sea men, small-breasted, lithe sea women, all crouching so that none of their heads rose above the level of Kor's. And they spoke to us with delicate, skewing gestures of their hands, as is the manner of this mute folk, and many of them laid their fingers softly on Kor, though not, I thought, in appeal or importunity. I sensed the gentlest of invitations.

*Kor, I think they want you to go with them! For your healing.*

As they had once taken Sakeema into the sea to sleep and be healed. If one could trust the accounts of Sakeema.

"I must go back to Seal Hold," Kor said aloud, and he began to struggle to his feet.

"Wait a moment, Kor, and think. They offer you rest, safety, in a place Mahela might not destroy." But even as I spoke I felt his outrage, his defiance, and I smiled.

"I am not yet ready to hide from Mahela, Dan!" He was the king again, hard and keen. "Nor am I done fighting. Be of some use, would you, and help me get onto my horse."

"You cannot ride!"

"How else am I to get back to the Hold? For a certainty I cannot walk."

The sea folk had stood when Kor had stood, and they swirled like water, making way as I brought Sora and strapped the riding pelt onto her, yet crowding around so close at all times that I could see by the greenish seawater shimmer of their skins. I kneeled and boosted Kor onto his mare with my shoulders, seating him sideward, so that both his legs hung down by Sora's left shoulder. Then I vaulted up behind him, taking the reins myself. Still the sea folk watched us, holding their pelts in their strange, long hands, and as we saluted them and rode away they gazed after us like lovers wishing to remember, as if they might not see us again.

We rode slowly in the utter darkness, and before long Kor groaned and sagged against my chest, and I struggled to hold him from falling with one arm while I guided Sora with the other. I was afraid that I would have to lay him belly-down across the horse, and I did not want that. He would want to come to Seal Hold upright . . . his pride wanted it badly, for by the time we reached the Hold he had revived somewhat and braced himself enough so that he was able to walk in with his arm slung across my shoulders. It was very late. Few folk were about to see him or greet me. A few sleepy sentries looked at us without comment. Horses raised long heads to gawk in the torchlight—

for the horses stood in a close herd in the great hall of the Hold for the night, so that raiders might not seize them.

I went at once with Kor to his chamber, to stay there with him, and he had a boy bring me food—seaweed, forsooth, and fish, and mussels pried from the rocks. Not food such as I would have savored a few seasons before, but I was grateful for it, and grateful that not even Pajlat with his Fanged Horse minions and his Otter River allies could cut Kor's folk off from Mother Sea entirely. They had tried, at first, to besiege Seal Hold, biding their time between the raids that burned the lodges. But since my people of the Red Hart had come to aid Kor, Pajlat had camped on one side of the headland only so as not to divide his force, freeing the way down to the sea. Also, he had attacked more fiercely. Times were hard at Seal Hold. But there was more food for me there than I had seen in many a starving day.

I ate hungrily, then lay down beside Kor and slept, for I was much in need of sleep. Even in my slumber I sensed that Kor was lying awake in pain, and more than once in that night I sat up and silently handbonded him, then went to sleep again. A haunted sleep, for Mahela's black cloud lay heavily on the night, and my dreams were troubled.

# Chapter Seventeen

The shouting seemed at first to rise out of the troubled dreams. Then I jolted awake. The Hold was full of echoing yells and footfalls.

"Raid," Kor mumbled, struggling to rise from his bed. The shock of his wound had made him weak, and he had managed only to prop himself on his elbows when I sprang up and pushed against his chest to make him lie down again.

"Stay," I ordered him. "Tyee and I will see to it!" I snatched up my weapons.

"Dan!" Kor exclaimed, something of moment in his voice—but there was no time. I ran out with the other warriors awakened out of slumber. In the haze of my dreams I had thought at first that the enemies were raiding the Hold itself, but not so. Sentries had given the alarm, and the sounds I had heard were those of Seal and Red

Hart warriors running to answer it. I ran with them. Someone at my side, a fair young Red Hart, cried, "The water!"

Karu. I could see her in the dim light outside, daybreak's light just graying the edges of the sky. And of course Pajlat would be raiding against the water supply, the cliff just back of the Hold where the rivulets trickled down into the stone troughs carved to catch them. If he could keep us from water, in a few days he would have defeated us. I ran that way, and Alar found her own way to my hand, and her light blazed far brighter than the clouded dawn. Something in her seemed to move me out of self, as often happened. I was no longer mere Dan, but I was Vallart, the hero out of that long-ago time of swords and glory, or even—something more, I was not sure what, and there was no time to think on it. Dawn was all shout and thrust and cut, batter, beating the enemies back. Close work, a confusion of knives and spears—I leaped to a stance atop the rim of one of the stone troughs, where I could slash at any enemy who came near, and from there I could see all who struggled. The raiders were mostly Otter. For the sake of stealth they had left Cragsmen and mounted Fanged Horse warriors behind. And stealth had taken them almost to their goal, but the Seal and my yellow-headed tribefellows of the Red Hart were pushing them back—

I came back to self at the thought of my tribemates, I was once more Dan, Sakeema's fool, looking out over the fair-haired warriors I had sent to this fray, some of them hard beset, and one—not there. . . .

Something had shaken Kor's voice. . . .

And then I heard the coarse roars and the cracking of whips as the Fanged Horse charged the headland, and I saw how Mahela's cloud lay like a black hand of doom over us all, and looking up, I saw flying just beneath the cloud a dark, sharp-winged bird. And I knew that all my nightmares had been better than this day.

The longest of days. Some of the old Seal women inside the Hold managed to bridle the horses and bring them to us, or we might not have survived. A few at a time, scurrying, they brought them out. One brought Sora to me—the only aid Kor could give me, that day.

After the enemy had tired of lashing and beating and stabbing at us and had at last gone away, on toward sundown, I walked into the Hold and went to look at Kor.

Lightheaded, I felt afloat in weariness and hunger and—grief. I found Kor where he lay in his bed, saw the fever-sweat glistening on his pale face, saw him open his eyes to look back at me.

"I wanted you to eat, and sleep, and eat again, Dan," he said softly to me, "before I told you."

And though it should not have surprised me—for many people die in fighting, and why not, then, my brother?—my knees gave way beneath me, and I sank down to crouch at Kor's side.

Tyee was dead.

Kor handbonded me and told me the tale. More than once he told it to me, speaking it softly, almost chanting it as shamans sometimes whisper-chant the legendary tales, and at last it came clear to me that it was Tyee, my brother the shaman and seer, Tyee the Red Hart king, for whom the thunder cones had spent their fire.

He had met death not in battle but on the trail to Seal Hold, not far from the Demesne, two days' journey up the Blackstone Path on the flanks of Chital. My people, rising at first light, found their king lying under a devourer, swaddled in its gray fleshy folds, completely hidden and very still.

They attacked the fell servant of Mahela with their blackstone knives—which did no good, for devourers are not hurt by knives of stone, no more than water is. And they tugged and wrestled at the monster with their hands. Perhaps because it was annoyed, or perhaps because it disliked daylight, the devourer lifted off Tyee, and he moved, groaned and came shakily to his feet—he had withstood it, for he was a worthy king, and in a night's long, silent battle Mahela's minion had not been able to take him into its maw. He stood straight and pale to watch it go. But whether out of ill humor, or because it had orders, the devourer swiftly circled back and struck him a blow with its thrashing tail, thicker than a man's thigh and far stronger than any warrior's arm. A heavy blow, an attack, it knocked him ten paces away from the place where he stood, over the trail's edge, over the lip of a crag and down the sheer mountainside, falling without a scream—perhaps the blow itself had killed him, had crushed his chest. My people had found his body on the rocks far below.

"The thunder cones blazed for him," I said to Kor, "and I feared it was for you. I went nearly mad with grief and shame, and now my shame is the more. *Ai*, Tyee . . . ."

"Shame?" Kor asked gently.

"Or regret . . . that I had ever gone on my fool's journey."

"But how could you have helped Tyee?"

"It is not that. I had no thought for him, Kor." I had been so taken up with fear for my bond brother that I had spared none for my brother in blood, my mother's son, Tyee. . . . Grief, heavy in me.

Some of my people had come into the chamber while Kor was speaking with me, the young yellow-braided Red

Hart warriors, man and maiden, looking taut and drained with much fighting. One of them, Karu, touched me on the shoulder. She sat beside me, the others sat close by me on the stone floor, clustering around me.

"That is how we also felt," one of them said. "Shamed."

"We had often scoffed at him," admitted another.

"And muttered," said Karu, "and wished you had stayed to be our king, Dannoc." She was looking levelly at me. That was like Karu, her courage, to face these things. "But how we missed Tyee when he was gone. We attended his body with greatest honor."

"And honored his word also," said Kor quietly, "and came here to fight for me."

My people spoke further, remembering the fires in the east, the sunrise like no other sunrise they had ever seen, as the thunder cones had shot forth blood-red flame and burning rock, fearsome even at the distance, and the rising sun had turned the smoke, spreading so that it seemed to cover the earth, the colors of blood and fire. They had shivered, watching, keeping vigil by their slain king, knowing for the first time that he had been great. They had gifted him with their ornaments, even the feathers from their braids, and raised a cairn over him, and kept watch for a day before traveling on in haste to Seal Hold.

"Mahela has erred, taking Tyee," said Korridun softly, with a keen-eyed, perilous softness. "His death has sent me warriors willing to die. It sent my bond brother on his way back to me many days before battle was joined."

Silently I scanned the faces of the Red Hart warriors. I did not know them as well as I once had.

"Who among you is a bold, swift rider," I asked, "and loyal, and courageous, to do as King Korridun may bid?"

"There are few enough of the curly-haired ponies left,"

Kor put in, catching my drift, "and they are footsore from the long journey, and many of them wounded. But there are some fanged mares we have captured."

"Better yet. The fanged mares are fierce and swift. But the rider must be as fierce, to master one."

Everything depended, so I thought, on this rider who would go to Tassida and give her his mount so that she could come to us. It should have been me, if I was "the seeker." But I could not leave Kor. . . . I heard what my people of the Red Hart had to say and looked long into their eyes before I chose my messenger. Karu, I thought at first, but Karu might be jealous of Tass in her heart. I chose a youth. Then in haste Kor and I told him his errand, and I saw him onto a fanged mare and off into the nightfall. Darkness would guard him from the enemies camped on the beach below.

I went in and stayed with Kor, and changed his bandaging, and saw to it that he passed water. Even in his agony mindful of his folk within earshot, he would not cry out, but afterward he lay the night in a stupor. I lay by him, wakeful with despair.

My grief colored my thinking, I told myself, grief and the shadow of Mahela's cloud, that all seemed so dark. But I had seen well enough how my people, mine and Kor's, were worn down with fighting, their numbers too few, many of them fighting despite wounds. I knew well enough what I should do. A bold attack, a raid on the enemy's camp at dawn or midnight, a sword to Pajlat's heart. . . . But I did nothing. Despair told me that such attempts could not succeed, but only send us down faster to death. Perhaps despair was right.

The next day dawned in brume so thick that warriors could not see the comrades within bow-reach of them. Voices rang like the speaking of spirits out of the fog. We of the Hold stood tense guard all day in the murk, but Pajlat did not risk the cliffside paths to attack. Perhaps Mahela took no pleasure in the combat when Korridun was not taking part, that she sent such weather. Or perhaps she had gone off to shadow Tassida again, and wanted the war to wait for her return. Or she had gone on some yet darker errand. . . . Afterwit tells me it was so, she had gone to keep Tassida from us by whatever means, for my soul knew she was absent, I felt the gloom lighten, my heart lighten somewhat during the respite of that day.

Just before nightfall the fog cleared away. There would be fighting the next day.

That night Kor was well enough to pester me to eat. And when, before dawn of the next day, I cursed Pajlat and got up out of my bed, Korridun rose to stand unsteadily at my side.

"You can't fight!" I exclaimed. For unless I guessed wrongly, there would be hard battle that day.

He snapped, "We'll see whether I can or not."

"I am not daring you! Kor—"

"I am the king!" he flared. "What, am I to lie abed when my warriors go to combat wounded?"

He was at least well enough to be mettlesome. My heart lightened, and something teasing in me rose to meet his peevishness. "Let me at least get some fresh bandaging on you," I said, and I started to reach for it. He struck my hand away. I smiled, for the blow was stronger than I could have hoped.

"I'll tend to my own hind end, thank you. Get out of here."

"Make sure you pass water," I instructed.

"Out!" Kor shouted, and I went. But to annoy him further, I readied Sora for him rather than letting him do it himself. With ill grace, and out of necessity, he let me help him mount. Then he rode out to see to the placement of his warriors—I stayed within the Hold, catching a mouse-colored fanged mare for myself, until I heard the cheer go up as our people saluted him. Then I joined him, and he and I rode to the headland's point to watch the enemy's preparations.

The Fanged Horse encampment straggled along the beach as far as I could see, and the raiders in their hundreds were preparing their mounts for war by tying on the tassels made of human hair and blowing into the mares' nostrils the powder made of dried fungus that was reputed to make the horses swift and fierce. On the fringes of the beach, under the twisted spruces clinging to the storm scarp, Otter River warriors tested the edges of their knives. The twelve of Cragsmen sat lumpishly, like boulders, widely spaced, as if they might fight with each other if they came closer together.

It would be a sharp battle, for though we on the headland held the higher ground, the attackers were far greater in number. Kor's folk had been few since Mahela had vented her wrath on them the winter before. The Red Hart were few since my father had wasted many of their lives.

"I hate this," Kor said softly to me, all spleen gone from his voice. "It breaks my heart. It is so senseless." His eyes were on his meager war host, and on the enemy below.

I nodded.

"Have you taken note, Mahela has not lifted hand against us, to take us to her realm? There has been no need for her to bestir herself. We are doing her work for her."

The realm of death, he meant. Mahela's work, the taking of souls.

"The world going down into the old hag's maw," Korridun said more harshly, "and we of the tribes, killing each other. It is horrible."

Pajlat and his raiders had mounted their fanged mares. Kor sighed. "Line of battle," he shouted, and he and I took our places at the center of it. He sat steady on his mount, his face grim.

Pajlat led the enemy charge, the hooves of the fanged horses thundering, their chests roaring, loud as the black storm that still coiled overhead. At the horses' heels swarmed Otter clansfolk on the foot, and the Cragsmen lumbered along with them. As for me, I loosed my bolt along with the other Red Hart archers, and most of us felled our targets, for we of the hunting tribe seldom waste an arrow. And half a twelve of feathered shafts thudded into the thick bisonhide shield Pajlat held tight to his chest. I tried the mercy shot to his neck, though not with any thought of mercy—I badly wanted to kill him. But my bolt missed, parting his hair rather than lodging in his throat.

"Ill luck!" shouted Karu from her curly-haired mount by my side. There was no time for a second shot. My Red Hart comrades were changing their bows for spears and knives, and I found Alar in my hand, and with a shout we kicked our ponies forward to meet the charge.

Host met host with a shock like that of sea turned against itself, like clashing breakers, sending spray of blood into the air.

It was a long, bloody day with no rest.

Alar wanted to kill the Cragsmen. It was well thought of, for there were few among Kor's followers who were fit to face those great hulks with their vicious blackthorn clubs, but I would not heed Alar. I felt I must stay by Kor. He was not yet well in strength, his face was pale, his eyes narrowed in pain. And everything seemed hard that day, as if ill luck squatted in the air, as Karu had said—she had her mount killed under her, though the thick, curly fur was often proof against fangs and knives, and she buried her stone blade to the hilt, then, in a Cragsman's leg before he howled and struck her senseless. I saw my former lover, Winewa, bring down another in the same way, and a small mob of Seal hacked the lout dead. I saw other Seal, with that inborn liquid grace of theirs, slipping into gaps in the enemy lines as lithely as seawater, spearing horsemen from the side, sending Otter scuttling back. But there seemed always to be more horsemen, more Otter, and I could not reach Pajlat to slay him, and Kor's breath came in tight, rasping gasps—I could hear him next to me.

*Another wound?*

*Cuts, nothing worse. Yet I seem—so weak—*

*Bleeding? Have you torn yourself open?*

*Curse it to Mahela, yes.*

Overhead, a chilling laugh, sounding even through the clamor of battle, and out of the bruise-black cloud swooped a devourer with a rider on its back. Mahela, in her human form, with her retinue of fell servants swirling around her. Thunder cracked and rain poured down, so dense that the world turned black and green, as if we were under the sea. We battled on, our feet and our horses slipping on wet moss and wet rock and mud. And my people of the Red Hart were afraid, I could see it in their cringing shoulders. Despite themselves, they flinched every time a devourer swirled overhead, flying low.

Mahela looked on, amused, diverted, delighted, dressed as if for a festival—her shimmering green gown floated and eddied about her as she flew on her demon steed, the skirt of it flowing down over her feet. And oddly, she looked beautiful, eerily beautiful, with the waves and torrents of her black hair and her fair white face, comely and daunting, nearly like that of—no, I had to be mad, thinking it. Battle bends the mind.

*Kor—*

His sword, Zaneb, fended off his enemies, but he was gazing up at Mahela with a peculiar look, at once intent and aloof. And mindspeaking him, I felt for a moment the surge of his feelings, and they were—as white and black as Mahela, and far more mad than my thoughts. Blood-hot. Moon-mad.

I wrenched myself away. No time, I told myself, there were enemies to tend to. Enemies pressing hard.

"Kor! 'Ware the foes that tread on earth!"

He lowered his glance to me. "Mahela has meddled, somehow," he said. "I feel it in her. We amuse her."

"I know it," I said sourly. I knew Mahela of old, and I did not trust her smile. I knew she would strike in her own sweet poisoned time.

# Chapter Eighteen

Only because darkness fell early under cloud and rain, forcing the attackers back to their camp, did we outlast the battle. And when Kor got down from Sora, with my help, he looked as pale as the wounded who were being taken, senseless, into Seal Hold—or the dead, who were being sent away, with blessing and apology, into the sea.

*Kor! Are you bleeding still?*

*Does it matter?*

*Hush.* I helped him to his bed—he could walk, though barely—and looked at the wound, and saw thankfully that it no longer bled. He had worn much swaddling, and it had stanched the flow. I saw to fresh bandaging, and he let me, tamely.

When I had finished he said to me aloud but privately, for my ear only, "Dan, we cannot hold them off for another day."

"I know," I told him. Kor was not one to cry despair. He spoke but what was true. We would not last.

Yet we had to. Unless we held them off until Tassida came. . . . The others Pajlat and his minions might enslave, but Kor and I would be killed, surely and none too gently. And then there would be no hope for anyone, no hope for the dying world, for he and I and Tassida never would be three. . . .

Should she come to us. I knew what the meddling was that made Mahela smile. I knew her dark hand lay heavy on Tass.

*My brother*, Kor thought to me. He also knew, he also remembered the larger battle, and all that he could not say in any other way was in those silent words.

"We must attack," I said.

We worked out the plan over food. Our aim had to be to take Pajlat by surprise, perhaps sleeping, and kill him—it went against our natures to think like brigands, but the thing had to be done. The Fanged Horse raiders would fight on after their king was killed, they would as soon fight as breathe, but their Otter allies might lose heart.

"And if there is one person whom I do not mind killing by stealth, it is Pajlat," I said. "Unless it might be Mahela."

Kor looked at me, and said nothing, for he was spent. He ate little, and afterward lapsed at once into a sleep that was more like a stupor. It fell to me to choose our warriors and speak to them. I took a turn at guard, then went and lay by Kor's side, wakeful, but glad that he slept.

Wanhope that I was, by the time I arose, in the dense darkness before dawn, I was telling myself that we would be able to hold our own at least one more day. But Kor was right. We did not.

The dawn attack let us manage it, bloodily, until three-quarterday, but otherwise did us little good. The enemy had seemed almost to be expecting us, as if some ill-wishing bird had told them we were coming. By the time the sun passed its height, we had been forced back up the cliffs we had braved in the dark, and Pajlat, curse him, still rampaged, nearly untouched. But I had wrenched away his long reach, his bisonhide whip, so that he fought on only with knife and maul. Kor had killed a Cragsman, dodging under the cudgel and driving for the throat, taking a glancing blow on his ribs and back as he did so, but no worse harm. I felt senselessly hopeful, so much so that when I saw the rider I felt at first an unreasoning leap of heart, as if I had seen Sakeema—

Bursting like a dayspring from between the mountain-side trees, leaping his horse into the battle, as I had done two days before, and the horse was a fanged mare, I knew the one, the sand-colored fanged mare Kor and I had chosen for our messenger to Tass. The rider, a tall and comely yellow-braided youth, but not the one we had sent for Tass—and my thoughts of god, king, savior, fell to ashes.

It was Ytan.

What curse rode on my back, that when I looked for Sakeema, I had to find Ytan? Sheer evil luck, worst of ill luck, the same perverse luck that kept my blade away from Pajlat's throat? Or was it Mahela's hand, heavy on me?

With that mad-dog, death's-head grin of his, and with thick bandaging still wrapped around the wounds Talu had given him, Ytan joined the nearest Cragsman and began with glee to fight. And though he would fight a Fanged Horse warrior if one were foolish enough to attack him, for the most part he turned his knife on his own tribe-fellows. He, Ytan, the one enemy I could not bring myself to kill. And the other Red Harts were as badly shaken as I was to see him raising weapon against them. Perhaps worse, for they had not encountered him since he had left the tribe. They faltered in their line of battle, and the Otter River people cheered, and Pajlat's horsemen roared like their fanged mares and pressed forward.

By nightfall, our enemies owned a foothold on the headland. On the day to follow, almost certainly, they would take the Hold. For Kor, an unpleasant death would follow. For the others, slavery at the best. Torture or death, perhaps. For women, the shameful torture called rape.

And soon after, world's end.

That night Kor and I walked out into the darkness, not willing to waste in sleep what might be our last hours together, even though Kor could not walk far. We spoke to those who stood guard on the portion of the headland that was left to us, and then we walked to the point and sat on the chill rocks, looking out over the greenly shimmering midnight sea far below.

It seemed to me that there was nothing of hope or solace to say, so I did not speak. But Kor said to me, "I feel so much regret in you, Dan, and I cannot understand why."

I sputtered as if ocean had slapped me and given me a faceful of seawater. I had left him and gone off on a fool's quest—"I left you just when you needed me most," I complained, "and to no purpose, and you cannot understand why I regret it?"

He smiled slightly at my tone—though I could not see him in the night and the murk of Mahela's making, I felt the smile in his mind. "Indeed I do not," he said. "Nor can I comprehend why you bewail the quest. It has gained us both much."

I snorted in disbelief. "I know how little it has gained me," I retorted, "and how can it have gained you anything?"

"But it did. More than you know."

This was a new tale to me. I hearkened, and when he spoke on his voice was very gentle, almost tender.

"It was not as bad for me as you believe, Dan, after you left. Small wonder that you think so, for you remember those times just before you went away, and they were the worst of my life. I was sunk in a pit of my own making. But when I saw you truly had to leave me, I made up my mind to be strong." He spoke but merest truth, as always. His words were clean of any plea for pity or praise. "I had to be strong. And I managed it better day by day."

"I am glad of it," I told him. "But I deem the pit was of Mahela's making."

"Scarcely, Dan. She did not make me pity myself, nor can any adversary, no matter how strong. It was of my own doing."

His honesty silenced me. He went on, he told me more.

His days had been spent in preparation for the war and siege that he knew must come. Even though he drove himself every day, working his people hard and himself even harder, so that he should have been lost in exhaustion by sundown, he often found that he could not sleep. And even though no vigil was any longer required of him, he often walked the headland during the night.

Kor said, "There was no time by day to think of anything but food and the fighting to come and the squabbling within the tribe. But at night there was a plenitude of time to think, and room. At first the thoughts were dark. And when my mind turned to you, none too kind." I felt rather than saw his smile, his quiet amusement. "But in the course of many such nighttimes, hard work by day and wandering by night, something began to happen. There is a—a wisdom in the night.

"It came to me as if out of the dark spaces between the stars. I felt very small beneath that vast sky, and it was a comfort in a way, that I felt myself not at the center of things. But sometimes I felt myself—I can scarcely describe it. I became part of the night, I was as vast as sky, as immense as sea, I was at one with the washings of the sea, and I was—yet myself. And in a dim way I began to understand what I am, both things at once. Small, yet vast. Fragile, yet—deathless. Dan, can you at all understand? Saying it, I feel mad."

I told him, "You're no more a madman than I am."

"That's dubious comfort, Dan!" Teasing, he moved to strike me lightly with his fist, then caught his breath and cursed. "Bloody hell! But I am stiff." At my side I heard his stirrings as he lifted himself and changed position to ease the ache of his wound.

"I will go back," I offered, "and get a cloak, a pelt, something for you to sit on."

"No. I am all right. It is a great thing, Dan, not to need too much softness any longer."

A quirk in his voice like the quirk of his wry half smile.

"Dan, you are so good to me—if you had stayed by me, you would have let me weep on your shoulder forever. Truly, you did me a favor by going away for a while and making me be strong. And an even greater one by coming back to me again."

He meant it. My heart ached so that I could not speak. After a moment he went on.

"I was not without companionship in the nights. Vallart came to me sometimes, out of the shadow-stars in the tidal pools."

"Alone," I murmured, remembering how I had seen Chal alone at Sableenaleb.

"Yes, alone. It felt nearly—he must have been very much like you, Dan. It felt as if you were here with me, in a way, all the time."

I said huskily, "I am grateful to him."

A long silence. I sensed Kor had more to say, and waited for it, and in time it came.

"One moonlit night I walked far down the beaches toward the greenstones and found a queer sort of living creature lying in the sand. It was a white-breasted cormorant—I saw it first by the flash of those white feathers, and then saw the glossy black of the rest of it glimmering in the moonlight. But it was far larger than any cormorant should be, nearly as large and heavy as a man, with a mighty beak the size of my sword. And though it darted its weapon of a beak at me and hissed at me to warn me away, it had no strength to move from where it lay. In the moonlight I could see the dark blot of the wound on its white breast."

"Kor," I said in horror, "it was Mahela!" Horror, because already I knew what he had done.

"Yes," he said with just a hint of his faint half smile in his voice, "I know. I knew it from the first, but pretended I did not, and I stood in the surf and netted fish for her to eat. But I would not let her have them until she grew civil and accepted them from my hand, instead of driving that heavy hooked beak of hers at me."

"By great Sakeema's blood," I groaned, "why did you not kill her when you had her at your mercy, and finish the task I had begun?"

"Only once since I have known you have I ever killed when I could offer mercy, and you may recall we both regretted it bitterly."

"Will Mahela have mercy," I demanded, "when she comes to make captives of us all?"

"For the matter of that, it is not Mahela seeking to capture us or slay us, but mortal warriors of the six tribes."

"But Mahela—"

"Let it go, Dan, please. It is the one thing in the world I do not expect you to understand."

Something—fated—in his voice, for all that he tried to keep his tone mild and wry. I said nothing more, but sat and listened to his tale.

After a while, after eating many fish, the large cormorant grew tame enough that he could stroke its glossy green-black feathers without fear. And as he touched it, of course, it changed, and there in the sand lay Mahela, naked, with a horrible wound marring one white breast, looking up at him in a way that was both piteous and seductive. But when she saw he was not surprised she was furious, and clawed at him, leaving bloody welts on his skin. After her fury had passed—when dawn made green streaks on the eastward sky—Kor carried her away to a sea cave, the same one where he and I had hidden our swords for a season while we quested to Tincherel.

"And she was too heavy for me to carry in any way but by slinging her over my shoulders, with her white buttocks to the sky, like earth's answer to the moon," he said. "And very little she liked it, but she had small choice in the matter, for she was not strong enough to walk, not even with my help." An odd, dark clash in his voice, a combat, of two things: his hatred for her, and his—

Mercy, I told myself, the mercy that made him help all who needed his aid.

He had carried her away and hidden her in the cave, hidden her from sun's burning rays and from his own people, others who might find her, who might not tender her such mercy as he did. He gave her his cloak to cover herself with, and left her, and was back before sunrise with food for her—food not much better than the raw fish he had already given her. "Little enough to spare at Seal Hold," he told her gravely. Then he left her alone to rest and mend through the day. But that night and every night to follow he returned to her, and sat and talked with her.

"Nothing but talk, Dan. And even that, none too agreeable. Mahela's tongue is even sharper than Tassida's."

"Then why talk with her?" I grumbled.

"There was wisdom in her, Dan, like the wisdom in the dark voids of the night. Much worth learning, only—bent awry. The same dim sense I had felt before, coming clearer. But before it was more than a whisper in my mind, like a distant song, she grew strong enough to fly, and she left me. I came to the cave one nightfall, and she was gone."

"Left with no thanks and no promise," I muttered.

"Of course not. She is the goddess."

Still, in the course of the long summer's wearing on, no storms had attacked the frail coracles with his people in them fishing on the sea. The season had favored in every way. No lives had been lost, many fish had been brought in and few had rotted in the drying. Gentle rains had fallen on the oat crop at fitting intervals, and many baskets of oats had been gathered and stored in Seal Hold.

Then, when all was ready for them, as if they had been summoned, the attackers had come, and the black tempest of Mahela's making.

"She has been toying with you, biding her time," I said bitterly. "Letting you bring in the fish, the oats. She wanted a worthy battle to watch."

"Perhaps."

"You know what she is, yet you do not entirely hate her?"

"How can either of us know surely what she is? There are depths to her, Dan, like the depths of sky. Deeper than greendeep. I have talked through the nights with her, and learned from her as I learned from darkness."

That odd battle in his voice again. . . . I knew I should ask what he had learned from her, but bowed my head to my knees instead, for I also was no stranger to the self-dug pit. Whatever knowledge he had found, whatever he thought Mahela had given him, or the night, it was to no avail, I deemed.

"All that you have learned, then, what can it matter if she yet lives? She will swallow us."

"It matters. Even if Mahela should take us both this moment, it matters still. And you, Dan—do you not yet know what your quest has gained you? Gained us all?"

I gave no answer, as suited the name of nothing.

A quiet. Off in the darkness somewhere, a warrior screamed as his wound was dressed. Overhead, a mutter of thunder. This was not the clean darkness of starry night. It was dense, and seemed to smother the world.

With a faint prodding edge to his tone, Kor said, "Dan. A tenday's night after you left me, last spring, I had a strange dream, so real I would have put my hand in fire for it. You came to me and sat by me where I lay sleeping—it was you, I could feel it to my heart of hearts, to the center of my being, but I could not see your face. There was a sort of sunsheen lightning playing about your head, and leaning over me as you were your face was darkened against that light. I badly wanted to see you more clearly, but I could not." His voice faltered, then steadied again. "It seemed the worst of mischance. But you were yourself, utterly, but also something more, and your name was Dan but yet something more, something uncanny, and it alone of all that I dreamed I could not remember when I awoke."

The strange name—I had nearly forgotten it. I had seldom thought of it since leaving the Herders, since turning back toward Kor, and the sound of it came dimly to my mind, like a distant voice. "The seeker," it meant. But the quest had failed. I had renounced the name, I had turned away from seeking.

"It's parlous dark, Dan," Kor said. "I cannot see you. Say your true name, Dan," he gently dared me, "and I warrant you there will be light for us to see by."

Though I could not have clearly said why, though moments before I would not have believed it of myself, that there was anything I would not do for Kor—it was a thing I felt I could not do, even for him. "Stop it," I whispered.

"I seem to remember a time," he remarked, "when a certain muttonhead kept calling me Sakeema, little as I liked it."

My head came up in protest. "And I was wrong," I flared at him, "was I not?"

*Were you?*

He mindspoke because he was trying to tell me something scarcely to be encompassed in mere words grumbled in the dark. A glance, the deep sea-changing glance of his eyes would have helped, but as I could not see him he touched me with his mind, as if he had reached out to lay a hand on my shoulder, and as I felt the touch I sensed a vast quietude, something within him more immense than the sea, as limitless as the nameless god. For a moment I stopped breathing. I could not speak, not even to mindspeak.

*Dan*, he thought to me with a hint of plea, *know yourself, and you will know me, what I am.*

He was Sakeema after all. Inwit knew, had always known. Yet not Sakeema, or not entirely. I felt the pain, the heart-deep ache of his wound. He was Kor. He was—god, yet going down to defeat. . . .

My mind was swirling like Mahela's accursed cloud.

*Dan, name yourself by your true name to me, accept it, and you will understand!*

I could not. "I am not what you think I am," I whispered, though I scarcely knew what that was, except to deny it.

*You called me Sakeema again and again—you, my dreamwit, and I should have known it was in some wise true. But I fought it and denied it with all my strength, did I not, Dan?*

"Please," I begged.

*You had no mercy on me when you went off and left me alone with my denying.*

"I am sorry!" I cried out, though there had been no anger in his mind, no desire for my contrition. Only the bare, blunt truth.

*But there is no need for sorrow. I suffered, it is true, but I found my way through it. I could have spared myself all the suffering if I had not been afraid to—to accept. Dan. . . .*

"What?" I whispered, and my hand went out into the darkness, met his and gripped. Warm touch of his mind thanked me for the handbond.

*Dan, it was—so simple. There was—something required of me, and I did not like that thought. A sacrifice. Perhaps it has already been taken.*

His cock, he meant. Though in fact all his life had been but one sacrifice after another, for his people, for me. . . . The torments Sakeema had suffered at his death could not have been much worse than those Kor had suffered for my sake.

*It is simple, Dan, truly. In your own time you would come to it, I would not need to urge you. But there is not much time, so I must ask you: Who are you? What is your name?*

I bit my lip until I tasted blood. The name he meant, I knew it well, knew the word, the shape and the sound of it. A few times I had taken it into my mouth and spoken it. But to take it unto myself—it was an enormity. Every part of me feared it.

For Kor's sake. . . . I struggled. There was a—a monstrous, nameless darkness that I had to face and accept. A dark agony, an ordeal, a price that had to be paid just for being . . . what I was. . . . And I had never wished to be anything but a hunter and a dreamer, a wanderer in the forests. What could be more glorious, I had asked Kor once, than to be a god and save a dying world? Why did he fight it? Now I knew why. It was worse than fearsome, it was—unthinkable. And even his hand-bond could not help me, my mind turned away from it like averted eyes, fled like a coney in the grass, I tried to see his face but everything was darkness, and I could not—remember . . . .

I was failing him yet once again. My head bowed, I groaned and I felt his left arm around my shoulders.

*It is something you have to do for yourself, Dan! Not for me, or for the world, but because you must, to be—what you are, who you are. Whole.*

But I could not, I truly could not. Despair lay too heavy on me, that night.

I was shaking, not with strain but with utter defeat, and Kor felt it, tightened his embrace around me, held me against his chest. "Never mind, Dan," he murmured. "Let it go. It doesn't matter."

I thought to him, *But you know—it does. And I—I am such a coward—*

"Hush. No. It truly doesn't matter, because of this: I will always love you. Beyond world's end, if need be."

# Chapter Nineteen

At first light battle was joined again.

The memory of that dawn reeks in my nostrils with the stench of dead horses piled below the cliff, Calimir somewhere among them. Who would have thought that the death of so mastered, so mute a thing as a horse could have doomed us? Yet I felt that all my hopes had fallen to ruin in the moment that Calimir died.

Always that reek, that stench of dead hope, when I think of the beginning of that day. That, and the taste of bloodthirst in me. I wanted to kill. I went to the battle bare-chested, with rage and defiance in my eyes. But I had no chance, that dawn, to aim an arrow at Pajlat's neck. Mounted on the mouse-colored fanged mare, I faced his minions but a spear's length away, with Kor at my side, while they were still no more than shadows in the murk, and already warriors were grappling almost before it was light enough to see.

Kor and I met each other's gaze in silence for a moment, handbonded in silence. We both felt that this would be the day we died, but it was not a good thing to say. Our grim comfort was that we would go together.

With a wordless shout we charged the mass of the enemy.

Sun rose red as blood over the eversnow, then disappeared behind Mahela's black hand. And blood splattered red on the headland below, and Zaneb and Alar shed much of it. Blood of Otters, the treacherous former friends of the Seal Kindred. Blood of Fanged Horse raiders. Kor and I were hard beset, but for a while we seemed scarcely to know it. If we had to die, we would take with us as many of the scum as we could, and to Mahela with us all. It annoyed us that we could not force our way to Pajlat, whom we chiefly wished to kill. Why could we not at least kill Pajlat? It seemed a cruel injustice that too many Cragsmen stood in the way. Alar seemed to grow wings in my hand, and the stone in her hilt burned yellow with her bloodthirsty joy, for there was nothing she loved better than to lop hands off Cragsmen, and that day she lopped many.

And Korridun's people of the Seal surged along with him, with me, wielding their shell-tipped spears. And not far away Karu, mounted on a slain comrade's pony, shrilled her warrior's yell. But they were too few, the Red Hart warriors, the Seal Kindred on foot led by dry-eyed, dark-faced Winewa who thought always of her lost child as she fought. They were perhaps half the number they once had been. And though we charged again and again, in the course of that long morning we were pressed relentlessly back.

Back. We would be forced back to the Hold, and the old women and little children cowering within it would flee to the deepest chambers, and some of the Seal warriors would go within and defend them for a while from behind barriers of stone. But not Kor and I. We would make our stand and die at the entry, side by side. . . .

And then somehow the swirl of combat came between Kor and me, forcing us apart. And slash and struggle as I might, I could not make my way back to him. There had been nothing left to us but to die together, and even that stark solace, it seemed, Mahela wished to take from us. . . . Like sea tide the battle washed between us, bearing us ever farther away from each other, and I began to be afraid. But I would not mindspeak Kor, for he was weakened by his wound, and I would not weaken him further with my own fear.

Mahela, the old meddler. I knew she had done this to us somehow—I seemed to feel the dark touch of her hand. And then her devourers, circling overhead, ever circling overhead, began from time to time to lash down with tails longer and thicker and more deadly than any whip of Pajlat's had ever been, knocking warriors dead with a single blow. Kor's warriors, always.

"To the Hold," I ordered the Red Harts who fought nearest me. "Tip arrows with fire, shoot yon monsters through the slots in the stone." I felt grimly certain that the devourers would not like fire.

I turned my fanged mare, protecting their retreat as best I could with the sword, taking wounds—though I knew they were lesser wounds than most of those suffered around me. Some shitbottom Otter pricked me with a spear in my thigh just above the knee. One of Pajlat's raiding scum placed a bleeding whip-weal on my head.

And then someone slashed my mare's throat from jawbone to jawbone, nearly severing her head, so that she sank stone dead to the ground beneath me, and I stood mountless amid hard battle.

And in the darkened air above me I saw the many greenshades dancing like the swaying spirit-dancers around the autumn soulfires, many more than the fighters remaining on the field below. And seeing them, I felt myself to be near death, far too near . . . I would die soon, and not at my bond brother's side. So many had died, too many. . . . I saw Tyonoc, Kela, Leotie, Tyee, greenly shimmering. My throat closed at the sight of Tyee bodiless in air, and my sword sagged in my hand.

"Fight, Dan!" His voice cracked like a lash. "My pigheaded brother, where is your stubbornness now, when your tribe needs it worst? Have our people come here to die for his, that you should despair?"

I lifted Alar and wielded her, but sluggishly. "Tyee," I whispered to the wind, "you were right, my brother. Sakeema lies dead somewhere, long since meat for worms."

"No whit!" My father's voice this time, angry. "Have I not told you Sakeema lives?"

"Then he is our betrayer," I said.

And Tyonoc said, "I have reared a fool." I had never heard him speak so harshly; it stung me, but thrust me deeper into despair. "A buffoon! You lunkhead, my son, do you not yet know yourself, what you are? Have you forgotten again your own name?"

And the dark cloud of Mahela lay over all the world, so it seemed to me, like a vast devourer of sky, swallowing me along with all the rest. And my limbs felt as heavy as if a devourer big as the world swaddled me. Alar flashed before my eyes, protecting me of her own accord, but it seemed to me that I saw only darkness, I felt as if I could scarcely move, could scarcely breathe, despair wrapped me so tightly in its chill embrace.

"Your name!"

I scarcely heard him. A devourer of my own making

had me, holding me in deathly swaddling, intent on taking me, I had to withstand it . . . and in that most lonely of struggles, all foolish fears fell away from me, all my terrors were gone but this most primal one, that I would be smothered, drowned, unsouled, lost—in the final darkness. . . .

Center. I had to center in self.

Amid darkness and battle clamor I listened for the stirrings of my own soul. It would have been easier to find a midge in the night.

I was—a Red Hart. . . . No, no longer. Not entirely. I was—a hunter. . . . No. Hunters kill the creatures of Sakeema, eat the meat. I was—a storyteller. . . . But all my tales ended in doom. I was—one who yearned for the god. But Sakeema was dead, or a villain, many times I had declared it to be so. Unto myself, then. I was—was—

I could not remember my name.

A devourer made of cloud gloom and bloodshed and my own desperation had me in its grip, and I knew I could not let myself be afraid, or I would be—no more. . . . But, oddly, I felt angry, furious. Hot anger ached in my chest, my shoulders. Why was this always happening to me, that I could not remember my own name?

Say the name, my son!"

I wanted to curse him, curse the world, curse fate. It was not fair, that I could not remember. Was not my name, whatever it was, blast it, was it not as good as anyone's? As good as Kor's, and Tassida's—

Something sang through me at the thought of them, some nameless passion. And out of the darkness within my own despairing mind came the faint, spiritous voice of a song.

*Two there were who came before*
*To brave the deep for three:*

*The rider who flees,*
*The seeker who yearns,*
*And he who is king by the sea.*

Kor, the sea king. Tass, the rider. And by my body, how I loved and yearned for them both.

I was the seeker.

I was the one who could love and quest forever.

I was Darran, Darran, Darran!

The name surged through me with a power such as the sun must own, rising. I shouted, I flung up my arms, and all was light, my own light. The skin of my face, my bare chest and arms, all parts of me glowed with a sheen as of yellow lightning, and I felt my long hair lifting like wings around my head, and in my hand I gripped the hilt of a shining sword. Stormwind was blowing, not Mahela's but my own.

Horses neighed in terror of me, threw their riders and ran away. Good, the creatures at least had saved themselves for the time. . . . The warriors who stood nearest me screamed like the horses or fell back with widened eyes. The Otters prostrated themselves, for they were a reverent folk, and clever. Darran would have slain them had they come in his way. I had been mistaken to think that Darran would not kill. For the sake of war, no, I would not. But for Korridun's sake . . .

There were things Darran could do, at once, to aid him. "Sylkies!" I called, my voice rising like thunder roar. "Sylkies from the sea, come to us!"

And at once I saw them, flowing like a freak tide up and over the lip of the seaside cliffs. The tall, loose-jointed, sharp-toothed sea warriors, wet and shining, naked but for the pelts they wore on their narrow shoulders, weaponless but for their own weirdness. They had needed only my word to let the uncanny wave of them wash into the battle.

They caught up the weapons of dead men in their long-fingered hands, they surged against the enemy. Their distant kindred, Kor's people, raised a shout and fought with new strength. Good. But Kor, where was Kor?

I had to come to him, quickly. I had been gone from him too long.

"Where is my brother?" I shouted to the greenshades hovering under Mahela's hand of darkness, but they did not answer me. I could no longer see my father's face, or Tyee's, or the face of any spirit I knew. Of their own accord they would not have left me, I felt sure of it. Mahela's tempest had whirled them away. Mahela would take away the world, when she could.

And though no enemy came near me, everywhere around me warriors fought with each other, stubbornly, stupidly, everywhere I could see the fighting, the blood, the dying. . . .

I could not see Kor. Fear squeezed my heart. In her fair womanly form, on a devourer's back, Mahela flew overhead and laughed. "Shoot me with an arrow, Dan," she mocked, and I saw her glance off toward the Hold, and I also looked that way.

Sakeema help us all.

Alone, Kor faced Pajlat at the entry of the Hold.

Alone, apart from the battle where the sylkies might have aided him—I myself stood nearer. And afoot—whether unhorsed as I was or by choice, Kor stood afoot, and Pajlat had just sufficient honor to meet him in like wise. Or perhaps it was the steep slope of sliding gravel that had decided him. Few horses could have kept their footing there in any event. Small disadvantage to Pajlat, for even afoot and downslope, he still loomed taller than Kor, lout that he was. I saw the flash of Kor's sword, the lift of Pajlat's club, half again Zaneb's length, and madly I plunged that way, through eddies of the battle.

Sakeema, if only my bond brother would not be killed before I could come to him. . . . Echo of a plea I had pleaded before.

When he was well in strength Kor made a fierce and canny fighter on foot, lithe, deft to evade and to take advantage. I think I would not have feared so much for him, even against a hulk like Pajlat, on any other day. But doom hung in the air, and Kor's wound had made him blood-drained and stiff, not able to move strongly or quickly or with his usual skill. Even as I thought it I saw him take a shrewd blow in the ribs that nearly felled him—I would not be able to come to him in time!

I roared aloud in rage and anguish, and lightning flew up from my flying hair, sun-yellow lightning that clashed with Mahela's of sea-green hue so that both burst into splinters and thunder. Warriors and devourers shrank back from the fire of my face, and Mahela's black fist of cloud grew battered and shapeless before the force of my own stormwind. No one dared face me, not even Cragsmen, but I cared nothing for my own power, I wanted only to save Kor—

But a warrior blocked my way. Before me, grinning his cold grin, dripping knife in hand, stood the one enemy who could defy me.

Ytan.

Like a flame burning in a still place I stopped before him. Overhead I heard a thunder-low laugh. Mahela was watching.

Ytan, my brother, born of my dead father, my dead mother. Of all my Red Hart family, the only one who remained to me. Ytan . . . and eerily in my own silence I remembered happy days, gone like a dream, when we were boys together and he would wrestle with me and sometimes let me win, when he would sleep by my side as the tan deerhound puppies lay on top of us both. . . . Gone as if they had never been. There stood Ytan, raising a blackstone knife to sink it into my throat, knowing full well that heart would not let me kill him—

And beyond, as if in a nightmare lightning-flash under a storm-black sky, I saw Kor crouching in front of Pajlat, white-faced, defeated, clutching his side, his own blood welling red between his fingers. And Pajlat held the stone blade with which to sever the head he would tie to his riding pelt—

I screamed, not a warrior's yell or yet a scream of fear but a cry more than half sob, and I raised my sword and slashed open from throat to belly the one who stood in my way. And Ytan fell, and the devourer within him flew out, gut-gray, and rippled up to circle with the others. I did not see, for I saw only Kor, Kor, and my heart was broken, for I had killed my brother, and even as I sprang forward I knew the moment I had tarried had made me too late to save my friend of friends—

I was Kor, with Kor, my own death loomed, for my heart was his heart, I felt his pain and fear. And though he did not move his mouth or turn aside his eyes as Pajlat lifted the knife, I, Darran, screamed aloud, and the scream formed a word.

"Sakeema!" I cried.

In greatest need I called on my god, and Sakeema came.

# Chapter Twenty

It was splendid, glorious, the young warriors told me later, to see her coming, bursting out of spruce forest on the back of the great stag, its antlers embracing her and the lovelocks of her tawny hair flying behind her with the speed of its running, the sword in her left hand—though she was not to need it—and her face, pale, from the pain of her injured arm perhaps, and achingly beautiful, and rapt, as if she had seen a vision. All the Otter River folk threw down their weapons and fell prone, hiding their faces when they saw her, for they knew that Sakeema had come to the battle, riding on a mighty stag, lacking only her retinue of wolves.

The Cragsmen and the Fanged Horse raiders fought on, for they cared nothing for Tassida on a red hart.

I had not seen, for my back was to the mountains, my eyes on Pajlat and Kor as I sprang forward, a few paces too far away. . . . But I felt the rush as something of shining red-brown sprang past me and bore down Pajlat in a single leap.

So it was that I saw her come, when Birc, the stag who had once been Kor's guardsman, when Birc sprang past me, harried Pajlat to the ground and held him shrieking there as he drove his antlers to the heart.

And Kor crouched yet alive, his head bent to his knees—I could see his taut back and shoulders, but not his face. When I kneeled by his side, he seemed not to know I was there. His right hand pressed tightly over his wound—I could not handbond him. Zaneb lay at his feet, her light dimmed.

"Kor," I whispered, and I put my arms around him, scarcely daring to touch him for fear of causing him further pain. His head turned toward me without lifting, but anguish would not let him open his eyes.

At a small distance, Tass sat swaying on her strange mount's back, reeling as if she would fall.

*Tass*, I mindspoke her, I could not help it, my heart was so full. *Tass, beloved, come quickly, heal him, the wound is deep, he will die!*

I saw her stiffen on Birc's back, and I went rigid in fear, gut-certain that she would bolt, that I had sent her fleeing from us again, fool, dolt, wantwit that I was, with no more sense than to mindspeak her—but she braced her one good hand against the stag's shoulder and pushed herself off him, landing with a small cry of pain before she came unsteadily over to where I kneeled, and then I knew that she had come out of fear and into courage, sometime on her hard journey to join us.

Tassida. The healer who would no longer flee. Kor, the king by the sea. And I, the dreamwit. The three of us crouched together, clustered like the three petals of a frail flower, while the battle swirled near at hand. . . . Even unhorsed as they were, the Fanged Horse raiders were taking a hard toll of the sylkies. They badly wished to break through to Kor, to me. A sea maiden fell, cut down by a whip blow—then Birc lunged and sank his antlers deep in a marauder's chest, tossed the man away amid a splattering of blood. He turned to the others, but they did not await him. Sea people and deer man fighting side by side, it was too much for them. They fell back.

Tass sheathed Marantha, kneeling by Kor.

He did not even look at her, so much was he taken away by pain. His face had gone gray, his eyes were slitted in pain, his body was knotted like a fist, fighting the sickening weakness of his mortal wound. Tass laid her left hand softly on his hunched and trembling shoulders, and at once his agony lessened—I could see how his breathing eased. His eyes closed more smoothly. But he had not moved his hands from the wound in his side.

*Kor?*

*Help me—help me lie down, Dan.*

Together Tassida and I eased him to the ground, and I slipped Zaneb into the sheath at his side. ''Try again, Tass,'' I urged her.

She cradled her broken arm in her left hand and laid her right hand on his chest, then placed the other beside it, and I watched, hand to my mouth. But there was small change. Kor lay and panted quietly in muted pain, and Tassida took up her arm in her hand again. Her pain, little less than his. Her pale face, very quiet, very beautiful, and in a low voice she said, ''Dan, he will mend, given time. I seem to be a healer, as you have said, but I am not yet a god. It was at least partly your tears, before, when all wounds were sent away without a scar.''

"It might have been," I told her. "I am Darran. But I know you, stonebearer, and you are indeed the god."

She stared, too weary or too much in pain to shout at me as she would once have done. "No more than you are," she averred.

Perhaps she understood, perhaps she said it to quarrel with me. But it was true. And she could have declared the same of Korridun.

"Look yonder," said a voice tight with pain—Kor's. His sea-dark eyes were open, gazing into the distance.

I looked, and felt my blood chill. The snowpeaks were stirring, melting, sliding toward the sea. Beyond the edge of the cloud, sky was darkening. Somewhere the sun was dying.

"Mahela has seen you coming, Tass," Kor added starkly.

"Tass," I demanded, "are you ready?"

Kneeling, I gazed levelly at her. She stared back at me, and I saw the muscles of her jaw move, she had tightened it so.

*Tass*, I mindspoke her, and then aloud I said softly but formally, "Tass. I am Darran, the seeker, and I have sought you long. Beside me is Korridun, the sea king. Have you also found self, and courage? If you are willing to venture, tell us now your true name."

She moistened her lips with her tongue, then whispered, "Tass. The rider."

For she also had misnamed herself, years before. She had called herself horseback rider, but she had been born to ride the stag.

Darran's inwit told me what to do. I took her right hand, the one that dangled helplessly below her splint, and I lifted Kor's bloodied right hand away from the wound in his side—he and Tass both cried out at me, I was hurting them both. And as gently as I could I guided their right hands together, sword scar to sword scar, so that they handbonded. Tassida's eyes opened wide with wonder.

"The arm," she said. "It has stopped aching."

The taut lines of Kor's face smoothed, and he made a small sound of amazement, for pain had left him. I wished I could let him rest, but there was no time. "Kor," I said urgently, "you have to stand. We must face Mahela."

Tassida's handbond gave him strength to do it. Together the two of them rose and stood side by side with reasonable steadiness, and I stumbled up to stand with them. Quickly I took her other hand in mine, sword scar pressed to sword scar. My whip cuts ceased to hurt me, ceased to bleed.

A soft glow from Alar, Marantha, Zaneb, from the three jewels, yellow, amaranthine, sundown red. Within the three of us, the stonebearers, a waiting hush. Nothing more.

A devourer swooped low overhead. On its back rode Mahela, gloriously gowned and silently laughing, as a cormorant will. "So, little daughter!" she called out, her voice wild and glad in the tempest wind, "I need not have feared you, after all! Your power is fit to save only yourself, it seems. Yourself and these two handsome cocks."

The mountains were leveling, dying with a roar louder than Mahela's thunder. Numbly I saw Birc standing near us to guard us, blood glistening on the tips of his antlers like the red buds of springtime on a bare tree . . . the trees would never bloom again, they were dying with the world. The very sun, dying. In the air the sounds of dying, warriors still striving on the headland below, fighting as if under an evil spell, in thrall to demons, their screams rising with the stench of death on the wind.

"Nearly all those yet alive in the dryland world are on

yon battlefield,'' Mahela jeered, ''and they can think of nothing but to kill each other! I will have them all before much longer, and you three may stand and watch, my chick and my cocks. And when all else is done, I will put out the stars as if they were slaves' eyes.''

*It is because . . . because I am yet afraid, that she can do as she will.*

Tass, mindspeaking, she who had never willingly mindspoken me before. And Kor also heard, as he should not have been able to hear, and he understood. *You are not so very much afraid,* he told her, and I could hear him as well, for we three were as of one mind.

*I am not afraid of yon gloating goddess. But—I am yet afraid of Dan.*

*But why?* I burst in. *Tass, I love you.* She knew with what ardor I loved her, and with what wise compassion Kor loved us both.

*Bold cock,* she thought to me wryly.

*I am not Ytan!*

Dead, dead, far too much death and dying, all was dying . . . did she know he was dead? Yes, I felt it in her, how she had hated him, how she was glad I—I had killed him, I had killed my brother Ytan. . . . Grief twisted my heart as I mindspoke his name, and I sobbed.

Tassida tore her hands away from me, from Kor, and strode off.

''Tass!'' Furious, thinking she was fleeing mindspeak or my sorrow, I ran after her. ''Bolting again?'' I shouted. ''There is nowhere left to go, wanderer!''

She gave me a quelling look and strode on. After a moment I comprehended that she was looking for something. Amid the many and many lifeless bodies of the battlefield, looking for one—

She kneeled and laid hands on Ytan's ghastly, hollow corpse.

"Tass," I breathed. It was a thing I would not have asked of her. Though indeed, once there had been a hacked and horribly mutilated body growing cold in my arms, and she had brought it back to warm and comely life. . . . Unsteadily, hands to his wound again, Kor came and stood beside me, perhaps remembering that same uncanny night. I put my arm around him to support him, and he stood as silent and awed as I.

Ytan did not move or breathe beneath Tassida's hands. Nothing happened, except that tears ran down her taut face and fell on his bloodied flesh.

"Tass," I whispered, begging for I scarcely knew what. For Ytan to live and be well, for her to win the victory, for world's healing . . . it all depended on her. This one fierce, shy wild thing of a woman, it all depended on her.

She looked up at me with the tears clinging to her face. Then she closed her eyes, and her tears stopped as she centered herself. For the long span of ten breaths she crouched by Ytan's side. . . .

His body filled, his wound closed as if it had never been. He stirred and drew breath under her hands. Sighing as if waking from sleep, he opened his eyes.

"Lady wolf," he murmured in wonder, seeing Tassida. Then he caught sight of me and struggled up, moisture in his eyes like rain in a blue sky.

"Dan—"

There was something he would have said to me, but there was a battlefield all around us, tempest screaming overhead, and beyond, the fir forests falling, the eversnow shaking and turning black under a darkening sky, and the crags crashing into the sea. Ytan looked wildly around him and burst out profanely at me, "Mahela take your cock, you jackass! Do something!"

"Well spoken, Ytan," said Kor wryly. "Tass?"

She rose to her feet, and her flesh glowed with a dark fire, and she silently nodded.

We took our places to either side of her—she had always come between us in ways that seemed all for ill, so why not now, for good? Her head proudly raised, she opened to us her two scarred hands. The splint burst apart and fell away from her arm. In that moment I felt all my hurts heal, leaving no scars. Kor lifted his hand from his side, and his wound was gone.

Light blazed out that was not the light of the sun.

Jewels in our swords, shining, or—us, the three. A storm of light combating Mahela's black storm, clashing with her darkness. The few warriors left alive on the headland cried out, and some of them dropped their weapons and flung themselves to the ground, hiding their eyes against that light. Blaze of yellow lightning: that was Alar's doing, or mine. Sundown glory, Kor's, and the fiercest stormfire, Tassida's. . . . But storm was all outward. Within us, the three, was a calm. And in the calm, a nameless, peaceful passion I can scarcely describe—we were Kor, Tass, Dan, but we were one, we were all handbond, all mindspeak, mindbond, the thoughts of any one of us belonging to all, the feelings . . . shared by all three. We were specks swimming together in the sea of ourselves, we were as vast as the sea, and nearly as strong: in that stillness and that passion there was great power. Immense as the sea. But it was not the power that filled our hearts, it was—Kor, Tass, Dan. It was love.

*Handbond is as nothing compared to this*. That was Kor, marveling.

*Darran*. It was Tass, thinking to me. *You sought the*

*god, but he was always with us. We are all Sakeema. Is it not so?*

*Yes,* I told her. It was more than a reply—it was affirmation, pledge, vow. We were healer, seeker, visionary. Three in one and one in three. . . .

This wonder, the passion, needed a name. ''Godbond,'' I whispered aloud.

The black fist of Mahela, the stormcloud, swirled and vanished, gone like smoke, like fog, before a strong, clean wind of light. And the devourers turned as insubstantial as brume, glimmered greensheen for a moment and were gone as cleanly as the cloud. Even their stench was gone. Only a cormorant remained, a large bird, bigger than any seemly seafowl, flying where the tempest had been. It glided down over the headland and alighted below the rocks, near the shore. Bodies lay there, I knew, but even the taste of the air seemed sweet, as if the reek of death were gone from it, as sweet as if it had been washed by springtime rain. And the storm of our own making softly subsided into fireglow.

*The sun,* Sakeema thought, the three of us all thought as one, and a glory of sunlight filled the sky.

''Mountains,'' I murmured aloud. ''I want the mountains again, the way they were.''

We all looked and felt each other's handbond tighten with joy, for there they were, beautiful in the sunlight, my beloved snowpeaks as they had ever been.

''Peace,'' Kor breathed, and weapons fell down, snatched out of warrior hands as if knocked away by a god's unseen finger. Those who yet lived on the headland shouted in surprise and awe, then stood still and looked around them as if just awakened, as if aware for the first time that there was more to the world than death and war.

But another shout, Ytan's cry of horror, turned my head around.

In the sea a mountain of water was gathering, a peak far taller than my snowpeaks, a great, eerie wave that reached into sky and quenched the sun! Looming, frothing white and curling, it upgathered as we looked, a might of water fit to drown the dryland utterly. Just above the lip of it circled a speck, an overlarge cormorant, Mahela, spiraling ever higher and higher, eagle-high, and the wave followed her, growing, upraising, towering, until all the sea must have been taken into it. From the headland, cries rose thinly, like the mournful cries of birds, from those who stood and watched it forming, but the wave itself grew in grim silence, tall and massive and powerful beyond belief or reckoning. Then with a roar louder than Mahela's thunder, louder even than the roar of melting mountains, it started toward us.

And within a few heartbeats Sakeema had found, we had found, the three of us, that we could save ourselves, godbonded, but no more. Even Sakeema was no match for the might of the sea. What Mahela could not take unto herself she would destroy. Wretched, maddening thoughts spun through me. My brother Ytan, just saved, to be killed again. And Birc, and the sylkies . . . perhaps not the sylkies. But yes, the curly-haired ponies and the fanged mares, and Tyee's baby beyond the mountains somewhere, and even the Herders and their six-horned sheep beyond the thunder cones at the beginning of the plains, they would all be slain.

Of all the creatures of Sakeema, only we three might remain. . . .

*Dan, Tass, forgive me*, Kor thought to us, and I felt a snap like a breaking bone.

He had sundered the bond! I cried out as the deed shattered through me, and my vision went black for a moment before I could see. By then he was arrow's flight away from me, running, swift as a hunted stag he was running down the headland toward the shore, onto the sand of the beach to meet the monstrous upgathering of the sea, and Tass and I could do nothing but cling to each other and watch.

# Chapter Twenty-one

It would strike like a falling mountain, and then all would be black, black and drowning deep. . . . Nightmare, the demon that had ridden my sleep since I had been old enough to dream, I had known even then that it would end this way, but I had sweated in fear and cried out in the dark merely for self. Not . . . world's end. Not . . . Tass, not . . . Kor. . . .

He stood spear-straight and very still on the shore, head held proud in some mad defiance but arms uplifted as if to show that he bore no weapon in his hands—laughable, to think of raising sword against the sea. Curling, reaching, huge, mountain-high and heavy, the warrior's arm of ocean hung over him, upraised, fist clenched against all that yet lived on dryland. My hand tightened on Tassida's to tell her of love. *Kor!* mind cried to him to tell him the same. Less than a heartbeat and that black blow of doom would fall on all of us—

Ocean towered, peaked, shivered, shuddering like a strong captive put to torture who will not cry out. Then with a deep and hollow inrushing sound it laid itself down, crashing back into its vast basin. Swift, low waves ran up the shore and lapped at Kor's feet.

And Mahela came skimming over the waves, her black wingtips nearly touching the water, until she stood in fair, womanly form by Kor's side on the shore, and I saw him reach out briefly, with one hand, to touch her.

For a moment Tassida and I could find no strength. Then with panic's whip lashing us we ran headlong, half falling, down slope and steep rock to Kor, where he faced the goddess.

Odd, Mahela's aspect. A bleak quietness in her, as if she had been defeated. Her shimmering green gown was gone. She wore a dead man's cloak picked up from the ground, merely a rag to cover her nakedness, and her bare feet showed beneath it, as if she were a captive. Yet something about the proud lift of her everpale face, also, as of victory. She looked only at Kor, and her gaze was rapt. She spoke only to him. "It is settled, then," she was saying to him as we came near. Her tone was calm, level yet tender, as if she spoke with a pledgemate.

"Not entirely, mighty lady. We must talk." In him, also, that same calmness and an ardent strength. No desperation in him any longer. Striving, yes, but not struggling against unthinkable odds. Something had indeed been settled.

"What can there be to talk about?" asked the goddess.

"There is much to be spoken of. You have a tale to tell us, Mahela. Say on. Speak to Tassida."

I tried to keep my jaw from slackening in an uncouth way. He commanded her?

The glance with which she answered him was that of an equal, challenging. She would not always obey him, that one! But this time she chose to do so. She turned her head. "Greetings, my little daughter," she said. "Greetings, Darran." She spoke to us with easy courtesy, as if we were tribemates meeting after a short absence, though I sensed that she had not wanted to take her gaze from Korridun.

I mindspoke, *Kor! What is going on?*

*Later, Dan.*

*Are you all right?* He, standing near me straight as a lance, looking as well in body as I had ever seen him. Godbond had done that for him. But for some reason I felt afraid.

*As well as you are. Or nearly. Hush, Dan, listen to her.*

And by my other side stood Tassida. "Why do you call me daughter?" she asked the goddess, her head lifted arrogantly, and I saw what I had many times seen but not wanted to know. Her face, which some inner struggle had made as pale as Mahela's but for the the faint brown sheen put on it by weather: face as like to Mahela's as Ytan's was to mine.

"My fiery little one," answered Mahela with an odd, stark tenderness, "I birthed you, just as I did Sakeema some small time before."

Tass stood as if another word could topple her. I took her hand to give her strength.

"Do you not yet know me, you three?" Mahela complained. "I am she who mothers all." Her smile, hard, as always, yet there was little edge in her. Her wrath seemed gone, blown out like stormwind, quelled like the sea. "Before dryland was, I was old, and I grow only younger.

I shaped the mountains, I wove the grasses and gave milk to the sky. I—"

"All-Mother?" I blurted, too astonished to be silent.

"Why should that so surprise you, Darran? You, my bold cock and murderer? Of course the one who makes life must rule death. What is life without death? Yes, I am she whose name men have forgotten, but to curse by it."

More like the All-Mother's halfwitted sister, I thought. All awkward, askew, awry. Yet. . . .

Yet who was I to call her evil? I, with the lightning storm in me that I scarcely understood? Dan the murderer, son of a murderer, brother of another?

There was small need of strength in Tass. She had long known dark things of herself, and I felt her wry acceptance as she thought to me, *It is better, perhaps, than being the get of a whore*. Her words when she spoke were bitterly amused.

"Did you fly down to the plains then, O mighty glutton-bird, and lay the egg that hatched me?"

"I birthed you in human form, daughter! As I had to, though I fought it as long as I could. There is great power in my creation, for what is beauty without power? The pomegranate, it does nothing but mutely speak of Sakeema, and by its mere being it is very puissant. The sundered fruit I could resist many years longer than the whole one, but when those two scoundrels stole them away to dryland, my thoughts followed perforce." Mahela shrugged, a whimsical action in that haughty goddess. The soiled cloak swayed around her naked shoulders.

"Who is my father?" Tassida asked.

"You have none. I needed the aid of no man to make you. You are nearly my double, little wolf. Nearly my self as I might have been."

I saw Kor intently watching the goddess. "Speak to Dan," he ordered when Tassida asked nothing more.

Mahela's eyes turned on me, eyes deep as the sea. "You are Darran. I know what you are, and I dare say I know what your question will be."

Kor, what was happening to Kor? But I sensed he did not yet want me to know. And there was something else, the one thing I cared about even more.

"All-Mother, why were you trying to destroy the world you have made?"

"I wanted at first only to take it away to my undersea realm."

"Is it not fairer," I asked with courtesy, more courtesy than I had ever showed to her, "much fairer, here under the sun?"

"Perhaps. You think so. You mortals, so willful."

Mahela was struggling to speak. Perhaps never before had she tried to explain to anyone why she had done what she had done.

"Too striving, too clever," she said. "Even while the world was yet young, you mortals grew to be too many, too mighty, crowding out the wild creatures, you with your castles and cities and your many weapons, sharp tools for cutting the forests, sharp plows for tilling the earth, ships for sailing the seas and killing the great whales. Shamans even drew plans for ships to sail the skies and drive away the birds. Nothing was ever enough. It is you who are the gluttons, not I."

I stood keenly listening. Mahela spoke of the time remembered only by Tassida, the time when Chal and Vallart had lived, generations before Sakeema.

"So you started to take away the kings," Tass said softly.

"Yes, and managed a sort of balance, for a while. But humans. . . ."

The life-giver shook her head in despair, and I began to see what it had done to her, the long struggle with this creature of all her creation most clever, most willful, most like her.

"Time and again I brought them low," she told us. "Human kind, they are so wrongheaded, so greedy, it breaks my heart. They must always be making war. The time came when they themselves helped me lower their great stone cities to the ground. Booklore and the ways of making metal weapons were forgotten, only you six small tribes remained, and I had taken away the tree of the god. But I knew well enough that in time the tribes would grow, and learn, and threaten again. I made myself servants—"

"To help you take it all," I said. I no longer hated her, but I saw she was a desperate, twisted thing.

She looked straight at me. "Darran, hear me: I never wished to destroy. I took into safekeeping what would have been destroyed if left here under sky for people to find a way to."

How was I to believe her, my longtime enemy, Mahela? Yet how not? I had never heard her speak so earnestly.

"It would have been better to take the humans, but even with the fell servants I could never gather them all, for they are willful. And always their numbers returned." Weariness in her voice when she spoke of that long combat. "I made up my mind that I would settle it for all time: safeguard my world, or destroy it, or accept my defeat. And I have been defeated." In some wise she had, and in some wise, she had not, inwit told me. I stood watching her uncertainly.

"You three would have lived, for you are Sakeema. But when Korridun broke the bond and confronted me . . ."

Her proud head bent so that her black hair flowed down. Her shoulders sagged beneath her bedraggled cloak. ''I could not strike. I could not kill him.'' She lifted her eyes and looked at him, a look of such naked need that I winced. ''Or you, little daughter.'' Her glance turned to Tassida, still full of longing. ''Or even, Darran, my bold cock, you.''

A long, awkward silence.

''There is the matter of my cock to be spoken of,'' Kor said at last.

*Kor!* Dismay jolted me. *Did it not heal, like the rest of you?*

''I am healed, yes,'' he answered me aloud. ''Whole, no. I am maimed. No better than a castrate.'' He turned to face Mahela, meeting her stricken eyes with a long, searching look. ''Will you stand by your bargain, mighty lady?''

I let that go by me with only a faint pang of unease, thinking only of—Kor, so unmanned, it could not be, I could not let it be! ''But you must be made whole!'' I stammered. ''We must try again. Tass—''

One look at Tassida's ashen face and I saw that it was no use. What godbond had not done, no power of hers could do for Kor.

He mindspoke me, *Dan, let be! Perhaps it is a blessing. Mahela can never again attempt to take self from me by that means.*

Like someone drowning in deep water, helpless, I felt the strong downward tug of doom. My breath came short, my eyes saw black.

''I will abide by my bargain,'' I heard Mahela say. She sounded as shaken as I. ''Korridun, I need you too badly to do otherwise.''

No sound, then, but the lapping of salt water along the shore. A terrible question echoing in that silence.

*Kor!* I begged.

"I am going with her, Dan," he answered me aloud. His voice, very quiet, very gentle. "I am going with her, back to the place she calls Tincherel."

It might as well have been the end of the world.

For a moment I could not move or speak. It was as if a mountain had fallen on me. Then, with a roar like falling mountains, a murdering madman's roar of rage and sorrow, I snatched out my sword and rushed at the goddess to kill her. Rage and grief of Dannoc, wrath of Darran and all the strength of godbond were mine. I knew Mahela to be a twisted, unnatural thing, no better than a devourer—why should she have Korridun? Godhead and fate and doom be damned. My face, my skin, my whole body blazed and crackled with lightning fury as I leaped at her.

Whether brave, indifferent, or frozen with fear, Mahela did not move. She stood straight and still in her huddle of dark cloak, awaiting me. But in a single leap Kor was there, between me and her, taking the warrior's crouch, ready to dart in any direction I might choose to get past him, though he had not touched a weapon. And I knew he would not raise blade against me.

*Dan, no!* His face as frightened, pale and staring, as it had been that first night I had stormed into his life with drawn sword. *As you love me—*

I scarcely heard him. I was berserk, and like a bull bison I charged him, knocking him flat when he would not yield to me. Mahela, right in front of me. Sword flashing in air, high-poised above my head. I would strike hard and true—

But it was Tassida I saw before me, Tass embracing the goddess, shielding Mahela's body with her own. "Dan, no!" she shouted aloud, horror on her lovely face. "You fool, it is my mother!"

And Kor was up again and had a grip on my arms from behind, pulling me back with all his strength.

I broke free of him—no one, not even Kor, could hold me back when I was raving. I tore Tass away from Mahela and flung her to one side. Very still, both fair and dark, the goddess stood before me. I lifted sword to smite.

*Darran!*

It was Kor, mindspeaking me by my true name. I turned toward him, for I could not do otherwise—and all my wrath pooled into sorrow at the sight of his face. I stood shaking, weak as a starving man, staring at him. In very truth, I was Darran and I could not save him, not even with the sword. He would not let me.

"I am to go with Mahela," Kor told me, quietly, gently, "and she is to let the dryland be while memory of this time shall last and beyond. Forever. It is a fair treaty."

"No!" It seemed to me most unfair, for his sake. "Kor, why?" I dropped Alar to the sand, I was pleading with him, or with whatever powers had control of his fate. "All you have ever done is give goodness. Why must it always be you who suffers torment? The—one who keeps vigil, the—victim. . . ." Memory of all he had done, thought of what he meant to do, harrowed me. I started to weep.

I hid my face, I could not see him, but I felt his touch—he put his hands on my shoulders. "Listen to me, Darran! We are the three stonebearers, you know that. Tass is the healer. You are—seeker, dreamer, but more, you will find out what you are. And I am, always I have been, the—the sacrifice. Of course it is I who must go. It is fitting."

"Fitting," I muttered, turning my face away.

This, then, was the ordeal. This was the dark agony of being Darran, to love such a brother and not to be able to save him. Kor himself was the price to be paid for the world's well-being.

"Dan, look at me!"

*Dan, you are making it harder for him! Cease those tears!* It was Tass, coming up beside me. I felt rather than saw her scowl.

*You do not understand!* I flared at her. *You do not know that—that chill and deathly place—*

*I understand well enough that you are hurting him!*

Truth in her, blunt and hard, like river stones. And hurting Kor was the one thing I had wanted never to do again. I centered myself, let tears go for a small while. I raised my head, looked into his well-beloved face.

He only looked back at me, silent, his chest heaving as if he had fought a battle. In his sea-dark eyes, a plea. Something I had to do for him before he—before he was gone. . . . By my side stood Tass. Somewhere behind, Mahela, very still. Around me, the empty world, vast sky, vast sea, shore silent but for the washings of salt water, mountains where no deer ran. I let it all go, let passion go and looked only at Kor, thought only of Kor, what I had to do for him—though I knew he would not ask it of me, he would never ask it of me again.

IF YOU FELT WHAT IS IN ME, he had told me once, IF YOU TRULY FELT ALL THAT IS IN ME, THEN YOU WOULD UNDERSTAND. And I had tried it, that closest of all bonds, and I had come close, but I had fled. I had failed him.

And this would be—my last chance.

*Handbond*, I mindspoke him.

He comprehended, and for a moment it was as if he could not move. Only his mind moved to touch mine, faltering.

*Heartbond. . . .* he thought to me.

*Heartbond came first. Yes, my brother, I know.*

His right hand left my shoulder, met mine. Fingers met, sword scars met, passed the grip. We did not need it for strength any longer, I noticed. The clasp was more for—for closeness.

Heartbond, handbond. Then mindspeak. But, beyond mindspeak, the mindbond without words.

I ventured.

No longer aware of my body. I was—soul, as if dead, a greenshade flying over the sea, or swimming in it, as shadowgreen as the greendeep, but I was—living, I was Dan, as vast as the sea, as limitless. Yes. That was the aspect that had once so terrified me, being without limit, without edge, a formless, boundless Dan opening into the vastness that was Kor as he opened into me, I could no longer think of him as other, he was a warm sea as vast as sky, welcoming me without a ripple, and what was the use of fear when I was so warmly afloat, gliding, drifting at my ease in Kor . . . and he in me? All that was in Kor was in me. All that he had ever known, I knew. All that he remembered, so did I. All that he . . . felt. . . .

His passions, I felt as my own.

I felt it, but even unbounded as I was I could scarcely encompass it, that surpassing great gift of his to me, to his world, that courage, that . . . love. . . .

He loved her. And I had wanted to kill her.

He loved Mahela.

Truly loved her, with a keen-edged, striving love that had been willing to combat her yet loved her none the less, a love as shining as his sword against stormcloud. A love so light and dark, so much a part of him that he himself scarcely knew it yet, but how could I not have known it? He had coupled with Mahela, and being what he was, he was then fated to love her. He was Kor, the master of mercy, the king by the sea.

Kor, within me and of me, like light in the sky, like salt in the sea.

As I accepted self I accepted him, all that he was, all that he felt, all that was in him. And I was willing to stay with him, formless in him, forever. No thought in me of pulling back, as waves wash back into the sea. No memory, almost, of my body, left—left outward, when we were all inward, Kor and I, and as immense as stardark, as limitless as the haunts of the nameless god. But there was a calling, voiceless, or a touch not of hands, something that mattered to me, and reluctantly I turned my thoughts from Kor to attend to it.

*Dan. Kor.*

Mindspeak. It was Tass.

Her arms around us both, she was gently, quietly calling us back, as gently as once she had eased our way back from the sea. And though I did not know when we had moved, Kor and I stood with right hands clasped but left arms around each other, tightly embracing, with our heads pressed against each other, so that when I came back to awareness of my body I felt first the warm salt wash of tears against my cheek, my own and his.

Kor thought to me, *Nothing can sunder us utterly, Dan.*

Not even death, or the abyss of the sea. He spoke truth, words that could have been tested by fire. I knew that.

Mahela stood watching us. She had not moved, or spoken scornfully to us, or tried to part us as she once had done, and she looked somehow frail in spite of all her power, standing there as she was in a cloak borrowed from a corpse, apart, with a small frown on her ageless, handsome face. And I saw that unwonted diffidence in her, remembered the lilt in her voice, the odd tenderness of her smile, and I knew why Kor had broken godbond and run to face the wave that could have destroyed the world.

She loved him, in her tortuous way.

"I can scarcely blame you, Dan, for not thinking better of me," she said quietly to me. "But be comforted. I am not your enemy any longer. I accept my defeat."

I stooped and picked up my sword, which yet lay at her feet. I sheathed the blade, then faced Mahela. "Great lady," I replied to her, lifting my head, "how can I think of you as defeated, you who will have Korridun?"

I could feel him there beside me, the touch of his mind against mine, his hand still gripping mine. And I knew how he had fought against his unwilling bond with Mahela at first as if against a doom, and how the battle had made him into a darkened, embittered mockery of self. It was indeed better, and fitting, that he should be with her.

*Yet I will miss you, Kor. The touch of your hand.*

The sea lapped at our feet, and on the sea a bright ship came sailing, the tall masts bare of sails, bare even of the banners that had once hung upon them. It was Mahela's dwelling from the Mountains of Doom, and it shone regally in the light of the sun dipping westward behind it.

What needed to be said could not be put in words. Tass touched Kor's hand, embraced him and kissed him. I held him hard for one last moment before slowly releasing him, and he turned to Mahela without a backward glance. Taking her hand, he guided her to a coracle. For the first time I grew aware that his people were silently watching from the headland, the beach. Elders and children, the nursing mothers and the few warriors who yet walked, all watching and silently weeping. And the Red Hart warriors who yet lived, and the Otter River folk, even the Fanged Horse raiders. And the sylkies who remained put on their pelts and gave him, sealform, a retinue as he sent the coracle away from the shore.

At the distance of the breaking waves Mahela spoke to us, her voice raised to carry to the reaches of the headland.

"Now hear me well, you mortals: I give up my creation to you for all time. No longer will there be a sanctuary in my realm beneath the sea. What you slay will be slain for all time. What you drive away will be gone. What you wreak will be done. If the sea grows more salt, it will be because I weep, but I will not lift my hand again."

She bowed her head, tightly shut her eyes, clung to Korridun's hand with both her own as if she were a captive pleading for his mercy. And with a surge and a sweet clamor the creatures came up out of the sea.

# Chapter Twenty-two

The joy, the grief of that day—it was godbond, I think, that had given me the strength to withstand such mingled anguish and exaltation as I had never known before, and have not since. Joy as keen, as vehement as the sorrow. . . . I stood watching my bond brother, in the coracle, ever farther away from me, and the creatures were coming back to the land.

The waves washed at my feet, and the creatures ran up onto the shore with the water. Ferrets and hedgehogs, wildcats, foxes, the little pika in their tens of tens, and—all of them, all! The great, sleek catamounts, the bears, the badgers, and the deer, fallow, red, gray, the spotted deer, all the deer in all their twelve kinds, even the blue deer of Sakeema. And the tossing of the waves was the tossing of tall heads, manes of spray, horses! Not the dun horses only but the beautiful wild horses of many colors such as had once run on the plains, black, bay, white and the colors of sunlight, neighing and curveting and cantering onto shore. And the birds, the peregrines, the eagles! Bursting out of the sea, taking to sky. And *ai*, the white antelope of the peaks, and the great maned elk, and the wolves, the wolves of wonder. . . .

Those who stood on the shore that day and saw it were to the end of their lives deemed blessed by all who spoke to them. And for generations thereafter time was reckoned from that day, the beginning of the renewed world.

All manner of clamor rose from the many sorts of beasts greeting each other, and the sweet clamor broke out from the watchers as well, seeing the creatures, the white weasels and gliding squirrels, the swans! So beautiful. And the bison plunging out of the sea. And after them—the people.

As if in a dream I heard Winewa's scream, joy so piercing that it hurt, as she saw her daughter, our daughter, toddling toward her. Karu sobbed with happiness and embraced a tribesman. All those whom the devourers had taken were being returned. The folk of the unknown tribes of the times before memory walked out of the sea, their rich robes trailing in the water, and stood blinking. Then slowly they smiled, or wept, and some of them fell down and embraced the ground.

I saw it all, for I was Darran, but I stood as if rooted, even as bison thundered past me, and I watched after Kor. Tassida stood by my side, handbonding me, but even she could not comfort me much.

Slowly, slowly, like a boat in a dream, the coracle bobbed away, but its speed seemed all too great to me. Far too soon to suit me, Kor reached the waiting ship, helped Mahela aboard and boarded in his turn. Then I could no longer see his body, his erect head, the dark cap of his hair. I let go of Tassida's hand, burst from my place like the hawks bursting from the sea, and I seized a gray horse—such power was in me since godbond, I grasped the mane of a mighty gray more beautiful even than Calimir, and I vaulted onto its back and sent it where I wished, at the gallop, though the creature was wild with gladness. Up the mountainside by the straightest way we went, at a speed as if we ran on flat land, yet the speed seemed not great enough to me, and I shouted for more. I was in a frenzy to reach a vantage where I could see far, very far, before the ship had sailed out of sight.

I stopped at last at a place where I could look out over the spires of firs, and I let the gray gallop away. In sundown light, the ship was a fair blade of sunstuff cutting the glistening surface of the sea. Then it was a smaller knife of blackstone, leaving behind it a widening gash . . . sea would heal from its sundering, but would I, ever? Then it was a chip of flint near ocean's edge. And then it was gone in the sunset, and I could not see it any longer, though I climbed to a higher crag and looked again, though I narrowed my eyes against the sky glory, seeking.

I sat down in the dirt under a gaunt blue pine, bent my head to my knees and wept.

Through sunset I wept as grievously as I had once wept over Kor's broken body, and my hands snapped the pine needles under my knees and flung them away, and my tears soaked into the forest loam, and my fingers crept into it as if to hide. As of themselves my hands took up some of the dampened loam and shaped it, the way old Ayol of the Herders had once shaped clay beside a dying fire. Then I looked at my hands and saw what I was doing and cried aloud with pain, for my longing for my brother was worse than ever—

And the lifeless lump in my hands turned into a singing bird as red as my heart, and it flew away arrow-swift into sundown, winging toward Kor.

Comfort in that, somehow. Comfort in the feeling of the earth in my hands. I shaped it again, and laid it down, and under my hands the moist earth turned to a small brown deer that looked at me with wide eyes before bounding away.

This was the thing I was fated to be, then. Darran. The lifemaker. The shaper.

My weeping lessened, and I made others. I made more deer, and great-eared foxes, and a falcon, and a new sort of small dog that sniffed me, waved its tail in thanks and trotted away. Until twilight had turned to a darkness soft with stars I made them, and then I sat with my back against rock, bone of mountain, and listened to the night. It was full of the good creature sounds, chirrings and whistlings, the pipings and rustlings of songbirds in the trees. Somewhere close at hand, grunt and squeal of quarreling pika. More distant, owl's call. A screech that stopped my heart—catamount scream, I had never heard it before. On a far slope of Chital, the cry of wolves, as sweet to my ears as singing.

At moonrise Ytan and Tassida came walking up the mountainside, following my plain trail. Alar glowed like firelight to greet them, but I could not hail them or look at them without heartache, because they were not Kor. When they saw me, Tass came and sat by my right side, took my hand. But Ytan stood straddle-legged in front of me.

"Body of our father, Dan! Are you still sulking?"

Plainly, he meant to rouse me, but I did not answer him, did not so much as look up, not even at Tass. In a moment Ytan kneeled and laid his hands on my shoulders.

"My brother, please," he said, "tell me what I can do to help, after—after I have done so much to harm."

Only such an appeal from ever-sour Ytan, I think, could have moved me to speak. "But it was not you, Ytan." I raised my head and blinked at him. "It was the devourer in you."

"Still, I—I remember, Dan."

By my side, Tassida snorted in exasperation. I was of like mind. "There is no need for amends, Ytan," I told him. "But if there were, do not folk in Seal Hold need your help?"

In starlight I saw the flash of his smile, and he moved to sit at my left hand. "Less than the person here, I think. Tassida has healed all who needed it, and brought all those who died this day back to life and wholeness. All of them, even the horses."

"Especially the horses," she muttered. I looked at her.

"You could not bring back Calimir," I said slowly.

She shook her head. Her voice was steady, the glance of her eyes, level into mine. "It seems I cannot help the longtime dead. Those whose souls have fled."

Only those whom the devourers took, Mahela's pets, had come back from her realm, Tass told me. Not those who danced over the eversnow. The dead were dead. Tyonoc. Kela. Wyonet, Tyee, Leotie. Gone, forever gone, like . . . Kor. . . .

"Think of what is saved, Dan," Tassida said to me softly, "not what is lost."

I laid my head back against rock and closed my eyes hard, but the stubborn tears trickled out from between my eyelids. There had been a sunrise, once, with Kor, when I had thought I might never weep again. How wrong I had been. I had thought he was Sakeema, that he would make all things right for me. Now I knew who he was, and what Sakeema was, and I felt as if I might never cease to weep.

"Dan," said Tassida suddenly, urgently, "look!"

Never had I felt less like opening my eyes, but this was Tass who spoke to me. I looked. The forest, starlit and dark. In white starform, and alone, Chal stood silently before me. By my sides, Tassida and Ytan kept still as the stones. This was an eerie one, neither truly dead nor truly alive. But I thought of him only as an old friend, and my heart ached for his sake.

"Your comrade," I said huskily to him. "Gone."

His sober, kingly gaze answered me.

"Gone, to—to be with Kor? My lord out of the past, I thank you. But I wish I could—bring him back to you. . . ."

Chal came and kneeled by me, placing his hand on my forearm, a starlight touch I could not feel. Silently that touch said to me, as he could not say, Be comforted. He asked nothing more of me. But one star-mote hand lifted toward Tassida and his eyes, deep as night, turned toward her—I felt her stiffen. For a moment she met that stardark gaze, then silently she did as Chal signaled her. She drew Marantha. She laid the sword down on the loam at my feet, earth dampened by my tears.

In the sword's pommel, an amaranthine jewel glowed. For a brief moment, an eyeblink, Chal laid his palm on the stone, and the light flowed through his insubstantial hand. Then the shadow-stars of which he was made seemed to swirl and swarm like midges, and he was gone. Tassida reached for her sword, but stopped her reaching hand in midair.

"Dan," she said in a hushed voice.

"My brother, look!" said Ytan.

Even before they spoke, even before I looked, I felt the fragrance, touching me like sunlight, lying on me as gently as mist of dawn. At my feet, where Marantha's pommel touched the moistened loam, a spire-shaped flower was springing up.

"Amaranth," Tass breathed.

Sweet flower of healing, Sakeema's blossom. And I knew to my heart of hearts that Kor was in some sense yet with me, as I was yet with him. I knew it to the center of my being. And weeping ceased as if it had never been.

As if coming out of a hurtful dream I stirred and looked at Tass. She gazed back at me tenderly.

"So the amaranth is a better healer than I," she remarked.

'You, who healed a battle's worth of dead and wounded?" A wry thought struck me. "You healed them all? Even Pajlat?"

"Even Pajlat," she affirmed softly. "I had to do all or none, Dan."

"Scum of Mahela," I muttered.

"Though I must admit," Tass added, "I did him last."

"By my wounds, I hope he has not started up the fray again." The thought brought me to my feet. Tass and Ytan rose to stand beside me.

"When we left," Ytan said, "he and his horsemen were riding off to hunt the bison."

I groaned at that.

"And the Cragsmen have gone back to the peaks," Tass told me. "But the Otter have stayed for the feast, and so have the folk out of the past. There is a mighty sort of din and dancing and passing of perry wine going on at Seal Hold."

I stared blankly, for it had not yet occurred to me that

there was cause for rejoicing. Ytan said, "Dan, come down. Everyone is asking about you."

There was peace in me, given by the amaranth, but it was a frail bubble, not yet ready to burst into joy. I shook my head. Ytan took my hand and lifted it in both his own.

"Dan," he said, almost pleading, "there is one brother yet with you."

I looked into his fair, moonlit face as if looking into my own, seeing how generous of heart he was, yet how fragile. How he flushed at his own words. When he spoke again, he had roughened his voice.

"You greathearted dolt," he said, "all the time you were seeking, I knew Sakeema was as close as your right hand. We all sensed it, we Red Harts. Tyee could have told you, but, lunkhead that you are, you would not have believed him."

"You will lead the Red Hart Tribe, Ytan," I said to him.

He gawked at me.

"Go down," I told him, "and join the feast, and tell my people, all of them, that I will come back at sunrise."

He let go my hand and went, leaving me on the mountainside with Tass.

I sat again where I had been. She sat beside me. I took the forest loam in my hands, shaping it, not quite idly, for I was Darran, and in my blunderheaded way I knew what I was about. The fragrance of amaranth was in my nostrils, and the touch of Tassida's body was warm against my side, and under my hands the moist earth turned to the fairest creature I had ever seen, white, a sort of fair moon-white antelope with but a single horn that spiraled like the lovelocks of Tassida's hair, and it had amaranthine eyes that darkly glowed. It stood before us with head and horn tilted our way, gravely looking at us both as if in blessing.

"Dan," Tass said to me in a small, stunned voice, "it is the creature from my dream."

I took her hand. "Look at the horn," I told her. "It is one, but it is two, entwined. It is our love. The emblem of our love."

The creature leaped up like joy and bounded up-mountain, where it stood on a high vantage, savoring the night.

Tass said softly, "Dan, if you wish it. . . ."

There was not much need for us to speak or even mind-speak, since godbond. We knew that we would be together for as long as this renewed world should last. We knew that we would begin as was fitting in a world of new life, and that it would be good, very good, on the mountainside in that sweetest of all nights.

"Indeed I do wish it," I told her, my voice hushed. "But first there is one thing more I wish to do."

Again I shaped the earth, and this time I thought not of Tass, or the amaranth, or the good night full of creature sounds, or of my beloved mountains—though all these things strengthened me as I worked—but I thought of the one who had given them back to me.

And then I lifted what I had made, and saw its grace, heard the haunting song, and I released it into flight, watched it fly to the sea, its wingspan as great as the height of a man.

"Blue?" Tass whispered in wonder.

All the colors of the sea were in its feathers, blue and moonsheen and shimmering green and dusky violet and gray. For it was of Kor that I had been thinking. The blue swan would swim on the swells of the sea and sing forever of Korridun.

''Blue swan of Darran,'' Tass murmured.

''Blue swan of Korridun,'' I told her.

For Kor was the sea king.

# Glossary

AFTERLINGS: followers, usually on foot.

AFTERWIT: hindsight.

AMARANTH: a healing flower that disappeared when Sakeema was killed.

AWK: leftward.

BLACKSTONE: obsidian.

BROWNSHEEN: copper-colored.

BRUME: dense, gray fog.

CACHALOT: sperm whale.

CARRAGEEN: a dark purplish seaweed.

CHOUGH: a small, insolent crow.

COMITY: innate courtesy.

CRAKING RAIL: a short-billed landrail of drab plumage, shy habits, and excruciating vocal abilities.

DREAMWIT: a visionary person, a mystic.

DRYLAND: the opposite of ocean. Refers to any land above water, not necessarily arid.

DULSE: an edible seaweed.

ERNE: a sea eagle.

EYE OF SKY: the dispassionate gaze of the nameless god.

FIRE TRUE: true enough to be sworn to by putting one's hand in fire.

FOGWATER: condensation.

FRY: recently hatched salmon just emerging from the gravel, the length of the first joint of a man's index finger.

FULMAR: a stiff-winged, gliding seabird.

GAIR FOWL: the great auk, a sort of northern penguin.

GANNET: a large, white seabird.

GLIMMERSTONES: agates.

GRAYMAW: a shark.

GRAYSHEEN: silver-colored.

GREENDEEP: ocean.

GRILSE: salmon returning from the sea to their native river; "summer salmon."

GUDGEON: a rather stupid-looking freshwater fish.

GUTKNOT: navel.

HIGHMOUNTAIN: alpine (as, highmountain meadow).

INDEEPS: penetralia.

INWIT: instinct.

JANNOCK: unleavened oatmeal bread.

KING: a tribal ruler of either sex.

KITTIWAKE: a small, short-legged, gentle-faced gull.

LAPPET: a breechclout.

LOVELOCKS: curling tendrils of hair.

MERKIN: a woman's pubic hair.

MOONSTUFF: silver.
MOON-MAD: temporarily passionate or out of control, with emotions running high, as if influenced, like tides, by the phase of the moon.
NAGSBACK: a shallow mountain pass.
NOGGIN'S WORTH: a little.
ORICHALC: a hard, golden bronze.
PARR: young salmon still in the brown freshwater stage.
PEAL: salmon returning from the sea to their native river, turning from silver to red.
PICKTHANK: a flatterer.
RAMPICK: a tree whose top is dead or broken off by wind.
ROUGHLANDS: the shadowlands.
SCANTLING: a toddler, a very young specimen of whatever species.
SCARROW: high, thin cloud.
SCARROW-FOG: a thin haze high in the sky that lets the sun show as a white spot.
SCOONING: skipping over the surface of water as a flat stone does when properly thrown.
SHADOWLANDS: the arid high plains beyond the mountains, the steppes or shortgrass prairie.
SLOWCOME: a slow-witted person or one who is slow to act, sometimes with a sexual connotation.
SMELLFUNGUS: a grumbler.
SMOLT: salmon in the final freshwater stage, turning from brown to silver.
SMURR: drizzle.
SNOW MOTE: snowflake.
STONE-BOILED: cooked in liquid into which hot stones are dropped to heat it.
STOUP'S WORTH: a lot.
SUNSTUFF: gold.

SWORDMASTER: maker, namer, and wielder of his or her sword.

SYLKIES: undersea folk who can take the form of humans or seals.

THUNDER CONES: volcanoes.

TONGUESHOT: the distance a voice will carry.

TROATING: bleating, as of a deer in rut.

TUMBLESTONE: a rock washed smooth by the action of water.

WANHOPE: a person who continues to hope against all common sense.

WHIMBREL: a brown wading bird, related to dowitchers, godwits, curlews, willets, and snipe.

WHURR: to burst from cover with a loud flapping of wings, as a partridge or a grouse.

WITCH WIND: hot wind that blows down from the landward side of mountains.

A prophecy comes true, and a new mythology is born . . .

# SISTER LIGHT, SISTER DARK

## *Jane Yolen*

". . . a wonderworker with words" *Joan D. Vinge*

THUS WAS HER COMING FORETOLD . . .

And the prophet says a white babe with black eyes shall be born unto a virgin in the winter of the year. The ox in the field, the hound at the hearth, the bear in the cave, the cat in the tree, all, all shall bow before her, singing, "Holy, holy, holiest of sisters . . ."

Jenna's birth was hard but normal. It was not until years later that her legend turned it into a miracle; a legend that she herself did not believe. Brought up as a priestess of the Goddess Alta, Jenna knew her destiny was to be a hunter and receive, at the right time, her Dark Sister, with whom she would share all. But destiny can go awry.

Jane Yolen's 100th published book displays yet again her intelligence, compassion and sensitivity. It is the first in a stunning new series which will chronicle the growth of a new mythology and the death of a culture.

"We shall hear her tales over a winter's evening of ten thousand years" *Gene Wolfe*

Also by Jane Yolen from Orbit:

HEART'S BLOOD
DRAGON'S BLOOD
CARDS OF GRIEF
TALES OF WONDER
DRAGONFIELD AND OTHER STORIES

FUTURA PUBLICATIONS
AN ORBIT BOOK
FANTASY
0 7088 8285 4

# THE THIRD BOOK OF LOST SWORDS: STONECUTTER'S STORY

## *Fred Saberhagen*

"An entertainment of high order" *Publishers Weekly*

A story of space, time and the Gods of the desert . . . and the Swords of Power.

The gods forged the Twelve Swords of Power; now the gods have been destroyed by their own handiwork. The Swords are loose in the world, falling into the hands of human beings, changing human lives for good and ill.

Young Kasimir was the custodian of Stonecutter, the sword which can hew mountains and split diamonds with equal ease – until he discovers Stonecutter has been stolen. His first ally in the search to recover the powerful blade is Magistrate Wen Chang, who is reputed to have mysterious mind-reading powers.

Was Stonecutter responsible for the three murders they discover evidence of along the way? Or for the strange missing man?

And will Kasimir be able to recover Stonecutter before it does irrevocable damage?

"Fred Saberhagen has always been one of the best writers in the business" *Stephen R. Donaldson*

*Don't miss:*

**THE EMPIRE OF THE EAST**
**THE FIRST BOOK OF SWORDS**
**THE SECOND BOOK OF SWORDS**
**THE THIRD BOOK OF SWORDS**
**THE FIRST BOOK OF LOST SWORDS**
**THE SECOND BOOK OF LOST SWORDS**

FUTURA PUBLICATIONS
AN ORBIT BOOK
FANTASY
0 7088 4308 5